Charlotte Davison lives with her husband in a sleepy Somerset village, close to the beautiful Mendip Hills. Its location and superb scenery have always been referred to as their happy place, where life takes on a steadier pace.

They are both retired and love spending as much time as possible with their wonderful family, friends and adorable cocker spaniel, Marley. They are very fortunate to own a lovely home in Brittany, France, where they like to spend holidays with family and friends.

Charlotte's career has spanned many organisations such as printing, construction and insurance but the most rewarding was within the prison service, working alongside the in-house senior probation officer. A challenging role but it certainly gave her an understanding into how life can be so very different on the inside.

She decided to write her first fictional book when everyone was enduring lockdown in 2020, giving her the time and inspiration to fulfil a lifelong ambition.

With great positivity and determination, when there is something in life that you want to achieve, then do it, challenge yourself and don't look back.

She has loved the connection with the characters in the book and believes they are an illustration of real life in so many ways. Charlotte hopes this novel will appeal to many readers.

Charlotte Davison

CATCH ME WHEN I FALL

AUSTIN MACAULEY PUBLISHERS™

LONDON * CAMBRIDGE * NEW YORK * SHARJAH

A CIP catalogue record for this title is available from the British Library.

ISBN 9781035819416 (Paperback)
ISBN 9781035819423 (ePub e-book)

www.austinmacauley.com

First Published 2023
Austin Macauley Publishers Ltd®
1 Canada Square
Canary Wharf
London
E14 5AA

Introduction

Catch Me When I Fall is about a happy and loving family who, when given the opportunity of a lifetime, decide to sell their house on the Somerset/Devon border and move to France.

They couldn't refuse the best for their children and live the French dream.

The family would experience awe-inspiring times, meet many different people from all walks of life but along the way, they would encounter tragedy and drama; romance would be just around the corner but not everything would go the way they had planned.

Chapter 1

Meg Johnston arrived home from work later than usual. As expected, traffic was horrendous. It was stop-start for the 8-mile journey and Meg felt highly stressed and tired after a busy day at work.

The village of Hampton Deverell, on the Somerset/Devon border, was once a quiet, sleepy and idyllic community place to live. Since the new road had been built, with a housing development, it had become jam-packed with a transport system, which had become more like the famous spaghetti junction.

The constant pollution of petrol and diesel fumes filling the air was taking its toll on many local villagers, including the elderly and those who suffered from chest complaints.

They couldn't understand why so many houses were up for sale but the reason was apparent; the village was different from what it used to be. It had become a commuter belt, not only for the locals but outsiders too and its peace and tranquillity had completely vanished.

The Post Office and Bank had closed and the local bus service operated only twice a week. Even the local primary school had been threatened with closure, with the nearest school at least 7 miles away.

Public amenities should be a priority, with more houses developing. They were at a total loss! "Where had our pretty village gone?"

Having three children under 13 years of age could be demanding, especially working as a full-time physiotherapist at Devonshire General.

Meg's husband, Simon, was an English and History Teacher at Wickham Junior School who also found life extraordinarily stressful. They both wanted the best for their children and that had to be one of the main priorities in their lives.

Family life was so hectic nowadays, there seemed to be no quality time; it's work, eating and sleeping. Weekends was for household chores, checking and marking school papers, football training on Saturday morning for the boys and Swim Club for Katie.

Both of them were a non-stop taxi service but this was what you did for your children or was it? There had to be a more straightforward way of life; all they needed to do was find it!

Meg and Simon loved running as a hobby and belonged to HDRC (Hampton Deverell Running Club), competing in local marathons for different charities, trying to fit this into their busy schedules as and when possible.

Simon was also a very keen cyclist.

After picking up her 6-year-old daughter Katie and 9-year-old twins, Freddie and Charlie, from the after-school club, they called at the local store for some shopping before making their way back home.

'Tea will be ready shortly,' Meg told them.

'Let's hope Dad will be home soon so we can all sit around the dinner table together.'

Reuben, a black and white cocker spaniel, was sleeping quietly in his basket, cuddling his favourite toy, snoring here and there after a long walk with his walker, another member of the family who needed more time with them.

Meg was busy preparing dinner when the phone rang.

It was Simon. 'I will be home shortly and want to discuss some important news with everyone.'

Feeling somewhat anxious, Meg rushed upstairs to shower before Simon arrived home. She quickly changed, brushing her wet hair into a ponytail. It was not long before Simon's car pulled into the drive and as he got out, Katie ran to greet him, giving her daddy a big hug and squeeze.

Katie was undoubtedly a daddy's girl. She helped him carry his briefcase whilst he brought in a pile of papers and as he put the documents on the kitchen table, he shouted out, 'Hi guys, I'm home.'

Simon had a huge grin on his face and Meg caught sight of this whilst dishing up the dinner.

'You look very smug,' she said.

'Let's wait until dinner is over and then we can talk.'

She poured him a glass of wine and the family all sat down together. After frantically finishing dinner, Meg could not hold back her curiosity anymore.

'Well,' she said, 'what news do you have?'

Simon was eager to tell everyone and went on to say, 'Can you remember when Phillipe Malin visited the school last October to teach our year five pupils French?'

Meg turned to the children with a vague look but then she remembered.

'Yes, he was over here for a term, wasn't he?'

'That's right. Today, I received a phone call from him, who asked if I would be interested in a teaching post at his school near Dinan, France.'

Phillipe had told him there was a great need for English to be taught in France and that he would be perfect for the position. Simon was very fortunate to speak French fluently, thus not presenting too many problems with the language for him, should he decide to take the offer.

Meg's mind went wild and was churning lots of ideas. A new life in France! This could be the opportunity they were looking for. Could it mean less stress, more time together as a family and a slower pace of life? Meg could only see the positives but as a family, they needed to discuss this further as to whether they should embark on this venture.

It was a lot to think about but it wouldn't take them very long to decide. Meg was looking nervously at the children, not knowing what their reaction would be; telling them that moving to another country wasn't like going on holiday.

It could be forever. It excited the children like this was a big adventure.

Katie said, 'Can we take Reuben with us?'

Dad was most adamant. 'Of course, we can. We would never, ever leave him behind.'

He lovingly smiled at Katie while announcing he was part of the family. Freddie and Charlie wanted to know if they could see their grandparents and the rest of the family and friends back in England and just as important to them, could they continue with the sport they both loved; football.

Simon replied, 'The family will always be important and we will certainly allow you to carry on with your interest in football.'

'All we need to do is find a club suitable for both of you and I do know lots of schools in France who have their very own club and no doubt if you are good enough, which I think you both are, then I can see there will be little or no problem in both of you finding the right club.'

Katie was looking a little more pensive.

'Daddy, do they have anywhere I can swim in France?' she said with a smirk.

Simon replied, 'Of course, poppet; they have many swimming clubs and Aqua Centres.'

Her face brightened and she said, 'Well, that's OK then.'

Breakfast in the Johnston household was always chaotic. Getting ready for the school run and ensuring the children had packed their lunches and sports kit was always a headache.

As usual, Simon was rushing out the door, making sure he would not be late for school, assembling a piece of almost burnt toast in his hand, kissing everyone goodbye and saying, 'We will talk again later.'

Three weeks later, everything was moving quicker than they all thought. The decision was made to move to France and begin a healthier and stress-free way of life. It could be the beginning of a new chapter in their lives or so Meg thought!

Easter had come and gone and everything was fast approaching. Arrangements were made for the move as soon as possible if everything worked out as planned. Meg had handed in her notice at the hospital and Simon had accepted a position at the French school, Saint Vincent, near Dinan.

It was agreed that Simon would sign most of the contract papers on arriving in France. The children were excited about the new adventure of moving to France and the thought of inviting their friends over to stay. They put their three-bedroom detached house up for sale and couldn't believe how quickly they had a buyer.

What a lovely couple! Both were artists who told us this was the property they had been searching for a long time. The couple were so excited when they finally found one close to their art studio.

Meg told them about their upcoming move to France and they wished them good luck but not before they handed a gift of a watercolour that was hand-painted by themselves of the stunning Exmoor Valley.

'Take this with you so that you will never forget your roots back in England.'

Meg thanked them for the most beautiful and treasured gift. Reuben was all checked out at the vet and they were just waiting for the Pet Passport to be delivered.

Simon's mother had died when he was ten years old and his father had died two years ago. With the money left to them from the sale of their home, they decided that this would help with the finance of the French property. Also, the money from the sale of their home, hopefully would give them enough financial support to start their new life in France.

Meg and Simon were frantically looking on the Internet for a property near the school and a couple had popped up that looked possible. Fortunately, Meg's parents, Liz and Mike Thomas, both retired, lived in the next village at Upper Fordham.

Mum and Dad had offered to stay with the children whilst they made all the arrangements necessary and booked a ferry to view some properties over a long weekend.

Spending three days looking around several charming Breton villages near the school, they found a beautiful stone farmhouse which suited their needs. They made an offer and it was just a matter of time before they could get an answer about as to whether the offer would be accepted.

Excitement was mounting and life was now getting hectic in the Johnston household; so much to think about and lots to do. Meg rang Simon at work on his mobile, revealing that the family who owned the farmhouse had accepted their offer.

'Wow, that was quick! I can't believe it! What a bargain!'

Meg pictured in her mind how it would look in a couple of years; redecorated to their taste and looking like a family Breton home. The house or farmhouse, whatever they want to call it, was old but certainly had a lot of character and that was what they liked about the quaint French properties.

With tender loving care, a few repairs and touching up paintwork here and there, they could make it look like a beautiful home. Everything now seemed in place. Meg and Simon signed lots of paperwork and all was completed and now up to date. A start date for Simon's teaching post at the school was emailed to him.

'Phew!'

Meg said to Simon, 'We must sort the children out with their schools once we arrive in France.'

As the children prepared for their last day at school, emotions ran very high. Saying their goodbyes to friends was hard and Meg knew that both she and Simon would also find it difficult too.

Meg kept saying to herself, 'We are not a million miles away, so please come over and visit us; everybody would be very welcome.'

They also kept reminding themselves that they would always have a place in their hearts for family and friends.

Charlie said with a chuckle, 'There is always FaceTime, Mum!'

She squeezed him and gently wiped a tear from the corner of her eye. It was now the end of June and the big day had arrived. In the distance, you could see the removal van with its two drivers, slowly but surely edging their way down the cul-de-sac, trying not to hit the stone wall in front of the house.

They did a magnificent job reversing into the driveway and the sound of the noisy engine quietly faded away as they parked the van with the utmost care. The children excitedly ran outside to greet the removal men and Katie told the driver:

'We are moving to France.'

'Yes, I know,' he said. 'I am coming with you too.'

'What, are you going to live with us as well?'

'Sadly not, just delivering furniture to your new home.' The driver tapped her on the head and hoped she would enjoy her new life in France and make lots of friends.

The van displayed a painted sign on both sides of the van saying, *just hopping over to France*. It made them all giggle and gave a light-hearted feeling about the move.

'A cup of tea, lads?' Simon asked.

'That's very kind; yes please, mate. Where do you want us to start?'

Simon showed them where all the boxes and furniture was and in no time, the van was loaded and ready to go. Meg began thinking to herself, that's the beginning of our new life in that van. 'Are we making the right decision?'

Once packed, they could squeeze nothing else into the van; the driver steadily and gingerly drove back down the narrow lane and onto the main road, where he took a right turn onto the new road and then onto the motorway towards the ferry in Plymouth.

A small congregation of family and friends had gathered outside their house to wish them good luck. There was joy but also a little sadness having to say goodbye to everyone but they knew they had made the right decision, not only for themselves but for the children too.

Their neighbours brushed back tears and told them, 'They would never have friends like us again.'

'Don't be silly, of course you will and please remember you must come to France and visit for a holiday.'

They put their arms around each other, had a group hug and held back more tears. The box of tissues held in her very shaky hand was nearly empty. Meg didn't envisage that leaving would be this emotional. Reuben seemed settled in the back of the car, the children were laughing and making strange noises as children do, so the journey began.

The skies above Hampton Deverell were beginning to blacken and it had started raining but within a short time, the sun was peeping through the fluffy clouds and the most beautiful rainbow was visible ahead. Meg turned around to watch the children giggling and chatting; they looked so happy. Both she and Simon wanted this more than anything for them.

They drove onto the ferry, walked onto the upper deck and waved goodbye to Plymouth in the distance saying, 'We may be back one day, who knows!'

The journey took about ten hours (car/ferry) from door to door. The children decided to fall asleep about 3kms from their new home. Typical. Reuben was up and looking around as if to say, "I haven't been here before," and looking very interested at the large expanse of green fields.

'We could walk for miles, Reuben,' Meg muttered as they drove up a dark and winding lane with trees on both sides. She nudged the children to wake up and told them they had arrived at St Helene. Katie wiped her tired eyes and cuddled her precious teddy bear Rufus, gripping him tight to avoid losing him. Charlie and Freddie couldn't wait to get out of the car and have a wander.

'Don't get lost, boys!'

It was dark and there were no lights in the village. It was undoubtedly rural. All they could hear was the sound of the occasional grasshopper. It was so quiet, certainly different from what they were used to.

Simon looked tired after the long drive but as he got out of the car, he put his hands on his hips, looked up at the sky and looked very pleased with himself. The French Agent had placed the keys on a piece of string, which had been pushed through the letterbox.

Simon was not sure they would hand over the keys this way back in England but it did give them the opportunity of not hanging around for the Agent. As they stepped out of the car onto a small courtyard, Simon gave them a loving hug and said, 'Our new home. I hope we will all be very happy here.'

The farmhouse looked old and tired, with its whitewashed walls looking a bit sorry with paint peeling off the green shutters around the windows. Somehow, it didn't look as bad as when they first visited; yes, it did need painting and freshening up and possible urgent repair of the half-fallen down drainpipe but all in good time.

Katie put her arms around her daddy's waist and just hugged and hugged him. The twins were more interested in the stream at the bottom of the garden.

'This is great for fishing,' Freddie shouted.

'Quiet boys, people are asleep in the nearby houses.'

He told them that everything would look different in the morning after a good night's sleep. Night skies fell over the farmhouse and Meg found Simon looking up at the clear starlit sky.

'Are you OK, darling?'

Simon replied, 'Yes, this is what our dream has always been about and I just want us all to be happy. Of course, we can now give more time to the children and ourselves. Once settled, we can start living our dream.'

Simon put his arms around Meg and both stood looking up at the starry night sky. As they entered the farmhouse rather nervously, not knowing what the state of the property was like inside, they could see that the property had not been lived in for some time. Luckily, Simon had a torch with him and beamed the light around the downstairs.

It is very dusty, Meg thought and cobwebs were a prominent feature. Simon searched for the fuse box to see if there was any electricity.

'I cannot promise anything but we may be lucky if I turn this switch upwards.'

Sure enough, the lights came on and he was able to plug the kettle into the switch on the wall, which meant Meg could make a cup of tea with the travel kettle which had been jammed in a plastic bag at the back of the car.

They had to manage with what was with them as they only had sleeping bags and pillows but this was quite an adventure for the children, who loved every minute.

They quickly found some food in the back of the car which required eating up and sat huddled together, extremely exhausted and ready for some very much needed sleep.

Chapter 2

After a strange and disturbed night's sleep, they all wandered down the squeaky stairs to the kitchen. Katie cautiously looked around, brushing away any unwanted cobwebs. There was plenty of work ahead.

Katie remarked, 'We need Nan and Gramps to help us clean up.'

'It won't be long before they join us,' Meg said to Katie.

'I hope so, Mummy.'

Meg could tell Katie was already missing her grandparents, so she tried to explain that they were not far away and could visit us anytime and that they could visit them too. She knew it would be hard for the children but they would surely adjust once they are settled and have made new friends.

'Is there a local bakery nearby?' Meg asked.

Simon answered, 'There is always a village or town in France which has a bakery/patisserie; well, almost every village anyway.'

Simon decided to jump into the car and drive down the little country lane to St Helene town centre, where he found a bakery. It wasn't far and he thought that next time, he would walk and take Reuben with him.

People were queuing for their baguettes and patisseries. The smell coming from the bakery was amazing. Simon entered the bakery rather apprehensively and asked for *'Trios baguettes et six croissants s'il vous plait.'* (Three baguettes and six croissants, please.)

Some of the locals turned around and started to stare at him a little, knowing he was a stranger in their village. He spoke and introduced himself in French.

'Bonjour, je m'appelle Simon et j'ai déménagé dans le village de Sainte-Hélène avec ma famille.' (Hello, my name is Simon and I have just moved to the village of Saint Helene with my family.)

Their friendly faces made him feel very welcome and some even patted him on the shoulder and said, 'We think you will be very happy in St Helene.'

Simon began chatting at great length and then said, *'Je voudrais vous inviter chez moi pour un apéritif le samedi après-midi, si l'un d'entre vous peut venir.'* (Est-ce que quelqu'un voudrait visiter ma maison pour un aperitif Samedi et rencontrer ma famille?)

'Oui, merci beaucoup.' (Yes, we would, thank you very much.)

Feeling extremely pleased, Simon hurried back to Meg and the children and told them he may have invited the entire village to their home on Saturday for aperitifs.

In total amazement, Meg replied, 'The whole village!' Her voice trembled as she wasn't sure she could cope with the whole village.

'Let's hope the weather is good so we can entertain in the garden.'

Meg began to think perhaps there weren't enough chairs to cater for the whole village, as she exploded with laughter at the thought. The baguettes and croissants were still warm and smelt heavenly; they prepared the kitchen table and sat down to their first breakfast in their new house, which they had decided to call "Fleurs de Pre".

The house surrounded by meadow flowers and beautiful shrubs with powerful fragrances, filled the air with a lovely aroma. Busying themselves, they then spent most of the day tidying up and cleaning and even had time to walk Reuben along the beautiful Breton countryside. The twins had made themselves a Tree Swing and were enjoying themselves.

Meg could hear them laughing, which was something she hadn't heard for such a long time. Children enjoying the lovely French countryside, less pollution in the air, just a mingling of the trees swaying in the breeze and the gentle trickle of the stream at the bottom of the garden. Absolutely heaven.

Katie came running into the kitchen with some flowers she had picked and placed them on the kitchen table. 'Mummy, this will make our house look beautiful.'

Meg picked her up and gave her the biggest squeeze ever. 'I love you so much, poppet and thank you for the beautiful flowers.'

Meg placed them in a jar she had found lying on the stone floor and she told her they would find a pretty vase once the removal men had come with the furniture and boxes. Katie and the boys seemed so happy and wondered whether this would last or was it, to them, like a big long holiday.

Walking around the garden, it was visible that there was a lot to do to get it back into shape, what with repair of the seesaw, perhaps a new swing for Katie and a new Treehouse for the boys.

'It won't happen overnight but we can at least plan for the future.'

There was enough land to grow their fruit and vegetables, possibly handing out some to the locals. Katie asked if they could keep some chickens.

Meg said, 'Well, we have enough land for them to roam.'

'Yes, but please let us keep them and not eat them.'

'We will see,' she said with a twinkle in her eye.

The small orchard near the stream at the bottom of the garden was bearing some lovely plums and apples. Meg caught sight of the most beautiful magnolia tree growing in the middle of the garden. It was truly magnificent; somewhere she could sit and relax with a book.

Meg could even do some sketches, as she used to draw a lot when she had the time. How wonderful, she could see peace here. Perhaps this should be called "Meg's Retreat".

The removal lorry arrived around 11 o'clock and they told us they had stopped at a transport café for breakfast after spending a very uncomfortable night in the back of the lorry. Although they seemed a little tired, they were accommodating; unloading everything and they even helped to move the heavy furniture with Simon's help to the bedrooms upstairs.

Still, lots to do at the house but more critical was sorting out the schools for the children; so the next day, they decided to take a trip to Dinan. They wanted the children to be together if possible and found a school just outside of Dinan, which took them until the age of 18 years.

They spoke with Madam Joubert, the Head Teacher at Saint Jean Distelle, who invited them to walk around the school with her. Katie was pulling on Meg's skirt and sucking her thumb nervously.

Madam Joubert talked gently to Katie, 'You will love it here, they even have an indoor swimming pool.'

Katie's eyes lit up. The sad look on her face now showed delight and excitement.

'Um, is this Daddy's new school, Mummy?'

'No,' said Meg, 'Daddy is at another school but he isn't too far away. Freddie and Charlie will be at the same school as you, so you will be together but different years. The bus will take Charlie and Freddie to school and back but

Mummy will take you and pick you up. You are a little young to be travelling on your own.'

The boys felt immensely grown up, giving Katie a boyish snigger. 'It's okay,' she said, 'It won't be long before I can catch the bus too.'

Freddie and Charlie were pleased to learn the school had its own football team and after-school matches were held twice a week. 'Wow that is more than at Wickham. I think we are going to like it here,' said Charlie.

After a discussion and a tour of two other schools, they decided with the children that Saint Jean Distelle School was their favourite. All done. School started September 15th at 8.30 am, finishing at 4 pm with a half-day on Saturday.

'What, school on Saturday?' The twins retorted.

'Yes, but there is no school on Wednesday and lunch is a two-hour break.'

Feeling a little happier, the twins decided that on Wednesdays they would go fishing together and if they could persuade Dad to put up a football net in the garden, they could practice their football skills. They also found a vet for Reuben close to St Helene; another item crossed off their list.

Meg wasn't too keen to find a job, deciding to enjoy time settling in and making friends and a home for the family before deciding her future in France! There was enough to do at the farmhouse to keep busy for many months. All that was left to do was to sort out a doctor for the family.

Meg wanted to talk with some locals on Saturday to see if they could recommend one. The skies looked grey over St Helene and she could hear thunder rumbling in the distance. Simon had just got back from making some final arrangements with the school before he was due to start after the French summer holidays in September.

Meg said to Simon, 'I think you have got back just in time, there is a storm coming and strong winds were fiercely blowing through the trees, so we decided to batten down the hatches for the night.'

A cold chill was in the air, so they sat around a welcoming fire, drinking hot chocolate and toast before preparing a hot evening meal. As they woke the following day, the sky was blue, with no clouds and the sun was shining. Raindrops glistened on the leaves of the trees from last night's rain.

Everything looked fresh. They could even hear the stream trickling at the bottom of the garden. Meg was thinking about how lucky they were. Would this last?

Reuben decided to sniff around the unturned soil and seek out anything that dogs liked to do. Digging up the garden was his favourite pastime, however. He had lots to explore and burrow in this garden, keeping him busy for quite a while. He was beginning to settle, just like them.

Chapter 3

Saturday arrived and they were getting prepared to entertain their guests from the village. It was a beautiful day and the garden was a perfect setting with so much space for making their new friends welcome. Meg wanted everything to look perfect; she even baked some tasty vol-u-vents and made a cake, with the help of Katie, of course.

'Mummy, we can put them on the pretty plates that Nanny gave us.'

'Good idea,' Meg said, as she carefully placed them on the kitchen table.

The guests were arriving and many were carrying flowers or a gift. This was a French tradition of welcoming new people to the village. Meg couldn't believe it! There must have been twenty or more people arriving.

'Do we have enough food and drink for everyone?'

Surprisingly, that couldn't have been further from their thoughts; with that, a very portly man drew up in 4 x 4 truck.

'Let me introduce myself. My name is Henri Pascall and I am the Mairie of St Helene.'

He explained his role in the village, stating that he was the main person they should contact in the event of any significant decisions. Henri had his office at the Town Hall in St Helene. He told us the duties of a Mairie are like that of a Parish Councillor back in England.

There was a lot of responsibility dealing with all matters involving crime and legalities concerning the village of St Helene. All towns and village have their very own Mairie. Henri was a robust-looking man, with lovely rosy cheeks but somewhat a little overweight (possibly too many French cakes).

He was in his mid-50s. His English was excellent, which helped her understand; although Meg told him she would be getting Simon to give her some more lessons so she could mingle within the community more.

They say, "When in Rome or, more appropriately, when in France."

'Please accept this from all of us in the village.'

Henri presented us with two large boxes of wine, a bottle of Calvados, apple brandy and very potent but very traditional in the Normandy region of France. He also gifted some cheese and plants for the garden with plenty of sweets for the children.

They were exceptionally grateful for their kindness and the talking and laughter of everyone was a delight to hear. Katie played with two little girls who were busy making daisy chains and playing with Reuben. Freddie and Charlie were making friends too, with a couple of the local boys.

The tree-swing was in full use but did need some attention at some point, together with an old seesaw which had seen better days too. Perhaps they could all help to restore the playthings, *possibly a project for the boys,* Meg thought.

Being introduced to so many different people throughout the afternoon, Meg was surprised at how much French she was talking; not enough to hold an entire conversation but she felt confident and pleased with herself.

By chance, a very charming person shook her hand and kissed her twice on the cheek. It was French etiquette when greeting people. *How lovely,* she thought. He introduced himself as Doctor Louis Bernier and said that he had a surgery in St Helene.

'You are most welcome to come along and visit us and perhaps we can help you decide on choosing your family doctor in the hope we can oblige.'

'Thank you very much, Doctor Bernier,' she would certainly give this some thought.

Doctor Bernier wished them much happiness in St Helene. He told her that Dinan and the surrounding areas had much history and once settled, they must visit the beautiful churches and chateaux. Every Thursday, a market in Dinan sold fresh fruit, vegetables, fish and local Breton produce.

'I am so pleased that I could come along today,' he said. 'I wanted to take advantage of the opportunity of meeting you and your family.'

What a kind man, she thought.

They stood speaking for quite a long time and he was very interested to learn that Meg was a physiotherapist back in England. She told him that she had studied at the University of Birmingham for several years before qualifying.

Simon had also studied his Teaching at Birmingham, which was where they had met. They were married two years later and had three children, Katie and twins Freddie and Charlie, who she would like him to meet.

She pulled up a couple of chairs and they sat chatting for ages about England and why they had decided to move to France. The doctor was keen to learn about English cricket and Meg told him that their local village back in the UK had an excellent cricket team and they always supported them when it was possible.

The doctor seemed extremely interested in the life they had left behind but said France was a good place too. Meg saw the children walking over and called them to meet the doctor. Dr Bernier shook both the boys' hands, giving Katie a peck on her cheek. She blushed and ran away.

'She can be timid,' Meg said.

The doctor laughed and they carried on chatting. Dr Bernier told her he had studied at the Leeds School of Medicine. He was there for four years and then returned to France to finish his medical training. He was a fascinating man and it was a pleasure listening to him but couldn't help wondering if he was married and, if so, why hadn't he brought his wife with him.

'Let me introduce you to my husband,' Meg said.

Simon was speaking with Henri Pascall and she could hear loud laughter (too much wine, she would say) but she was able to catch Simon's attention. Turning his head to acknowledge the doctor, he strolled over to greet him.

'Simon, this is Doctor Bernier, he has a practice in the village.'

They both shook hands and chatted for a while.

'Let me fill your glass. Red or white, which do you prefer?'

'Oh, red, please.'

Katie came rushing out of the house with her plate of homemade vol-u-vents and chocolate cake. Katie didn't want the guests to go away hungry after she had made such an effort. Delicious was the reply from many!

'Did you make these yourself?'

'I had some help from Mummy.'

'Well, you certainly know how to cook!'

Meg couldn't believe the time. She glanced down at her watch. It was 6.30 pm and the guests were still busy talking and laughing. Doctor Bernier reckoned that he had to leave because he was off to a meeting with the local Cycle Club but didn't go without reminding them of a visit to his surgery.

'I hope you aren't driving, Doctor.'

'No, it is only about 2 kms to where I live, not far at all.'

Also, he had a glass of wine or two, maybe three, so it was undoubtedly the right decision. When Simon heard that there was a Cycle Club near the village, his eyes lit up. Simon had always enjoyed cycling and it was something he could pursue here in France, for sure.

'I am certainly going to find out the name and location of the Club,' he said excitedly.

Reuben was stretched out on the lawn behind. Having so much garden to run around was total bliss. He would run, flop down and run again, so different from England, where he only had a 30-minute walk each day by his walker and if time allowed, a walk by them if they were not too busy. Here, he could walk and run whenever he wanted—he loved it and his tail never stopped wagging.

Meg felt quite pleased with the day's outcome after meeting a lovely lady called Danielle, who was slightly younger and ran the village's local florist. She called out and said, 'Meg, bring the family to my house for drinks, I am not far away and live just outside St Helene.'

'That would be lovely,' Meg replied.

Danielle gave Meg a card with her telephone number and told her she would love to offer her the same hospitality that both Meg and Simon had. With a very flushed face, Meg replied, 'That is so kind of you, we would undoubtedly love to accept your kind invitation.'

The locals were now beginning to leave after a lovely afternoon and evening and again, more kissing but this was France; this was what they did! Katie was rubbing her eyes and Meg knew she was getting exhausted. There was chocolate cake around her mouth. Meg gently washed her hands and face, changed her clothes and put her to bed. Katie fell asleep in seconds.

After clearing away the debris from the garden, the boys and Simon helped with the tidying up in the kitchen and feeling very tired, they sat around the kitchen table.

'That was a very successful afternoon and evening, don't you think?' Meg said. 'The children have made friends and we have too.'

Reuben was snuggled up in his box and fast asleep. What a day! Sunday morning, they all awoke to feel fresher but knew there was still a lot of work ahead. They were lucky to have a sunny and warm day, which meant a lot of work in the garden.

The garage was still packed with boxes and required unpacking and sorting. Katie seemed very happy playing in the fields with the dog and the boys were in the process of trying to fix the seesaw and Tree Swing, keeping them busy and out of trouble for a while!

The church bells were ringing in the distance and Meg could see some of the villagers walking past the house, possibly off to Sunday morning church prayer. They turned to her, smiling and waving, shouting out 'Bonjour Madame Johnston.'

'Bonjour,' she replied, also waving to the friendly crowd.

On Sunday mornings, the Cycling Club got together for a ride out. There must have been twenty riders or more, all in brightly coloured yellow and blue jerseys. From the corner of her eye, she could see Simon standing in amazement; hoping that he, too, one day, would be able to join the Club.

After a couple of weeks, they were getting the house into some sort of order with many boxes unpacked. They were all loving their new home and Meg was going to make sure it would work for all of them. However, she was feeling a little homesick but wasn't going to say anything to anyone as she hoped it would pass.

The signal for her mobile wasn't brilliant but she got 3 bars, so decided to give Mum and Dad a call.

Mum answered, 'Hello love,' she said. 'How are things?'

'Perfect Mum, we have got the house straight but now the garden needs a lot of work.'

'You have been busy!'

'Sorry, Mum, the signal isn't perfect and I can't quite hear you; what did you say?'

'You have been busy,' she replied for the second time. 'Dad is down the allotment but I know he would want to have a chat. I could get him to ring you later.'

'Yes, of course. The children miss you both, so I wanted to know if you and Dad would like to come over and visit soon.'

Meg didn't tell her mum she was homesick but felt much better by speaking to her on the phone. As she said goodbye to Mum, her voice trembled slightly. It was just hearing her voice and knowing she was far away. She had that feeling back again. Homesickness was bloody awful but she was determined to get through it. It won't last, she kept telling herself.

The boys were helping Simon in the garden and repairing the drainpipe, which needed urgent repair before they had more heavy rain but lo and behold, they had it fixed in no time. Meg decided to take Katie into town, which had a weekly market and have a good look around.

They found that they could park the car without any problem. No parking meters here; just park where you can—no charge. *This was great,* she thought! And as they were walking through the town, they passed Danielle Fleuriste.

Could this be where Danielle has her flower shop? Meg gazed through the window and saw a dark shadow in the background. It looked very much like Doctor Bernier; he was busy chatting to Danielle, who was putting up a lovely posy of fresh flowers. He was a good friend of Danielle and Meg had this desire to go inside but thought otherwise.

They quickly walked away but considering all the time, 'Should we have gone in and said hello.'

However, it did remind her that they still had to visit Dr Bernier about possibly registering for his surgery. They walked around the market and bought some mussels.

'How do you cook these, Mummy?' Katie asked.

'Clean and wash them thoroughly and then pop them into a big pan with some wine, onion, a little garlic and chopped bacon.'

'Would I like them, Mummy?'

'Try them and see.'

Over here, the traditional dish was Moules et Frites. (Mussels and Chips.)

'Shall we have them for tea?' Meg asked.

Katie thought for a moment and nodded her head. 'Yes, please.'

They also bought some fresh fish and vegetables—everything looked so fresh and inviting. She could have spent a fortune. So much assortment of everything. The vibrant colour of the aubergines, juicy tomatoes and rosy red apples. Delightful. Walking back to the car, she felt a gentle tap on her shoulder. It was Doctor Bernier.

'Bonjour Madam Johnston.'

'Bonjour, Dr Bernier.'

He was carrying the most beautiful bunch of flowers.

'How lovely, are they for anyone special?'

'My sister's birthday is today and hope to visit her this evening and surprise her.'

Meg told him they were gorgeous.

'Danielle, who runs the florist across the road, is a good friend and she always puts together a lovely selection of flowers. Thank you again for a lovely afternoon last Saturday—it was so nice to meet you and the family.'

'It was a pleasure to meet you too,' she answered. 'We were hoping to visit your surgery shortly.'

'Well, why not come along on Friday evening after my surgery finishes.'

'Let me check with Simon but that should be okay,' Meg replied with a slightly nervous tone.

They stood talking for a short time in the busy street. Meg felt a warmth surround her, which she couldn't explain. Louis started talking to Katie and could see he appeared to have a lot of time for her. He went on to say that he had a niece, Alice, about the same age.

'I'm six, nearly seven,' Katie told him.

'Alice is six years old too, so I could bring her along to meet you one day.'

'I would like that. We can play in the garden on the seesaw if Daddy fixes it for me,' she said in a slightly harsh tone.

He chuckled at her remark. Meg longed to ask if he was married but couldn't pluck up enough courage. Perhaps he would think she was being too curious. It was getting late, so they said their goodbyes and told him they hoped to meet with him on Friday evening at the surgery.

It was nearly dark by the time they arrived back at the house. It would appear they had carried out all the jobs and even the seesaw had been repaired to Katie's satisfaction. Simon and the boys had lit the log burner and although it was only the end of July, the house was old and quite damp.

They were still determining how old the property was but could only think that it could be around 80 years old, judging by other houses in the area.

Katie bounced through the door and said, 'We have Moules et Frites for tea.'

'Whatever is that,' Freddie said in astonishment.

Katie shouted out, 'They are small black shellfish found on the rocks and we need to wash them well.'

Meg put them into a large bowl for washing before cooking. Of course, they knew frites is French for chips, which made it alright! Chips are chips, wherever you are. They were cooked just like the recipe and went down extremely well with some crusty French bread and a glass of white wine. Tasty, was the verdict by all.

That same evening Meg's mobile rang. It was Dad.

'Hi Dad, how are you? I spoke to Mum earlier and she told me you were busy down the allotment.'

'I was but we definitely need some rain for the beans but other than that, the vegetables and fruit bushes are coming along fine.'

'Would you and Mum be able to come over and visit?'

'Of course, love. I have a couple of hospital appointments at the end of the month but as soon as that's over, we can book a ferry and we will be on our way.'

'That's great, Dad; I know the children are missing you and I can't wait to show you and Mum the house and garden.'

Meg asked Dad if he could give her a hand sorting the garden out. She had the strange sense that he was smirking slightly at Mum on the other end of the phone.

'Let's see what is involved but I should be able to help you. I will need plenty of cups of tea,' he said laughingly, 'and I had better bring over some gardening tools too.'

'We don't appear to have many forks and spades, Dad, so that would be great.'

They then started to talk about all sorts of things, the kind of things you talk about when you are missing someone. They just kept rambling about nothing important but she knew she didn't want to put the phone down; she just wanted to keep talking. Meg was undoubtedly missing Mum and Dad and couldn't wait for them to book the ferry.

'It has been lovely talking to you both; please let me know when you are coming over and we can make all the necessary arrangements. Simon and the children send their love and once we have the house phone and Wi-Fi connected, there should be no problem with the signal and we will be able to FaceTime. Goodbye Dad, I love you lots and see you soon. Love to Mum. Bye-bye.'

They were getting ready to visit Dr Bernier at the surgery when Katie decided to fall in the garden and cut her leg. There was blood everywhere and Meg was getting a little concerned. The cut looked quite deep but Simon picked her up, took her into the kitchen and bathed her leg. She was frightened at the sight of the blood on her dress.

'It's alright, darling; we will have your leg mended in no time.'

Meg put a dressing and plaster on her injured leg and once she couldn't see any blood, she calmed down. Meg lifted her off the table and as she hobbled across the kitchen, she said, 'Perhaps the doctor will look at my leg.'

'I don't think we need to bother him, poppet, he will probably say it will soon get better and what an excellent job Daddy has done.'

'No, I must show him my leg; he is a doctor.'

They stood still and quietly chuckled to themselves. Anything for attention! Freddie and Charlie were teasing Katie about her leg.

'Don't be mean, boys,' I told them. 'She had a nasty fall and was very frightened.'

'Such a softie,' Freddie replied. 'I didn't cry like that when I broke my arm while riding my bike last year.'

'Be kind to your sister, Freddie,' who quietly sighed and walked away.

It was getting late and they all got into the car, hoping they were still on time for their appointment with Dr Bernier. They arrived, slightly out of breath, after rushing and making up some time.

'Bonsoir la Famille Johnston.'

They all gathered in the reception area and looked around. It was very similar to their doctor's surgery in Hampton Deverell. They slowly walked over to the receptionist, who shook their hands and gave them a tour of the surgery. They were all very impressed; they even had a small A & E Unit (something like a walk-in centre back home).

After a short time, Dr Bernier joined them and asked what they thought about the surgery. Simon responded by saying it looked very friendly and well organised. Dr Bernier was one of three doctors and two nurses assisted him. Being very impressed with the set-up, they decided to register.

They filled out the necessary paperwork with the receptionist's help and were offered tea and biscuits afterwards. Everything seemed perfect and exceptionally well laid out. Dr Bernier shook their hands and wished them all well.

As they were about to walk away, Katie ran over to the doctor, saying she had fallen in the garden and asked if he could look at her bad leg.

With a gentle gaze and smile, he said he would. 'Quickly, come with me.'

He beckoned a nurse who came over and held Katie's hand. Katie looked very pleased with herself, with everyone fussing around her. Afterwards, she came out of the treatment room with a giant grin on her face and sucking a lollipop.

The nurse had checked her leg and changed the dressing and all was good, with no broken bones. The nurse gave them a wink and they thanked her for her time.

Chapter 4

It had been two months since they arrived in France and they were beginning to live the dream. Meg was beginning to tackle homesickness and had gotten through some difficult moments but it was getting better. Simon and the children were just loving France. She was hanging out the washing when the phone rang.

It was Mum. 'Hello, how are you?'

'Is everything okay?' Meg said.

'We are considering joining you for a couple of weeks if you will have us!'

'Of course, Mum, we would love that. Has Dad had his hospital appointments?'

'All good and under control.'

'Brilliant, when are you coming?'

'We will catch a ferry from Plymouth on Tuesday, arriving with you around teatime.'

'The children will be thrilled and I can't wait to tell them. Simon was hoping you would come out before the autumn so we can get planting with some vegetables and Dad could advise us on where, when and what to grow.'

Meg could sense an air of excitement in Mum's voice as she said, 'Dad would love that.'

'Looking forward to seeing you both on Tuesday. Love you lots, Mum.'

She ran into the garden to tell Simon and the children that Nan and Gramps were coming over next week to visit. Katie jumped up in the air with excitement. The boys said they would show Gramps the stream at the bottom of the garden, where hopefully, they could do some fishing.

Gramps loved fishing but did mainly sea fishing in his day. He once had a small fishing boat moored on the Devon coast and in his younger days, would go out and do some mackerel fishing.

When Meg was a little girl, she remembered going out with him and bringing back the mackerel. Mum would gut and cook the fish for supper. She didn't think Dad had done much fishing since his brother died, except on the odd occasion.

They would do everything together and just loved getting the boat out and sailing around inlets and bays around Salcombe. She wanted everything to look spic and span when Mum and Dad arrived. The bedroom next to Katie's had new bed linen and matching curtains.

It looked pretty and on the day they arrived, she had asked Katie to pick some wildflowers from the field behind. They had some scorching days, which meant Simon could paint the shutters around the house and wash down the walls.

'Looking good, Simon,' Meg called out.

Cream walls and green shutters. Over the front door, a beautiful jasmine was growing and little yellow flowers were starting to bloom. The contrast against the newly painted walls looked terrific. She was feeling so happy.

Reuben was lying in his favourite spot in the garden under a shady bush next to a gorgeous magnolia tree, which was in full bloom and looking magnificent in the summer sunshine. The garden was all fenced off and safe for the children and dog.

A little gate at the far end of the garden led to the stream and where the boys played and did a spot of fishing with the Tree Swing overlooking beautiful views across fields.

Perfect! Meg couldn't wait to show Mum and Dad their "little piece of France". It was a very exciting household on Tuesday. Having spent most of the morning cleaning and ironing, everything was looking welcoming for their arrival.

She even had time to make some cakes. Katie was in charge, as usual, supervising every move. Simon and the boys went into the village for the bread and then on to an enormous Hypermarket to stock up on provisions, which sold everything from a stamp to a washing machine.

'What time will Nan and Gramps be here, Mummy?'

'About 6 o'clock,' she said, 'so we must have everything ready and have evening dinner prepared.'

'I can help Mummy but first, I must go and pick some flowers for Nan and Gramp's bedroom.'

Katie skipped into the garden and Reuben followed. As she opened the gate, Reuben dashed down the garden and without looking, straight into the stream. The stream was running quite fast from the recent night's rain.

Katie shouted, 'Reuben, come back here,' but he looked back at her and wandered on, not taking any notice of her call. At this point, he was swimming—the water was getting deeper. Katie didn't know what to do.

She called out, 'Mummy, Mummy, come here quick, Mummy.'

Meg could not hear her as she had music playing in the kitchen. Simon was out shopping with the boys. Nobody could listen to her call for help. Katie ran as fast as she could to the house and called out to Meg.

'Reuben is in the stream and I can't get him back.'

They raced down the garden but Reuben was nowhere to be seen when they got there. Meg and Katie were frantically calling Reuben, their calls getting louder and louder and still no sign of him. Suddenly they could see he had managed to climb up a muddy and slippery bank.

He was shaking the water off and panting. They managed to get hold of him but Katie, who was still crying, said, 'You naughty boy, don't do that again. We thought we had lost you.'

He looked at her as if to say, "What is all the fuss about? I only went for a swim!"

She picked him up and cradled his wet body, which was covered in bits of green weed and not smelling too good but clutching him tightly, all the same, never letting him go. They walked back to the house and bathed Reuben washing the muddy, watery, slimy mess off his furry body from the riverbank.

He seemed happy enough but Meg snapped at him and told him not to go to the stream on his own again. He looked up at her with such saddened eyes as if to say, "What me!"

Meg couldn't be mad at him for long. She wrapped him in a towel and dried him whilst Katie returned to the field to pick her flowers. As Katie raced back home, she saw her daddy and the twins getting out of the car; they had bought enough shopping and food to feed an army.

'Hi sweetie, you have been busy picking flowers, haven't you?'

'Yes, they are for Nan and Gramps. I need to tell you something, Daddy. Reuben has been very naughty. He jumped into the stream and I couldn't get him back.'

'Is he okay?'

'Yes but he needed a bath because he was smelly. I told him he mustn't do that again!'

With a smile, Simon gently put his hand around her shoulders and walked into the kitchen with several shopping bags and the twins carrying several bottles of wine. Everyone was getting excited at the arrival of Nan and Gramps and it wasn't long before they could hear a car.

'I think it's them,' cried out Katie.

She was so excited; she couldn't wait to greet them. The car turned into the drive and there was a look of delight on everyone's face. Gramps got out of the car first, followed by Nan.

'We are so pleased to see you.'

'Did you have a good journey?'

'The crossing was calm and the journey from the port to here was trouble-free. The roads differ from England; at least you can move without too many traffic jams.'

'Come inside and I can show you around once you have had a cup of tea or something stronger.'

'Tea would be lovely, dear,' Mum replied.

Simon hugged his in-laws, rarely would he call them Liz and Mike, they were Mum and Dad to him too. Meg was busy making a pot of tea. In the meantime, Simon had poured them a Breton aperitif called Kir, which was very popular in this region of France.

'How lovely, we could get used to this.'

They all sat down to supper and chatted happily for a couple of hours. Katie was bouncing on Gramps's knee and tugging at his cardigan.

'Gramps, come outside and let me show you our See Saw.'

'Later, my dear, it would be better to show me the garden tomorrow when we have more daylight.'

'Of course, Gramps.'

She then snuggled back down on his lap and cuddled him. Nan loved the flowers Katie had picked and their scent filled the bedroom with an air of soft fragrance. As Meg looked across the kitchen table, she held her mother's hand and said, 'It is so lovely to have you both here.'

Meg wanted to tell her Mum how she had missed them and how homesick she had felt but she bit her lip and held back. She had to be brave not only for herself but for Simon and the children. The children had gone to bed but Meg and Simon were still chatting with Mum and Dad and it was now getting quite late. Dad had yawned several times and he was slowly closing his eyes.

'Come on, time for bed everyone, we can help you unpack tomorrow.'

They all wandered upstairs; Reuben followed into Katie's room, found his spot on her bed and nestled down for the night. The following day, they were all up bright and early. Simon had gone to the bakery for bread, the shower and bathroom were in constant use and Meg was busy preparing breakfast.

'Did you sleep well, Mum?'

'Like a log,' she said. 'Dad fidgeted a little but he always does in a strange bed.'

One good thing was that she was so tired, she didn't even hear him snore. The smell of freshly percolated coffee greeted everyone and the aroma of the fresh crusty bread and croissants smelt heavenly. Everyone sat around the kitchen table, munching on breakfast and deciding what they should do today but Katie couldn't wait to show Nan and Gramps around the garden. Dad was quite eager to get outside and take charge of the garden.

'There is quite a lot of work to do but we will do as much as we can whilst we are here.'

'Yes please,' Meg quickly replied, without stopping for breath, 'but there is plenty of time.'

Mum and Dad had a few days to recover from their journey and it wasn't long before the weekend was upon them.

'Would you like to visit some local places of interest? There is so much to see and do here and as the weather is good today, we could have a picnic.'

'How lovely,' Mum said. 'Can I help you with anything, dear?'

'All under control, Mum.'

The boys were in the garden playing football and Simon was making a couple of phone calls whilst Katie was helping Meg hang out some washing.

Meg then grabbed some drinks from the fridge, packed the car and shouted, 'Is everybody ready, shall we go?'

As Gramps was getting into the car, he said to Meg, 'I think you have enough food in the basket for a week, we are only going for the day?'

Everyone laughed and so their journey began. Dinan is a medieval city with plenty of exciting places to see.

'We would like to take you to see Les Ramparts De Dinan.'

Most of the streets in Dinan were cobbled and very quaint. Katie found a sweet shop and as she pulled at her mum's skirt, she asked if they could go inside. She hadn't seen a shop before with so many different sweets.

'Can we have some, Mummy?'

'Of course but only a few. Just pick a few of your favourites.'

The children returned from the shop, clasping their bag of delights. Afterwards, they all strolled alongside the Ramparts and onto the Chateau de Dinan. After much walking, the children started questioning when they were going to eat.

Meg said, 'If we slowly walk up the hill, there is a lovely view overlooking a beautiful river and we could have our picnic there.'

They found the most beautiful spot for lunch and the warm sunshine made it all perfect. They sat, watching hand gliders pass by and Charlie said, 'I would love to do that.'

With fear on Nan's face, she shouted out, 'That looks dangerous—it's a good job they are wearing crash helmets!'

With his usual infectious laugh, Charlie remarked, 'Nan, they are not riding motorbikes.'

Katie was busy finishing off her much-loved piece of chocolate cake. Dad was asleep on the travel rug and Meg was taking in the beautiful scenery with her Mum. Simon and the boys were kicking a football around; all Meg wanted was for this to go on forever—but nobody could see into the future and what it brings.

She didn't want anything to get in the way of giving their children the best start in life. Having arrived back at the house; Reuben sniffed around for his tea and gently flopped into his basket. Finishing a rather late dinner, Simon went over to the post box outside.

Inside was a letter addressed to him. As Simon opened it, he raised his eyebrows. 'Wow,' his hands trembling, 'they have asked me to join the Cycle Club,' he said, his face beaming with delight.

'When,' Meg said with interest.

'Whenever it suits me. Tour de France, here I come!'

Little did she know how this was going to change their lives forever.

Chapter 5

Mum and Meg decided to visit the local Garden Centre and buy some plants. Katie wanted to plant some sunflower seeds, saying they would grow very tall and she would have to keep watering them.

'I will, Mummy, I will.'

When they arrived back, she could see Dad in the distance, hoeing and he seemed to be enjoying himself, whistling as he worked.

'A cup of tea, Dad?'

'Yes please, dear; hoeing is thirsty work!'

'Put a hat on your head; the sun can be very hot during midday.'

Simon was busy pruning back some bushes and trees. Meg shouted to him, ''Don't touch the magnolia tree, that is my tree.'

He turned his head towards her, smiled and said jokingly, 'Well, then you can look after it.'

The children played happily and Reuben was lying stretched out on the lawn. She ran into the house to fetch her camera; she wanted a photo of her family looking so happy, a moment she would always treasure. They could now make a go of living in France.

She just needed the children settled at their new school and everything else, hopefully, would be put in place for a happy future ahead. The garden looked lovely and Mum and Dad had worked very hard. Meg thanked them and told them she would certainly look after it and keep the weeds away.

Dad laughed and said, 'That's a job in itself! There should be plenty of vegetables later and I want to see some photos.'

'Of course, Dad, I will send you some; I will even send you a video so you can watch them grow.'

They all started laughing and at this point, Meg was beginning to feel homesick again, knowing Mum and Dad were catching the ferry back home the next day. Mum wanted to stay longer but said, 'Perhaps next time.'

Simon came into the kitchen with greasy hands. She asked him what he had been up to and he said, 'I was checking out the bike and making sure it is roadworthy.'

She could see the excitement on his face at the thought of riding with the local cycle team.

'When is the Cycle Club out next'? She asked.

'Not sure, possibly next Sunday.'

With the weather a little changeable, a soft breeze was developing into quite a strong and blustery wind when they decided to take a family drive to a pretty little beach along the pink granite coastline. The children wanted to climb the rocks and do some rock pool fishing.

'Let's wait and see what the weather is like when we get there.'

Meg remembered there was a lovely little café overlooking the nearby harbour where they could stop for refreshments and possibly a crepe.

'I can feel my tummy rumbling already,' Gramps said.

It wasn't long before the waves were lashing against the rocks and the seas looked quite stormy and rough. The small fishing boats swayed back and forth and it started to rain heavily. They hurriedly walked along the rocky footpath towards the café.

The smell of crepes cooking made them feel very hungry. As they all sat by the window looking out at the rough seas, they began warming their hands around hot cups of tea and hot chocolate.

When they reached home, Mum and Dad decided to finish their packing. Meg didn't want them to leave because she knew she would miss them again. This was the most challenging time for her, saying goodbye and knowing it would be a while before they came over again. As they were leaving, she asked them to ensure they rang when they arrived home.

'Of course, we will and thank you very much for having us.'

They waved goodbye as they drove steadily down the drive onto the country lane and out of sight, heading for the port. It was late afternoon when Meg saw Phillipe (the teacher from the school) strolling up the path, calling out, 'Bonjour Meg, Bonjour Phillipe.'

He asked if Simon was around.

'Let me take you out into the garden, where he is busy cutting the hedge.'

They both chatted for a while and stood gazing at the garden. Meg ran down and asked if they would like something to drink.

'That would be very kind.'

She hurriedly rushed back with some chilled lemonade and told them she was just about to take Reuben out for his walk, leaving the men discussing timetables for the start of the new school year. When she got back, she saw Simon pumping up the tyres on his bike.

'Just going for a short ride, won't be long.'

As he got on his cycle, Meg shouted, 'Don't forget your helmet, you are not going anywhere without it. Anyway, tea will be ready in one hour or so.'

'Thanks, love. See you in a bit.'

Sometime later and burnt offerings for tea, Simon arrived back.

'Sorry, love. I had a puncture on the roundabout into the village just outside Plancoet.'

'That was a long way,' Meg said in amazement.

'Only 15km there and back. I had to try the bike out. It went well, apart from the puncture, which could happen to anyone at any time.'

'I know but next time take your mobile so I can track you. You are unsure of the roads around here and I get worried. Katie was crying asking where my Daddy has gone.'

After Simon comforted Katie, she then presented him with some burnt Spaghetti Bolognese.

'Where's Charlie and Freddie?'

'Oh, a friend called and they went to the park to play football. The boy's Dad plays Petanque (French Boules) there and a competition is taking place.'

Simon asked if they wanted to go along and watch a game. Reuben looked up as if to say, "I am coming too."

There was still warmth in the evening sun as they idly walked the 1.5km to the park. They were greeted kindly by some of the locals who knew them from their garden party. 'Come over and join us for a drink.'

Meg sat down with a couple of ladies.

'Sorry but my French is still a little shaky, so I may be a little slow in understanding.'

'Don't you worry dear,' one lady told me. 'We will help you as much as you want.'

How kind, Meg thought; she really wanted to practice her French. Everyone, including Simon, would be highly pleased with her effort if she tried harder.

Simon was busy talking to the Mairie. Whenever she saw Henri, he always had a glass of something in his hand! Lovely man, though.

He said to Simon, 'I hear you have been invited to join the cycling club?'

'Yes,' he said with excitement in his voice. 'Do you ride, Henri?'

'You must be joking. What, me on a bike, at my age and my size? Not likely!'

Henri asked Simon if he had ever played Petanque.

'No but it looks a little like the game Bowls played back home in England.'

'Not quite the same but just as good. Would you like to play?'

'I thought you would never ask,' Simon said jokingly.

Simon appeared to be enjoying himself and when the game finished, they all patted him on the back, declaring he played very well. I could hear Katie talking and playing with a little girl.

'Mummy, this is Olivia. She is going to my new school too.'

They walked together, holding hands and skipping happily through the long grass. After a lovely evening meeting some villagers, they walked back home, feeling happy and somewhat tipsy. They opened the front door and as they walked into the hallway, Meg looked into Simon's eyes and told him she loved him very much saying, 'Please never leave us.'

'Not a chance,' as he looked down at her and said, 'I love you too. We have three wonderful children and there is nothing in this whole wide world I could wish for more.'

Feeling a little drunk at this point and perhaps it was the wine talking, she could tell they were both speaking from the bottom of their hearts. They kissed and just stood holding hands before wandering upstairs to bed. Quietly closing their bedroom door and making sure the children were fast asleep, they nestled into each other's arms and made love.

It was beautiful and a special moment. She couldn't remember the last time they were this close. As they fell asleep, they tenderly held each other tightly.

Chapter 6

September had arrived and a slight mist fell over the farmhouse and the leaves began to fall from the trees. There was a chill in the air but she could just about see the sun trying to shine through on this autumn day. The children were all very busy getting ready for the start of the school term.

Breakfast was leisurely for a change because everyone woke up early and the boys' didn't want to miss the school bus. Simon was waiting for his lift from Phillipe, who lived not too far away and kindly said he would pick him up, as he had to pass their home on his way to school.

'You could always cycle to school,' Meg told him with a sarcastic grin!

Simon stared at Meg, realising she was only joking as he picked up his briefcase. He was dressed so casually, no one would think he was a schoolteacher. Jeans, sweater and trainers. *They didn't dress like that in my school days,* Meg thought to herself!

Outside, the sound of a car horn was beckoning for Simon. She kissed him on the cheek and said, 'Do you have everything?'

'Yes, I think so.'

'Good luck, darling.'

There was a slight nervous look on his face as he waved goodbye and the car sped off into the distance. The boys were excited about starting a new school but Katie was a little tearful and needed support and encouragement, telling her everything will be alright.

'Don't forget you will be meeting your friend Olivia,' Meg told her.

Eventually, she stopped crying when Meg told her she might have a swimming lesson later in the week. She must admit sadness came over her as she remembered her first day at her new school but this was different. They were experiencing a new school and a new country and she must admit, this was going to be a challenging time for all of them.

The school bus arrived on time and Charlie and Freddie couldn't wait to board the bus and start their first school day.

'Enjoy your day, boys,' and Katie gave them a little loving wave.

They both shouted, 'Bye Mum, bye Katie,' and waved out as the bus slowly drove away down the country lane.

All packed and Katie was almost ready; all that was left to do was to fetch her packed lunch from the fridge. Meg started the car engine and off they went. Arriving at the school gates, Meg was pleased that Katie had already caught sight of Olivia and they started chatting away. A lady walked over and introduced herself as Esme.

'I'm Olivia's mother.'

'Nice to meet you. I'm Meg.'

Esme could see Meg was a little apprehensive about leaving Katie but she put her hand on her shoulder and invited Meg back to her house for a cup of coffee. Meg told her she had her dog, in the back of the car.

'Bring him too,' Esme remarked.

Meg could see the boys arriving at the school and running around the playground, looking happy and making new friends. Meg kissed Katie as she walked off, holding hands with Olivia.

'Mummy will pick you up at the end of your school day!'

A teacher was standing at the entrance lining up the children for a head count before going inside and disappearing out of sight. Walking back to the car, Meg saw a green van parked on the grass verge outside the school. She thought there were two people sitting inside the vehicle but wasn't sure.

It looked shabby, dirty and covered with mud. She took no more notice and went to get into her car. Adjusting the front mirror, she saw that the green van was ready to drive away. A strange feeling came over her and she felt a little unsure about the vehicle.

It wasn't right somehow. The two people inside were staring at the school. Indeed, something appeared very odd. She followed Esme to her house, which was not far from the school; in fact, it was within walking distance but now the mornings were getting darker, it was best to take the car down the narrow country lane to the school.

Meg entered Esme's house, where there was a log burner glowing.

'Would you like coffee or tea?'

'Coffee, please,' Meg replied.

They both sat chatting and Meg told Esme about her life and job in England. Esme went on to say that she was living on her own with Olivia. Not knowing if there was a man in her life or if she was married, Meg could sense some despondency emerging from her body language and a trembling mouth when she started to talk about Olivia's father.

Meg quickly changed the subject. 'Let's go out for a run tomorrow if the weather is good.'

'I would like that-it has been a while since I have had a good run out.'

'That's settled then, trainers to the ready.'

Having looked pleased with the thought of going for a run, Meg thought she may have made her happy in some small way. She was a couple of years younger than her but could sense some apprehension in her life and could tell she wasn't ready to talk about it.

As Meg walked to the door, she turned and said she would see Esme later when they picked up the girls and was really looking forward to the run tomorrow. Meg couldn't stop thinking about the green van parked outside the school, which looked very out of place.

'Will the van be there when I pick up Katie later this afternoon?'

The rest of the day went very quickly and everything she had planned didn't happen. Meg did, however, manage the washing and prepared the evening meal. It was almost four o'clock and time to pick up Katie. She couldn't wait to get to the school to find out if the green van was there.

As she pulled up, she could see Esme. She waved at me and they walked over to meet the girls. The girls ran out together and Katie fell into my arms. She showed me drawings she had done and was excited about her first day at her new school. We said goodbye to Olivia and Esme and began to drive back home. No green van! Oh well, it could have been parked innocently.

Meg's mind was possibly working overtime and thinking all kinds of strange thoughts. The boys arrived home about 20 minutes later by the school bus and Simon came home a little later. They all sat down together and talked about the day.

Meg was very impressed with how the children had experienced their first day at a French school and knew that before long, Charlie and Freddie would begin to speak much more French and she hoped that Katie would too, possibly with some help from Simon.

She didn't mention the green van parked outside the school to Simon. He would probably laugh at me. The next day, Meg was all geared up in her running kit for a short run with Esme. She dropped off Katie as usual at the school. It was her second day and she was excited and couldn't wait to meet up with Olivia.

'She is my best friend, Mummy. We even sit next to each other and eat our lunches together.'

'That is lovely, Katie but make sure you make friends with the other children too.'

'I will, Mummy but Olivia speaks to me in English most of the time and I can understand her.'

Meg did wonder how she could speak such good English. That, too, was somewhat puzzling her. They both had a run around the village and back which was about 7km taking about one hour. They returned, puffing and panting but still feeling good, considering they both hadn't ran for a while.

'That was a good run, Esme,' Meg remarked with sweat pouring down her face.

'Yes, I enjoyed it and perhaps we can we do it again sometime?'

'Of course, we can!'

As Meg was walking back to the car and feeling good but tired after the run, she still couldn't help thinking about the green van. Could she be wrong about seeing a green van outside the school yesterday morning? Perhaps she was overthinking it but as she did, to her surprise, she could see in the rear-view mirror, a vehicle approaching very fast behind her.

It overtook her on the country lane quite dangerously and to her astonishment, it was the green van and heading straight towards the school. She was on her way to pick up Katie and as she arrived, she could hear the school bell ring and saw Katie running towards her and she was crying very loudly.

'Mummy, Olivia has gone!'

'Gone, what do you mean gone, Katie?'

'A man and a lady came to the school and took her. He said he was her Daddy but the lady wasn't her Mummy!'

Meg was aghast with horror, Katie was uncontrollable and she didn't know what to do next. Esme was on her way to pick up Olivia and Meg didn't know what to say to her. As she glanced around, she could see Esme walking up to the school gates and rushed over to her.

'Esme,' I shouted, 'Katie has just told me that her Daddy and a lady had taken Olivia from school.'

Esme looked shocked but she didn't appear surprised. They walked into the school and spoke to a teacher waiting for Esme. If somebody had taken Katie, Meg would have run as fast as possible into the school but Esme didn't seem to be in a hurry.

'Is there anything she is not telling me?'

The school was going to ring Esme but everything happened so fast and there was some concern in the teacher's voice.

'I understood it was Olivia's daddy, so I didn't overthink it. Olivia even shouted out, calling him Daddy.'

Meg interrupted and said, 'Perhaps we should we call the Police?'

Although Esme was upset and sobbing, she had a definite tone to her voice and said, 'No, I must deal with this in my own way.'

Meg looked rather strangely at her, as she knew if her little girl had been taken even by her father without her consent, she would undoubtedly have gone to the police.

'You must,' she told her. 'They can search for her, especially as he took her without permission.'

'Meg, let me handle this. I believe I know Olivia's whereabouts!'

'Are you saying then it was her daddy who took her?'

'Yes. It's a long story. We aren't married and our relationship didn't work out. He just left us without saying anything; packing up his bags one day saying he was leaving us. No questions, no answers, no goodbyes! His name is Greg and is Olivia's biological father.

'We were living together in what I thought was a relationship going forward. I couldn't believe what was happening to us at the time and always thought he would come back home and everything would be alright.

'Days, weeks, months, he never got in touch with us, not even a phone call to see how they were or asking about Olivia which I thought was very strange. He loves his little girl and would do anything for her. That is why this whole scenario doesn't add up.'

Esme told me that she had heard from a lady in the village that Greg was staying in a caravan just outside St Laurent, about 10kms from Dinan and living with a woman but this lady didn't know anything about the woman, not even her name.

Greg had been seen in the local market several times with her and they had been sighted laughing together. Esme couldn't believe she had never bumped into him. He certainly kept a very low profile. Esme went on to say that she knew he would eventually want to see Olivia and that on several occasions has been seen looking through the school gates and by chance, a couple of times he has been caught speaking to her.

'She had told everyone that he was her daddy. There was no attempt to take her and all seemed very innocent because they were both laughing and joking together. Olivia seemed very happy talking to him but this was the first time he had gone into the school and taken Olivia without my consent,' Esme said with panic in her voice.

'This isn't right Esme,' Meg told her. 'You both need to sit down and discuss parenting arrangements and of course, you must decide your future. You can't go on like this, it is not fair to you and certainly not fair to Olivia. He just cannot go into a school and take her out without your permission. He left you and therefore, you should be in total charge of your daughter.'

'Yes, you are right. I will try and get in touch with him and do my best to work things out.'

There was still a lot she was not telling Meg and there was so much hurt in her voice. Meg kept thinking what she would do if this happened to her. She took hold of Katie's hand and said to Esme, 'Please make sure you get Olivia back and if there is any trouble, you must go to the police.'

'Thank you, Meg but hopefully there will be no need for that.'

They drove back home and Katie was still extremely upset and said, 'Will she be at school tomorrow, mummy?'

Meg didn't know what to say to her, except that she hoped she would be. The boys were already home when they arrived back.

'Where have you been, Mum?'

Katie was unstoppable, she couldn't help but tell them everything about how Olivia had been taken from school by her daddy.

'Can he do this?' Charlie said.

'No, not really but there isn't much we can do about it.'

Eyebrows raised; the boys searched the fridge for food.

'What time is tea, Mum?'

'If you have any schoolwork, I suggest you get on and do it. Tea will be ready once you have done all your homework.'

Fortunately, Simon was home a little later than usual, which gave her more time to get on with dinner. Arriving home, he looked tired, as he went upstairs for a shower. Feeling refreshed after his shower, Meg poured him a cold beer and told him the events of the day.

Dinner over, they sat down to watch some TV snuggling up on the sofa with Reuben. Meg was almost falling asleep when the phone rang. It was Esme. 'I just wanted you to know that I have seen and spoken with Greg and we have had a long chat. He wasn't hard to find as he was staying on a caravan park not too far away and the dirty old green van gave its location away.

'Olivia was with him and the woman was there too. She grinned at me and left us to talk. Olivia seemed happy enough as she was watching television and he had given her a cooked meal.

'We talked for ages and decided that for the sake of our daughter, they had to make permanent arrangements if he wanted to see her. I pleaded with him not to take Olivia again this way without my knowledge. "I just wanted to see her," he said. "We must be grown up about this!" Esme told him that he just can't go ahead and take her like that. "I know I did wrong and it won't happen again." I have now brought her back home with me and she is very tired and sleepy. I am keeping her home from school tomorrow, so could you please tell Katie.'

'Of course,' but Meg felt something was still not quite right.

Chapter 7

A couple of weeks had passed and Simon enjoyed being part of the St Helene Cycling Club.

'Do you know, Meg? I have clocked up almost 150kms since belonging to the club.'

'That's great,' Meg said.

'They hope to do a short tour in the New Year, so I mentioned I could be up for it.'

'That's fine but is the bike up for it?'

'A few adjustments here and there; otherwise, not too bad for a ten-year-old bike or perhaps I could consider investing in a new one.'

'I don't know about that,' Meg replied.

It was now late October and the bright sunny mornings were now beginning to cloud over, with the warm summer days almost leaving them. As Meg drove to the market to do some shopping, she could see that lots of people were getting ready for Halloween, with pumpkins already being displayed on the stalls.

It would be a good idea to have a party to celebrate Halloween. Perhaps she could ask some of the children's school friends and friends from the village. Simon had cut down some hedges and large shrubs from the garden and there was enough to make a vast bonfire, which was an excellent way to get rid of all the rubbish.

They had always celebrated Halloween back in England and she was surprised to see they marked the occasion here as well. It was a couple of days before Halloween and they were all busy carving out pumpkins. As luck would have it, she found some masks and hats at the bottom of a box, which had yet to be unpacked.

She also found some angel hair (fake cobwebs), which she admitted had seen better days and placed it around the front door entrance. Everything was beginning to look scary and creepy, well the children thought so anyway.

To her surprise, quite a few neighbours and school friends from the village turned up. One lady told her she had never been to a Halloween party before and told me that the English certainly knew how to celebrate.

'We certainly do,' Meg told her with a giggle.

Pumpkins were alighted all around the garden, the children wore masks and Katie wore her witch's hat. She was so excited even little Olivia came along and joined in the fun.

'You can wear my hat if you like, Olivia; I can find something else,' Katie replied happily. Esme had brought her along and apologised because she could not stay and could she pick her up later?

'Not a problem.' Meg asked whether Olivia would like to have a sleepover. 'I can bring her to school with Katie tomorrow if that's alright.'

Olivia jumped up with excitement, 'Please Mummy, let me stay.'

'Well, if you don't mind, Meg, as there is something I need to do.'

'Please don't worry; we will look after her.'

As Meg walked over to speak with some of the villagers, the smell of the smoke from the bonfire filled her with her childhood days. There was something about standing around a bonfire, eating a jacket potato in the cold night air, wrapped up warm in coats, hats, gloves and scarves.

She began thinking about her youth, remembering how life hadn't changed that much. Little things in life are the real thing that signifies importance and the memories will always remain forever. It was at that point Meg began, once again, missing Mum and Dad and hoping soon, they would make a return visit to see them all.

It won't be too long before Christmas and she knew they were planning to come over then. As she turned around, she could see that everyone was enjoying the fun, laughter and food. The children were making scary noises, hiding behind the bushes. Another party success by the Johnston's!

Now that everything had settled down for Olivia and she was back happy at school; Meg thought she would visit Esme in the hope they could go for a run together once again. Unusually, Esme seemed to drop her daughter off at the school gates and rush back home.

Perhaps she was busy with her mobile hairdressing or was she trying to avoid me? Meg thought she would call around and see her and invite her to her house for a coffee soon, although she may leave it for a while and let Esme get in touch with her when she was ready.

It was an exciting day for Katie as she was looking forward to her school swimming lesson; perhaps when she was a little older, she may decide to do competitive swimming and compete in local gala events.

'Who knows!'

The twins were busy with school life and to be quite honest, she didn't see much of them until they came back home at teatime. They had quite a lot of homework and played quite a lot of football for the school team; especially now that they had been promoted to a higher league at school-Charlie was their goalie and Freddie played in defence.

Meg felt so proud of her children, mainly because how they had settled into their new life. She couldn't ask for more. Esme had been on her mind for some time now and Meg couldn't wait for Esme to contact her, so she decided she would call and see her. She knocked on the door but Esme took quite a long time to answer.

'Hello,' Meg said, 'how are you?'

'Good thanks, come in.'

Her English was pretty good but Meg couldn't quite understand certain words as she seemed to be gabbling, so she asked her to speak just a little slower. She quietly muttered something as Meg ventured into the kitchen.

Meg thought she said, 'I have been busy lately.'

She then asked her if she would like to come for coffee after school.

'Thursday would be good for me, Meg!'

'Great, it's a date then!'

Meg did, however, find the courage to ask how she had been coping since the trouble she had with Greg.

'I'm fine, Meg,' but as she looked down, she could see her arm was severely bruised and she was holding her side slightly.

'How did you get that bruise on your arm, Esme?'

'Oh, that, it's nothing. I stumbled into a door, that's all.'

Meg was not convinced and couldn't help thinking Esme was not telling her everything. Perhaps this was why she took a long time to answer the door; slowly walking as if in pain.

'Can I look at your side, as I do have relatively good nursing experience from my training as a physiotherapist?'

'No, I am perfectly alright, please do not trouble yourself,' but Meg could see she was hurting inside and out.

'I would be much happier, Esme, if you would get your side checked out.'

'I will Meg, I will.'

They had agreed to meet on Thursday for coffee and Meg was hoping she would seek medical attention sooner, rather than later. Could Greg have done this to her? She wondered if Esme was strong enough and ready to return to her mobile hairdressing and whether she was telling her a white lie to cover up something more disturbing.

Meg wanted to get to the bottom of this without appearing too inquisitive. She just wanted to be there for Esme as a friend. She told her she would have the coffee pot ready on Thursday morning.

Esme struggled with a laugh and said, 'I will be there.'

Meg decided to drive into the town and pick up some shopping. As she walked over to the Boucherie (butchers' shop), she felt a soft tap on her shoulder. It was Dr Bernier.

'Hello, how are you?' He was dressed in casual clothes. It looked as if he had been out for a run. His sweaty tanned forehead and damp hair were a giveaway. 'It's my day off and I wanted to get a couple of things for my journey next week.'

'Are you going away?' Meg muttered.

'I am taking my niece, Alice to Bordeaux for a few days.'

As they talked and walked, they passed the florist.

'Do you like flowers?' He asked.

'My favourite are roses,' Meg said with a cheeky grin.

'I shall have to see what I can do!' As he stared into Meg's eyes, they both stood silent for a moment.

Meg then said with some nervousness in her voice, 'I hope you have a safe trip to Bordeaux, Dr Bernier.'

'Please call me Louis; we know each other well enough for first-name terms.'

Meg was thoroughly enthralled by his remark, which sent her heart beating fast. What was happening? Every time she saw him, she turned to jelly.

Come on, Meg, snap out of it, she thought to herself.

As they were saying goodbye, Meg asked him if he goes running often.

'Yes, I do; I belong to the St Helene Running Club.'

'I like running too,' Meg said with eagerness in her voice.

'Well, if you want, I can register you for the club when I return from Bordeaux.'

Meg beamed with total excitement.

'I would like that very much!'

As she was driving back, she began to feel like a total wreck.

'Louis Bernier, what are you doing to me? I am married with three children, for heaven's sake. Was this infatuation? I hope so.'

The winter nights were certainly drawing in and it was dark by four o clock. She was planning their first Christmas in France and hoping to invite Mum and Dad over for the festive period. The children would love to see their Nan and Gramps again and it would be lovely if they could be altogether for what she hoped would be a Joyeux Noel (Happy Christmas).

Thursday morning and she had arranged a coffee morning with Esme. It must have been around ten thirty, when she saw Esme at the entrance of the driveway. She still appeared to be in some pain as she slowly ambled up towards the house.

Meg opened the door and asked, 'Are you okay?'

She reached out and grabbed her hand for some guidance as they walked inside.

'How are you feeling?' She said she felt much better. Um, but Meg wasn't quite so sure!

'Sit down and I will get you some coffee.'

They sat and chatted for some time before she learnt the truth about Greg. Greg was in the Royal Navy and had been all over the world. He was 32 years of age when leaving the Navy and they met when he came to France on holiday. They travelled to the south and Greg would spend quite a lot of money in the casinos, losing more than he won.

They were having a good time, meeting friends and living the good life but it wasn't long before she fell pregnant with Olivia. At this time, Greg decided to move over to France permanently. He was undoubtedly very protective over Esme whilst she was pregnant and she couldn't ask for more.

Life was good for a short time when Olivia was born but money was scarce. Greg was working at a local garage, repairing and servicing cars. He would come home at night tired and didn't want to help much with the baby. He would get annoyed at the baby crying and didn't give her any rest time when perhaps it was needed.

It would make her angry and bad-tempered and saying things she shouldn't have said. They would argue and life became unbearable. Greg would lash out at her, hitting and shaking her. She felt he was taking his anger out on her because Olivia was always crying. It got to the point where she had enough.

'You either stop your hurtful ways or you leave both of us,' Esme told him.

He would turn around, smirk at her and tell her it was her fault she got pregnant. Esme was tearing up as she was describing her life with Greg. Meg had all these thoughts going on in her head. How could anyone do this to such a sweet person? Esme was 5ft nothing and mostly skin and bones. How would she be able to defend herself?

Meg sat there just listening to her and feeling such trepidation. She said that one day he came home from work and said things would change and that he was very sorry for how he treated her. He told her he would seek help and get some counselling to help with his anger issues and bad behaviour. Esme explained to him that she could help.

He turned and said, 'I think I will need some support, Esme.'

'Of course, I will be here for you no matter what.'

Life continued and they were good, especially when he became Manager at the local garage. The boss put him in charge of three men, which was the kind of authority he needed. He adored Olivia and would take her out for walks, play with her and read her bedtime stories and even take time to give her a bedtime bath.

Esme was now thinking everything would be good with hem and he was seeking help for his anger. But how wrong she was! It wasn't long before his anger would emerge once again.

'Why is he doing this to me? What have I done?'

She didn't seem to have any answers and nobody she could turn to. Her family lived in Paris and the friends she did have at the time somehow didn't believe in her. What was she going to do? Then one day, out of the blue, he just came home from work, left some money on the table, said goodbye to them and just walked out of the door, never to be seen again.

In total amazement, Esme didn't know what to do. Her only thought was for Olivia and how was she going to tell her that Daddy had left them.

'Oh no, Esme, how awful! How did you resolve the problem?'

'I did nothing. I was hoping Greg would return but never did, until recently when they agreed to meet and discuss Olivia. I could see the proposition I was giving him wasn't what he wanted to hear. He wanted the best of both worlds, wanting to see Olivia when it suited him but I told him my life had changed and I didn't want him in my life anymore.

"What about our daughter?" he said in an outraged voice.

"You should have thought of that when you left us!"

'At this point, he slapped me around the face, pushing me to the ground, continually hitting, stamping and punching me. I thought several times I was going to die. Eventually I got back up, feeling extremely shaky and faint.

'He gave me a weird glance and with a suppressed laugh, he then walked away, out of the door and that was the last time I saw him. I just kept thinking to myself, when will this end!'

'But Esme, haven't you ever had the courage to go to the police?'

'Oh no, Meg, I was fearful for myself and Olivia too. I didn't want anything to jeopardise that. I know now that was wrong but at the time, all I wanted was to make sure he wouldn't come back and hurt us. The physical and mental abuse was starting all over again.'

She told Meg that she had to work everything out for herself making sure she was doing the right thing for both her and Olivia.

'You must have gone through hell, Esme.'

'Well Meg, it wasn't the best time of my life I can tell you!'

Meg said that she would always be there for her if she needed help in any way and never be afraid to call day or night.

'Thank you Meg. I am very lucky to have you as a good friend.'

Chapter 8

December was quite busy for them and there was so much to do to get everything ready for the festive season. Mum and Dad were coming over the week before and many activities were taking place at the school. Simon was helping the drama group with a play put on by the pupils at the school and Katie was making paper decorations to display in her classroom.

Meg was filling up the freezer with goodies as you do at this time of year. Simon was getting the Christmas tree from Henri Pascall who had contacts and supplied most of the villagers with trees.

'Not what you know but who you know,' he told Simon.

Meg spoke with Simon and asked if she could ask Esme and Olivia over for Christmas. She believed they would be on their own and the thought of that made her feel sad. Simon was aware of what had happened during the past weeks with Esme and her partner and was only too pleased that she had thought of her this way.

'Of course, you can darling,' he said, 'but you had better speak to Esme and make sure she hasn't made other arrangements.'

Meg couldn't wait to speak with her and ask if she would like to spend Christmas with them. Esme was saying goodbye to Olivia when Meg approached her. She told me that her parents and brother live in Paris and it was always difficult to visit because of the distance and cost.

'I know one day I will have to endeavour to make an effort but now I cannot face them with my problems.'

'I understand and because we wouldn't want you to be on your own, the family would like to invite both of you to spend Christmas with us.'

Her eyes brightened and a slight smile grew into a very pleasing and happy face. 'I don't know what to say!'

'Yes would be a good start,' Meg said laughingly.

They both stood there smiling as this was the first time in ages that Esme looked untroubled and a radiant glow filled her sad face once again. Christmas Eve, Mum and Dad had settled in to celebrate the festive season with them and the children were helping Simon decorate the tree and erect the lights in the garden.

It was going to look lovely, Meg thought. She wanted it to be special for their first Christmas at Fleurs de Pre. Mum was busy stuffing the turkey and Dad was chopping wood for the fire. Meg was busy making trifles and preparing tasty little entrees.

Her iPad was playing Christmas carols which she had downloaded and they all had the Christmas spirit, as they say. Suddenly, there was a knock on the door. It was Dr Bernier!

'Bon Noel,' Meg said with a slight giggle.

'I have just popped in with a bunch of flowers and a Christmas message.'

Meg didn't know what to say.

'You did mention you like roses, so I thought a rose for a rose!'

Meg must have gone blood red but she could see he was only being friendly; well, she thought he was! Again, she was feeling a slight nervousness between them. It was a nice feeling, nevertheless. Meg asked if he would like to come and have a Christmas drink with the family.

'If you are not too busy.'

'Not at all, please come in.'

She introduced Louis to Mum, who had breadcrumbs stuck all over her hands. She brushed her hands down the sides of her apron before shaking hands but he just leaned over and kissed her on both cheeks.

'What a lovely gentleman,' Mum muttered quietly. 'Delighted to meet you,' she said.

Dad entered the room carrying some logs for the fire and Louis helped him balance the logs before some fell to the floor. They both shook hands and introduced themselves. Meg then asked how Louis would spend Christmas. He told them he was spending it with his niece, Alice and excitedly said he was taking her to the ice rink in Dinan, which was only in operation during the festive season.

Many locals took their children for a skate around during Christmas time. It had become trendy for all ages and it also gave the town some income to help towards the year ahead.

What a great idea, Meg thought.

She could take Katie and the boys; knowing they would enjoy it. Not too sure about Simon, though! She then asked Louis about his trip to Bordeaux.

'We had a great time and Alice loved being taken to the Zoo de Bordeaux Pessac, where she saw the big cats, wolves, giraffes and pandas. We also took a boat trip down the Garonne. We saw so much in such a short time with still plenty to see and do, so I am planning to revisit again one day.'

As Louis was edging towards the door, he wished them all a good family Christmas and told Meg he hoped he would see her at the Running Club.

'Yes,' Meg said with much delight. 'I shall need a run after all the food consumed over the next week or so.'

As he walked away, he waved and wished the family Bon Noel. Meg replied in her not so French accent, 'Bon Noel Louis.' Wow that was a surprise; she didn't expect to see him today.

Louis had given her a bunch of lovely roses, which Katie immediately put into a vase and placed on the hallway table.

'Why did he give you roses, Mummy?'

'I don't know, Katie. Perhaps. Daddy will get the message,' Meg said with a sarcastic grin.

Simon and the boys finished decorating the garden and came into the house, feeling cold and hungry.

'Was that the doctor who just popped in?'

'It was,' she said and Katie couldn't wait to tell her Daddy that the doctor had brought Mummy some flowers.

Simon smiled and said, 'I wanted to come inside to say hello but I was muddy and I wanted to finish the lighting before it got dark.'

Mum had made some homemade soup and they all sat down to a warm and welcoming lunch, with the smell of Christmas food circling around the kitchen. It was going to be the best Christmas ever.

Meg left Mum in charge of finishing the washing up and Dad sat in the chair with a book but it didn't take him long to fall asleep. His book fell to the floor and he was well away. They decided to take the dog for a walk as darkness began falling. It was starting to get frosty and a little icy underfoot with the temperature now falling below freezing.

Perhaps it may snow, Meg thought.

That would make it the perfect Christmas. They were gone about half an hour, returning with red noses and you could see their breath mingle into the cold night air. As they entered the warmth of a lovely home, they heard the boys and Katie sat laughing with Nan and Gramps.

Both were now awake and feeling refreshed but soon to be tired again by the constant antics of Katie and the boys wanting Gramps to play games. Katie asked Gramps to read to her and all Meg could see was the enjoyment on his face when he was with them. The love of a Gramps with his grandchildren is precious— you can never, ever take that away.

She decided to give Esme a ring saying they were looking forward to seeing her on Christmas Day. She told me she was feeling a little tired but was napping on the sofa whilst Olivia was playing with her doll's house. Meg felt some concern whilst they were talking but Esme reassured her everything was okay.

'We are looking forward to spending the day with you,' she replied softly.

Later that evening, they placed the children's stockings alongside the fireplace and everything looked very Christmassy. After a short time, Mum and Dad went upstairs to bed and both she and Simon sat in front of the fire just thinking about their first Christmas in France.

Did they make the right decision? At this moment, they both said to each other, 'I think we did.'

Downstairs, the aroma of the Turkey roasting in the oven was just like the old days when she was young—these were the things she remembered about her childhood and she wanted the same for her family. She always said Christmas was about family.

The sheer delight as the children walked downstairs on Christmas morning took her breath away. To watch her loved ones enjoy the festivities of Christmas, opening their presents, the love and joy which descended on their little faces was priceless.

Even Reuben was tenderly chewing on his new bone and strutting around the house with a new fluffy toy. Mum, Dad and Simon were swapping presents.

'Not more socks,' Simon replied with a giggle.

'You can never have enough socks, my dear,' Mum replied with hilarity in her voice.

Just around midday, the doorbell rang. Katie ran as fast as her little legs would carry her, nearly slipping on the tiled floor in the hallway and with an excited voice, she couldn't wait to open the door. Both little girls were so pleased to see each other. Meg could see that Esme had been crying and looked very pale.

'Are you OK?' She asked her.

'No, not really. Greg came over early this morning to see Olivia and asked if he could spend the day with her. I told him that would not be possible as they had made other plans. I didn't tell him where we were going; just in case Greg decided to come over and cause a scene.

'He wasn't pleased and pushed me to one side and let himself into the house. He could see Olivia playing happily with some toys and tried to coax her into going with him.

'She cried out, "Mummy, why is Daddy here?"

"It's alright, Olivia, he just came to see you on Christmas Day."

'He gave Olivia a present, kissed her on the cheek and rudely pushed past by, leaving without saying a word to us. Meg, I think he is going to attempt something awful and I am terrified! What should I do?'

'Let's all sit down after lunch and whilst the children play, we can talk about how to tackle this terrible situation.'

'Thank you, Meg; I don't know what I would have done without you. I have nobody else I can turn to!'

They spent the rest of the day eating and drinking lots of wine as the children played happily in the other room. Mum and Dad decided to go upstairs for a nap after drinking a little too much wine. It was now an excellent time to speak with Esme about Greg.

She appeared happier after their little talk but agreed that it was for her to resolve their differences and that it may be worse if they became involved. Feeling sorry for her, they told her they were there if she needed them. She smiled and there was evidence that she was feeling a little less anxious after their little chat.

Esme left with Olivia later that evening. Meg told her to ring when they arrived home as she was still worried for them both. What if he was waiting for them when they returned to their house?

Simon placed his hands on both Meg's shoulders and said, 'You must let her sort this out herself. I don't want you getting too involved just in case he could become violent.'

'I know Simon but what if he hurts them? I would never forgive myself if anything happened and I wasn't there to help them.'

Fifteen minutes later, Esme phoned to say they were both safely home. A sigh of relief escaped Meg but she told Esme to make sure she locked all the doors and windows just in case he decided to return.

Christmas was over and Mum and Dad had now travelled back to England and were experiencing their typical English winter weather—rain, wind and cold temperatures. They had cold, sunny, frosty mornings but the crisp days meant they could get about and discover parts of the region they hadn't seen before.

The children were due to return to school in the middle of January so they could enjoy some quality family time. Meg was running relatively low on provisions, so she popped into the market and as she walked past the florist, she could see Danielle waving.

'It has been a long time since we last met,' Meg said.

'Yes, it has,' Danielle replied. 'Why not bring your lovely family over one evening after I finish here at the shop and I will cook supper. It would be my way of introducing you to St Helene and I will invite a couple of friends I know who would like to meet you and your family. Let's say Saturday at 6 o'clock.'

'Sounds perfect!'

Meg was looking forward to some lie-ins before everybody went back to school. She hadn't slept too well since Christmas possibly because she was worried about her friend and kept repeatedly saying to Simon that she was getting quite concerned about them.

'Do you think they will be okay?'

Simon wavered slightly before answering, 'I think so,' but she questioned his remark by saying everything can change and he may harm them both with all that anger he seems to carry.

'I know, darling but as we told her, we can only help if she wants us to.'

Meg always felt at ease when she was with Simon; he would always put her mind at rest. She looked up at him, kissed him and said, 'I love you so very much.'

'What me?' Turning, he said, 'I love you more.'

Chapter 9

Brittany was experiencing some of the worst winters they had ever had and Meg couldn't believe it; heavy snow was forecast. She was told that it was quite rare for Brittany to have snow, due to its mild climate, so it could be said that they had brought the British weather along with them.

It was extremely cold and early mornings were very frosty and icy. *Climate change has a lot to answer for,* Meg thought. Simon was busy chopping wood yet again for the fire and planning his timetable for the next term. She quickly decided to take the children out of the way so he could have some peace.

She remembered Doctor Bernier talking about the ice rink in Dinan and thought maybe the children would like a visit before it closes at the end of January.

Meg shouted, 'I am going to take the children to the ice rink.'

'Good idea! Have a lovely time and I will have a meal ready for you when you return. Drive carefully, it could be icy out there,' but as he spoke, she noticed gentle snowflakes falling to the ground.

She called out, 'See you later—we won't be too long.'

They arrived at a packed ice rink and were in the queue, ready to get their boots, when they saw Esme and Olivia.

'Hi there, fancy seeing you here!'

Esme was busy watching Olivia and holding on to her very precariously as they skated gingerly around the rink. Meg, too, was holding on to Katie though the boys were finding it relatively easy to keep their balance but she called out to them in a witty tone, 'Please be careful; you aren't Torvill and Dean yet!'

Out of the blue, Meg could see Esme talking to a man. That's him—it must be. She remembered a resemblance to the man in the green van. It was Greg and they were laughing altogether and looked very happy, which surprised her.

She skated over and Esme glanced at her and whispered, 'Having talked at great length, decided they will get back together again. He told me he was a changed man and would never hurt me again and have to think of Olivia at a time like this.'

Meg couldn't believe what she was hearing. After what he had put her through, she would forgive him and give him another chance. She was at a loss to know why. Oh well, not her business and hoped she was doing the right thing. Meg hugged her and told her that if she wanted to talk or even go for a run later in the week, give her a call.

'That would be lovely,' she said in a calm but declining voice and perhaps then she could enlighten her on how everything had changed. As they left the ice rink, the snow fell quite hard. The children were so excited about seeing snow.

'I didn't think they had snow in France,' Freddie said.

'Snow is rare in Brittany, so make the most of it, kids.'

'Mummy, we can make a snowman when we get back.'

'Perhaps!'

All she wanted to do was sit in front of a glowing fire and get warm. It was very treacherous driving back. The windscreen wipers were finding it difficult to clear the snow but they eventually got home after what should have been a thirty-minute drive, took over an hour.

When they arrived back at the house, the snow was thick and she could see Simon peering through steamy windows, looking out for them. He opened the door and greeted them with open arms.

'I was worried you were finding it difficult to drive through the lanes with the snow getting deeper.'

Simon put his arms around them all and wandered into the kitchen to the smell of a casserole cooking in the oven.

'What have I done to deserve a wonderful man like you?'

The children didn't even take their coats off before they ran out into the garden and began making their snowman and Reuben decided he would help too. Meg called them and said it was getting rather dark, so hurry up. Handing Katie a carrot for the nose, she placed her scarf around the neck of the snowman.

'What do you think, Mummy?'

'Looks lovely; now come along and have some tea.'

It was bitter cold and Meg told the children there was a good chance the snow would still be there in the morning. They sat and chatted around the kitchen table. Katie was excited at seeing Olivia at the ice rink and Meg started to explain to

Simon about the body language emanating between Esme and Greg, as if nothing had happened.

They appeared to be enjoying themselves, laughing and joking with each other but was this for the benefit of Olivia? She was deeply concerned. What was going on?

Simon then interrupted and said, 'Letting them get on with their own lives would be best. If that is what Esme wants, then there is nothing more we can do or say.'

'I know but it is getting to me.'

'How can you treat someone like that one day and then the next, everything is alright? I don't understand!'

'The trouble with you, Meg, is that you are so caring and thoughtful but you must remember not everyone is like you. She will soon let us know if she needs us or wants help. Don't forget you haven't known her for that long; you just happened to be there for her when she needed someone to talk to.'

Of course, he was right, he always is. The next day I could hear the children calling out. Where had all the snow gone? The scarf was lying semi-frozen on the ground and the mushy carrot was lying close by. Katie looked sad at the sight of their melting snowman.

Meg thought the snow was here to stay for a little longer but the light rain and the warmer temperature had started a slow thaw. The roads were still extremely treacherous and very icy but the sun was beginning to shine through the trees.

'Well, kids, no more snow for a while.'

'Ah! It was fun whilst it lasted.'

Walking back into the house, she saw snowdrops popping up through the hedgerows. They looked so pretty; she knew spring was just around the corner.

'Remember, everyone; we are going to Danielle's tonight for a meal.'

'Haven't forgotten,' Simon shouted out from upstairs.

They were all looking forward to meeting some of her friends. Arriving on time at Danielle's, she was standing in the doorway, ready to greet them. They all did the French thing, a kiss on each cheek—such a lovely greeting. They stepped inside a lovely warm room with beautiful flowers arranged throughout the house.

Meg supposed if Danielle was a florist and could display them beautifully, then there was always an abundance of flowers in her home. The white orchids looked stunning in the hallway on the dark wooden sideboard, giving out a magnificent aroma which filled the air with an exquisite perfume.

As they sat talking, there was a knock on the door. They could hear laughter when Danielle greeted them. Meg instantly knew the couple were English. Danielle ushered them into the room and introduced them.

'Ruth, David, please meet Meg and Simon.'

They both stood up and shook hands. They told us they had no children and had been living in France for the past eight years. They appeared to be a lovely couple but were a little older than us, possibly in their mid-60s. Both were retired and living the good life. They owned a house on the other side of Dinan in a little village called Lanvallay.

'We love it here and wouldn't go back to England now or ever. The lifestyle is second to none, with no more frantic running around. Easy life and very stress-free.'

Meg looked at Simon and they knew this was one of the reasons they left the UK and said, 'We couldn't agree more.'

Simon told them he was a teacher and their future here in France as a family had so much more to offer them. They were very interested too in my occupation as a physiotherapist. David asked in a comical tone if Meg could massage his troubled back.

'Why not,' I laughed out loud, knowing the wine was beginning to have its evil way with me, before settling down to a delicious meal. They sat chatting for ages before it was time to go. The children were looking a little bored with all the talking and Meg wanted them to have a couple of early nights before school started again on Monday.

Having exchanged phone numbers, they arranged to meet up at some point. Thankfully, Simon only had one glass of wine so that he could drive us home. Meg, on the other hand, not so good and Simon knew she had far too much and would suffer the next day. He was right!

She did suffer the next day—the sound of the breakfast dishes being pushed around the table, the dog barking, children arguing.

'My head is like a spinning wheel,' she said.

Monday morning and everyone had to be on top of things because it was the first day of the new school term, everyone was busy bustling around the house, hoping they didn't forget anything. Katie was feeling excited at the thought of seeing Olivia. How smart they all looked and so grown up in their uniforms.

Simon rushed out of the door when he saw Phillipe and he looked back to say, 'Have a good day at school, kids and we will catch up later this evening.'

As Meg approached the school gates with Katie, she turned to me and said, 'Mummy, where is Olivia?'

She hadn't arrived and Katie wanted to wait for her. One of the teachers came over and whispered to her that Olivia would not be coming back to school. They had left for England. What left for England! How, why, when! So many questions I needed answers to.

Katie looked back at her on the school steps and was tearful at the thought of not seeing Olivia. The teacher quietly led the children into the school and Meg just stood in the playground in absolute amazement—what on earth was going on?

Were Esme and Olivia in trouble? Esme hadn't even rang her to let her know her plans. Was she forced into a decision by Greg? Meg despaired at the thought. Hoping Esme would ring her at some point or make contact. Greg had family in England; perhaps they thought they could start a new life there.

However, she did feel very uneasy about the whole situation. She decided to go to the caravan park where she knew Greg was staying and taking matters into her own hands, chose to drive to St Laurent.

Meg found this neglected-looking caravan at the far end of a field which she thought could be where Greg and the woman were staying. Luckily, as she drove up alongside, she could see someone's shadow walking inside.

She nervously strolled up to the van and knocked on the door. A lady opened the door ajar and began speaking in French.

'Bonjour,' she asked her if she spoke English and she said just a little. She looked somewhat shabby-her long unruly hair looked like it hadn't seen a brush in ages and her dressing gown needed a wash and had seen better days. She looked pale, holding a half-lighted cigarette and looked very surprised to see a stranger knocking at her door.

Having made some conversation, she did, however, reluctantly ask me inside. There were dirty dishes on the side and the caravan didn't look like it had seen a vacuum in days, let alone a duster. Meg asked if she and Greg were together.

'No, just friends. I was just someone he could lean on when he was troubled. He had become challenging and very reticent, just staring out of the window and not engaging in talk with me at all. Then one morning, he just got up and left, saying nothing, not even a note. *Same old tactics,* I thought. His passport was missing, all his clothes and some money had gone too.

'I remember him saying to me a few days back that he was missing his daughter and intended to get her back no matter what. Greg told me that sometimes he would lose his temper with Esme, sometimes uncontrollably and would resort to hitting her.

'What upset him the most was when Esme screamed out loud and Olivia was in the other room. She had come out, shaking and crying, telling her Daddy to stop.'

Poor Olivia must have been very frightened. Why would he do such a thing? She thought Greg felt very remorseful and wanted to make it up to them. He did say he loved Esme but couldn't help his uncontrollable temper, which he always seemed to take out on poor Esme.

The woman then said that, reading between the lines and different things he had told her, assumed he had taken them both back to England to try and sort things out and hopefully start a new life.

Meg kept thinking to herself, what she was being told didn't seem right and she was hoping and praying they were not being taken anywhere by force. Are they in danger? She began to feel terrified and distraught. She remembered Esme telling her that he had physically abused her and on a couple of occasions, she had to seek medical help.

Meg was beginning to feel very frightened for Esme and Olivia's safety. There was no way someone could change and become a different person in such a short time. On the other hand, perhaps Greg was trying to change for the best and there wasn't any need for concern. Meg stepped back and turned to the door, thanking the lady for the information.

'You have been very helpful!'

What a day! She needed a strong drink to calm down her nerves and returned home feeling slightly anxious, somewhat bewildered and bothered by what the woman said. Reuben was barking as always when he heard a car driving up to the house.

She just sunk back into the kitchen chair and sat drinking a glass of wine with Reuben at her feet, staring out the window but she couldn't help wondering whether Esme and her little girl were in trouble. She needed something to take her mind off the dilemma she was finding herself in, so she wanted to check to see if the doctor had registered her at the gym as he had said he would.

Meg went online and her name was there. All she had to do was activate and confirm her name and address and her card would be waiting for her at the gym.

Training would be difficult as she hadn't done much since arriving in France except for a bit of running with Esme, so although she was looking forward to working out, she was a little apprehensive but a short run should do the trick.

The next day was going to be hard but she was up for it. With a little run to get her in the mood, she strolled to the gym. Inside, she was met by a receptionist who showed her where she had to go. It was huge inside, much bigger than the one back home in Hampton Deverell but fewer people were participating, so Meg didn't feel intimidated in any way.

Speaking with a Trainer who asked her many questions about her health, gave her an exercise sheet to follow. Working on the exercise bike for around 10 minutes, then the treadmill for 10 minutes, finishing up on the bench, was certainly doing the job!

'You are good! Keep it going and you will soon be up to 30 minutes for each exercise.' Feeling exhausted and sweaty, Meg knew she had worked out but she had to admit she was feeling great. She drank two bottles of water and needed more. She went to the café and suddenly felt someone tapping her shoulder.

'Hello Meg,' a voice said.

Turning around, she saw it was Louis Bernier.

'Oh, hello,' Meg apologising for her sweaty look and thanking him for getting her registered at the gym.

'No problem, I hope you enjoy it. I am working at the hospital for the next two weeks, so I am taking advantage of a workout beforehand.'

'Oh, do you work at the hospital often?'

'Yes, quite frequently. I put in four 10-hour shifts monthly, which helps out with the staffing issues they have.' He then asked if she would like a drink.

'That's very kind, yes, please!'

Bumping into him like this was beginning to become a habit. She still didn't know whether he was single, married, divorced or what. Oh, how she would like to know. *It was nothing more than curiosity; um or so* she thought.

As the weeks went by, although she was keeping busy with getting the house straight and going to the gym, the garden had to wait a little bit because of the weather. She was speaking to Simon about how she would like to return to work. She wanted to continue her physiotherapy here in France if she could.

She was missing regular contact with people, especially now Esme was not around. Part-time would be good to fit in with the busy household schedule.

'Why not?' Simon said. 'It may be a good idea to find out more about whether your diploma is accepted here in France first though. They have a system which is not quite the same as ours back in England.'

'Good idea, I will go online and possibly pay the hospital a visit and find out more information.'

Chapter 10

Sunday morning and Simon was preparing for his cycle ride with the Club.

'How far is the next cycle ride?' Meg asked.

'I expect they will cover around 20kms but the weather is a prominent factor. The wet roads can be dangerous, especially along the narrow country lanes.'

It sometimes worried her when Simon was out on the bike. The speed they travel in the group was frightening and they all seemed to be cycling very close. Her thoughts then turned to Mum and Dad and she decided to ring them to see how they both were.

'Hi Mum, how are you?'

'Not too bad but Dad has a chest infection and is off to the doctor tomorrow. I have told him to take things easy and rest.'

'Good but is he ok?'

'With some antibiotics, he should get over it.'

It was now Meg wished she was back home with her family. She felt utterly useless not being able to be there with them.

'You mustn't worry, dear. Dad will be okay. The winter has been quite bad for us, it has been bitterly cold with lots of rain and it has been very windy. There has been some flooding in the village.'

Mum went on to say that she hadn't seen rain like this in a long time. Meg told her they had snow in Brittany and the children loved it.

'I expect they did,' Mum replied. 'How are the children getting on at school?'

'They love it and it is surprising how quickly they all pick it up.'

She told Mum that she was considering returning to work as a physiotherapist, possibly a part time post. Mum then suggested that sometimes the local Sports Centres, gyms and even doctor surgeries need Physiotherapists.

'I will certainly give this some thought.'

They seemed to talk for ages and told her to take care of Dad.

'Don't worry, he is in good hands! I will ring you and let you know the outcome.'

'Please do, Mum!'

As Meg put the phone down, she felt a tear trickling down her cheek. She was worried about Dad who suffered from asthma and a chest infection could be serious. Wouldn't it be lovely if they decided to sell up and come over to France and live?

She would be on hand for them as they get older and she knew the children would be over the moon. Talking with Mum, she decided to make some enquiries at the gym to see if there were any vacancies for a physiotherapist. She had even decided to visit the local hospital in Dinan.

She knew different countries have different processes than they have in England when looking for work, so it was worth trying. She drove into Dinan and saw the arrows marked for the hospital. She made her way to the other side of the town and followed all the signs. The hospital was huge. It had many buildings within the hospital grounds.

Meg could see the sign for physiotherapy but thought it better to go to the main entrance. Many people were bustling around; it seemed extremely busy but then hospitals always are. The building looked quite old but inside it had a very contemporary look—a lovely visiting area and a café where visitors could sit and relax.

Walking towards the Reception desk, I heard a voice shout out, 'Meg, is that you?'

She turned around and it was Dr Bernier.

He asked, 'What are you doing here? Is everything alright?'

Meg told him she would like to know how or where she could get some information on part-time work.

'I have good qualifications but I wonder if they would mean the same here in France as they do back home in England?'

'Come with me, let's walk over to the café and perhaps they could chat. Would you like a cup of coffee from the vending machine?'

'I would, thank you!'

They sat talking for a while and he told her they were very short of all kinds of nursing skills, especially in the physiotherapy department.

'Let me see what I can do! I may know someone who could help you.'

Leaving the hospital grounds, he asked if Simon was up for the cycle ride on Sunday.

'He enjoys riding with the club and is getting excited about the tour next month from Dinan/Nantes and then Nantes back to Dinan.'

Louis told her they would be covering around 200km and it will be a complex cycle ride but hopefully enjoyable. They needed more training so that Sunday would be a test for them. Tell him to get a good night's sleep the night before.

Louis was finishing his shift at the hospital, so they walked back to their respective cars together. Looking exhausted, he told her he hadn't slept for two nights due to a hefty work schedule. 'I need some sleep as I am looking forward to having Alice tomorrow.'

'That will be nice for you.'

'Thank you. I enjoy spoiling her and spending time together.'

What a powerful bond he had with Alice and she couldn't help thinking he treated her more like a daughter than a niece. He was indeed very kind and thoughtful towards her.

'Perhaps one day we will get to meet Alice,' Meg said.

They both agreed that before the bad weather settled in, they would arrange for the two girls to meet with each other. After my sudden meeting with Dr Bernier, driving back I inadvertently missed the turning to St Helene.

A beautiful cottage was for sale and nestled in a pretty little hamlet. She got out of the car and wandered over to take a look. It would be perfect for Mum and Dad. They hadn't shown any interest in moving to France but she noticed how much they loved it here when they visited them at Christmas.

She decided to take some photos to send them to her Mum and Dad. The back garden was manageable and not too big, with a courtyard to the front. It was just big enough for them. The house seems to have been renovated inside and out so she took the details from the information board outside to make some enquiries.

Meg looked at her watch. Goodness, it was nearly 4 o'clock and she had to fetch Katie from school, arriving just as the children came down the steps. Katie ran over to her and they drove back home, chatting all the way, like they do.

Dinner was later than usual as the boys had football training and Simon wanted to ensure his bike was ready for the Sunday cycle run. Meg thought to herself that he was spending more time in the garage than anywhere else. She couldn't complain; he just seemed to be so happy.

She took him out a cup of tea and said, 'Dinner will be ready in an hour.'

'Ok, love,' having told her he had nearly finished checking the bike.

'Is the bike OK then?' she asked.

'Yes, it is in tip-top condition.'

She wandered back into the house to finish preparing the dinner. The boys came in from football training, dirty and muddy. She shouted, 'Take those boots off and leave them on the porch for cleaning.'

They took off their dirty kit, ready for the washing machine and went upstairs for a hot shower before sitting down at the dinner table. Life was beginning to feel somewhat chaotic but in a good way. Always something to do but she wasn't complaining as it was nothing like back home with the constant traffic congestion and volume of people.

They were now experiencing a change in their lives and the things it had to offer a family like theirs. They were doing what they wanted but in her heart, she always knew they would always be there for friends and family back in England should they need their help. They are English, after all and nothing would change that.

Simon was up and about early for the early morning training session with the cycle club. They all sat down to a good breakfast and wished him good luck.

'You are going to need it,' Charlie said.

Freddie was a little more sympathetic. 'I am proud of you, Dad! I want to join a club like yours one day.'

'Perhaps when you are a little older, son!'

Simon kissed them all goodbye and off he went on his ride.

Katie shouted out, 'Have a nice time, Daddy.'

'Thank you, Poppet.'

Meg decided to give Mum and Dad a ring and show them the photos she had taken of the cottage for sale. Meg decided she would ring Esme to enquire if she was alright. The clouds were moving very quickly and she could see patches of blue sky peeping through. She hoped it didn't rain, mainly for the cycle club training.

Nothing worse than cycling in the rain. Meg poured a coffee and sat down to make her phone calls. She phoned Esme first, hoping she was available for a chat. The phone rang for a long time, so she just left a voicemail.

'Hi Esme, its Meg. I wanted to give you a ring for a catch-up. If you pick up, please ring me back. Hope to talk soon. Bye.'

She then decided to phone Mum and Dad. She rang their number and after a few rings, Mum answered the phone.

'Hi Mum, how are you?'

Mum sounded anxious and there was some apprehension in her voice, something Meg hadn't heard before.

'Dad isn't feeling too good again. It could be another visit to the doctor tomorrow.'

'Oh no, please tell me he is going to be alright. I wanted to speak with you and show you some photos but it may not be a good time.'

'What photos?' Mum asked.

Travelling back home the other day I took the wrong road. As I was about to reverse, I came across a pretty cottage with a board outside and it was up for sale.

'Perfect, I thought for you and Dad. I know you haven't given any thought to moving out here but I know Dad hasn't been too well recently and having you near us and enjoying a better environment with less pollution could be so much better for you both especially with Dad's asthma.

'The house has been lovingly restored and I did take a nosey look inside and it has the most beautiful kitchen, although the garden is a lot smaller. Would you like me to send you more photos?'

'Sounds lovely, Meg; I would like that. We will need to come out and see the house for ourselves.'

'Mum, it is so charming and I can see you and Dad there relaxing and not far away from us. It couldn't be better. Now tell me, how is Dad?'

'I don't know until we see the doctor but fingers crossed that he will be back to his usual self with the right meds.'

'OK, Mum but please let me know what the doctor says, won't you?'

'Of course, I will. How are the children?'

'They are good and Simon is out training with the team, getting ready for his 200km bike trip next month.'

As she put the phone down, Meg couldn't help thinking about Dad. All these miles apart. She was now beginning to get quite worried about Dad's health and kept thinking to herself that moving here could be the right decision for them.

By lunchtime, the sun was shining through the shutters in the kitchen, the garden was looking beautiful and Dad's handy work in the garden was paying off. Flowers and shrubs were popping up here and there; how lovely they looked. She decided to take a book and sit under the beautiful magnolia tree, Reuben at my feet, Katie playing happily on her new trampoline and the boys playing at the bottom of the garden.

She couldn't be more relaxed. Tiny white and pink buds were just peeping through the enormity of this tree. In a few weeks, the tree would be stunning. This is Meg's place where she could sit, dream and listen to the songbirds— peace in abundance.

Meg must have fallen asleep when she felt Katie tapping her on the shoulder.

'Wake up, Mummy!'

'What is it?'

'Daddy has just got back. He looks hot and sweaty.'

As he walked his bike up the drive, he wiped away his forehead and shouted out, 'That was a hard cycle ride, not too sure if I am fit enough!'

Looking worn out and extremely tired, she decided to run a hot bath where he could have a long soak and recover.

Meg jokingly said, 'You have to admit, you are not getting any younger.'

In Simon's usual jovial tone, he said, 'Is 50 old?'

Having laughed together, he turned around and said, 'What would I do without you, Meg?'

With a loving grin, she closed the bathroom door behind her and walked downstairs. She kept thinking that this was only a quick training session, compared to the one he would be doing in a few weeks. She just hoped he was up for it.

Looking down at her phone, she could a missed call. It was Louis, so she quickly rang him back.

'Sorry, I missed you but is everything okay?' Meg asked.

'Good, thank you Meg.'

'Did the training session go to plan?' she asked.

'It was slightly challenging,' but Louis remarked, 'Simon was brilliant and kept up with the team.'

Meg told him that Simon was now recovering in the bath, having a very long soak.

'Good for him,' Louis said. 'He surprised us all. Tell him from me he was outstanding, keeping up with us all.'

'That's very kind. Thank you. He will be pleased to hear that.'

'So he should be,' Louis remarked. 'By the way, before I put the phone down. Would you be interested in a part-time job at the surgery? We are in desperate need of a physiotherapist in the clinical room. Our top lady is going on maternity leave, leaving us very short of staff and I remembered our conversation at the hospital and thought this may suit you.'

'It sounds perfect, Louis. I am very interested.'

Meg was thrilled at the chance of being given this opportunity.

'Why don't you speak with Simon and get back to me?'

Meg didn't know what to say. It would suit her perfectly! Meg had now been working at the surgery for the past couple of weeks and enjoying every minute. The people were lovely and very friendly. She was getting a lot of help and advice from Louis.

There was a treatment room where she could work one to one with her patients. She loved it! It was only two days before Simon went on his cycle tour with the club and Meg was frantically running around putting together all his equipment. Anyone would think he was going on a tour around France.

Meg asked, 'Simon, are you getting nervous?'

'Not at all,' but she could tell he was.

His facial expressions said it all but she knew he would love every minute once the tour set off. Meg could hear Simon on his mobile talking to someone. It was Louis Bernier. They were making some final arrangements before the big day.

She was feeling a little apprehensive about his cycle ride but knew this was something he always wanted to do and she wasn't going to stand in his way. He had always dreamed of doing something like this and she was so proud of him for taking this challenge. She could hear the phone ringing in the distance and as she rushed downstairs, she could hear Charlie speaking. 'Mum, it's Nan; she wants to talk with you.'

Charlie handed her the phone and Meg could sense something was very wrong.

'Mum, what is it?'

In a very agitated voice, Mum said, 'Dad is in hospital—his breathing got very bad this afternoon. I didn't know what to do, so I called for the ambulance.'

'That was the best thing to do, Mum.'

'They have taken him to Devon County and I am at the hospital now.'

'Oh no, what have the doctors said?'

'They are monitoring him and giving him oxygen—he is now back in a ward and resting.'

'Please keep me updated, Mum and I will phone you later tonight. Send Dad our love and let him know we are all thinking of him.'

Meg then told her Mum not to worry, he was in the best place and they would do everything possible for him. Meg put the phone down and ran upstairs to tell everyone. Not knowing whether to tell Simon before his trip, she thought if she delayed telling him, he wouldn't forgive her as he, too, was very fond of Dad.

The pair of them were very close. She couldn't wait to phone Mum back later that evening and she tried to take her mind off things by helping the children with their homework and making sure Simon had packed his kit and maps.

It was almost seven o'clock and she couldn't wait anymore. She rang Mum at home but there was no answer. Perhaps she was still at the hospital, so decided to ring her mobile but still no response. Looking across at Meg, Simon could see Meg was distraught.

'No news is good news, love,' he said.

'I know but I feel helpless and we are so far away.'

'Just keep ringing on the hour. All we can do is wait!'

Not long after, the phone rang; it was Mum. She sounded tired; her voice seemed shaky. 'Are you OK, Mum?'

She took a long time to answer and said the doctors wanted to do more tests. Hopefully, tomorrow when he has rested.

'What sort of tests?'

'They want to do some blood tests and another ECG.'

'How is Dad? Is he awake?'

'Yes dear, we couldn't talk because he had been fitted with an oxygen mask and you could see he was getting restless and struggling to remove it. Just like your Dad, thinking he knows best. The nurses just wanted to make him more comfortable.'

They talked for ages before Mum said she was going home but coming back to the hospital in the morning.

'Alright Mum, I will ring you later when you have more news. Love you, speak soon.' She put the phone down and Simon could see she was distressed and tearful.

'How is he, Meg?' Simon asked.

'They don't know but are doing some more tests tomorrow.'

It was around eleven o'clock the next day when Mum rang.

'How's everything?' Meg asked.

'The doctors have completed their rounds and Dad is sat up without his oxygen. After some short tests, they have told us that Dad could be suffering from COPD.'

Being a physiotherapist, she knew this could be serious. Chronic Obstructive Pulmonary Disease. Her heart sank but she knew Dad was in the right place and getting the right meds.

'The ECG shows that it has affected his heart, so he will have to take things very easy.'

'At least now, Mum, we know how we can now look after him.' It was at this point Meg shouted, 'We need to be closer and I want you to move over here.'

'I can't think of anything like that now, Meg.'

Meg replied, 'Everything can be sorted out when Dad is feeling better.'

'It sounds like a good idea and Dad and I had given it some thought when you first suggested a move.'

Meg was shocked to hear that Dad was going home later that day but with the proper medication in place and the care of Mum, she just knew he would be alright. The day had arrived and Simon felt excited, although a little nervous about the tour. He had undoubtedly got himself fit for the ride and was looking good.

They all drove to Dinan and assembled outside the Town Hall for the start of the race. It had been very well organised with Henri, the Maire of St Helene and other officials in attendance to send them off.

Louis came over and said, 'We will look after him.'

'You better,' speaking with a slight giggle.

Meg could see Henri standing nearby in the crowd shouting and waving to the cyclists with immense pride. An official of the Cycle Club waved a flag and they were off. She had to keep reminding herself this was not a race but a tour.

They knew how capable each cyclist had become during the lengthy training sessions but she kept thinking that Simon was not as experienced as the others, which bothered her somewhat although from what she had heard he wasn't that bad! A bell rang out, the flag was lowered to the ground and the cyclists were off.

'Good luck,' everyone shouted.

Walking back, she saw that Ruth and David, the couple they met at Danielle's, were there to wave the cyclists off. Meg stopped and they stood chatting.

'You must be very proud of Simon.'

'Oh yes, very,' Meg replied. 'He has always been a keen cyclist and now living here in France means he has the time to achieve his ambition.'

Walking away, they tapped me on the shoulder and said, 'They hoped to see us again soon.'

Meg felt her heart pounding fast—she wanted everything to go well with no mishaps. She didn't want to show concern to the children, so hands in pockets, they wandered back to the car and drove back home. The children shouted, 'Shall we make homemade pizzas for tea!'

Katie rushed through the front door, grabbed her apron and took charge of the pizza making. 'Pizzas for tea, everyone,' she shouted out.

The next day, they all woke early. She couldn't help wondering how the tour was going.

'Will daddy ring us and let us know how he is?'

'He has his phone with him—he may even FaceTime.'

Three excited children couldn't wait to hear from him. Reuben was playing happily in the garden and as Meg looked around, she could see Danielle strolling up the garden path.

'Bonjour,' Meg said and with a chuckle, she returned the greeting. She wanted to see if Meg had any news from the team.

'Not yet but I hope Simon will ring later.'

She was carrying a bouquet.

'Especially for you, Meg.'

'How lovely, thank you very much! They are gorgeous and the smell is so beautiful. Come inside and I will make a drink whilst I put them in a vase.'

They sat and chatted for almost an hour, putting the world to rights or so she thought. Meg had told her the news about Dad and how she would love them to live here, having felt so helpless when he was so ill in the hospital.

'I know the feeling,' Danielle said. 'Both my parents live on the border between France and Belgium, some 300kms away and there are times when I would love them to be closer.'

She told her jobs there were few and far between and she had to be brave and decided to leave the town she had lived in for most of her young life for a better chance of finding work. Always wanting to travel but of course you need money to do that, so here she was.

'At the young old age of twenty-four, I arrived in St Helene, working at the local florist shop. If I could earn some money and work hard, then my dream to travel may come true one day. I rented a flat above the shop and my wages paid for my rent and food. Soon afterwards, I had a phone call from my mother, who told me my grandmother had passed away. We were very close and at this point, I just wanted to go back home.

'My mother told me that I should stay with the plans I had made but would obviously want me to attend grandma's funeral and of course, I wouldn't have missed it for the world. A couple of months later, I had a letter in the post telling me that my grandmother had left me a large sum of money.

'I was shocked and kept looking at the amount; I couldn't believe it. I had never had so much money in my life. I decided I wasn't going to waste it and it was not long afterwards that the florist shop was up for sale and I had the chance to buy it. I snapped up the offer and became the new owner.'

'Hey, Danielle, that is amazing! Your luck turned good in the end.'

'It certainly did and it meant that I could then get out of the flat and buy a small place of my own, where I am now and very happy.'

'You have a lovely home; all you need now is someone tall, dark and handsome to look after you.'

'One day perhaps!'

As Danielle was leaving, she said, 'don't forget to let me know how the team are doing.'

'I will. Hopefully, he will ring me this evening.'

Walking back to the house, Meg could see spring flowers popping up through the uneven ground and in the hedgerows; bluebells, primroses, daffodils, such beautiful colours. It must have been around six o'clock when the phone rang. It was Simon.

'Hi guys, how is everybody?'

'We are good, how's it going?'

'Yes, everything here is going well. We covered 70kms today and we are on track for a good day tomorrow. However, I did get a puncture but got it repaired quickly and off I went again. I don't think I am one of the fastest, so many keep overtaking me but the solidarity and harmony of the team makes it all worthwhile for me. At least I am enjoying every part of it.'

'Well, that's all that matters,' Meg told him.

The children chatted away with him and said he would hopefully face-time tomorrow evening.

'We shall look forward to that. We all miss you and please be careful.'

Meg kept thinking to herself that it wouldn't be long before the team were back home and Simon pushed his bike up the drive and came back to us safe and sound.

Chapter 11

Today was going to be a good day, Meg told herself. Having cleaned the house from top to bottom, she was preparing everything for Simon's arrival. It didn't seem they were waving him goodbye four days ago; how time flew, only another day and he should be back home.

The children were quiet for once. The boys sat in their bedrooms doing their homework and Katie quietly played dressing her dolls. Meg poured herself a glass of wine, put her feet up and sat staring at nothing in particular. She must have dropped off to sleep and was suddenly awakened by the phone ringing.

'Hello,' Meg said.

'Is that Mrs Johnston?'

'Yes, who is that?'

'It's the police.'

Meg started to shake; 'Ugh, can I help you? Is there anything wrong?'

'I am sorry to tell you but your husband, Simon Johnston, has been involved in an accident.'

'Is he ok?'

'I'm afraid he has been taken to hospital in Nantes by air ambulance with serious head injuries and is in critical condition.' The voice on the other end of the phone asked, 'Are you still there, Mrs Johnston?'

Meg just stood numb, speechless, not even thinking straight. Eventually, she said, 'Can I see him?'

'The Team Manager is here; let me get him to speak with you.'

With that, a very familiar voice came to the phone. It was Louis Bernier.

'What has happened, Louis? Is Simon going to be alright?'

'Meg, I am off to the hospital now. Simon hit the crash barrier at a very fast speed. He is unconscious and we don't know anything more yet.'

Louis asked if anyone was with her.

'Only the children!'

'Please stay where you are and wait by the phone. I will get back to you as soon as I have more news.'

What was she going to say to the children? She felt sick. She wanted to be with Simon but had no way of getting there because there was nobody to look after the children Perhaps Danielle would come over!

'Yes, that's what I shall do.'

Her mind was like fog; this was always something she feared when he was out cycling but she never thought this would happen in a million years. She now felt herself panicking, knowing she had to be with Simon. He would want me there.

Meg decided to wait until Louis phoned her back before making any decisions. At this point, the children hadn't been told about the accident but as soon as she heard positive news, Meg knew they had to be told. The phone rang and it was Louis. He said they had taken him to surgery. He had a severe bleed on the brain, together with multiple injuries.

'I need to be with him, Louis.'

'Of course! I will stay at the hospital until you arrive.'

He gave her all the details and then rang Danielle and told her what had happened and asked if she would stay with the children. It was hard having to tell the children but Meg told them to be brave for daddy. He was going to be alright and that he had a nasty bump on the head.

What else could she say? Danielle arrived, hugged them and said everything would be okay.

'I hope so, I hope so.'

'Don't worry about the children; they will be okay. Just keep me informed.'

Not looking back, Meg rushed out the door before getting into her car. She felt lost and there was a long drive ahead, not knowing who or where she was going and what lay ahead. She drove as fast as possible to the hospital and as she entered the swing doors, she could see lots of nurses and people bustling around but her mind was only focusing on one thing, Simon.

With a pounding heart and a blank mind, she didn't know what to expect. Everything was a blur and all she wanted to hear was good news and that she would have her Simon back home once again. Walking up the long and cold corridor with its clinical white walls, pushing through an emergency door, Meg could see Louis in the distance, waiting for her.

He was still in his full cycling gear and was looking pale and concerned as she ran up to him. He cradled her in his arms.

'Louis, is he going to be alright?'

'We must wait and see. They are doing all they can for him.'

Meg started to bombard Louis with so many questions and to her surprise, he was ready with answers. He told her that the roads were wet and he skidded into the side of a barrier at quite a fast speed.

'I was ahead of Simon when the accident happened and didn't know anything until a team car came alongside and said there had been an accident and the race was being stopped immediately. It was at that point I knew something awful had happened.'

Meg interrupted and said, 'But Louis, I thought it was just a leisurely tour with the club, not a race.'

'Well, we thought so too but some of the cyclists wanted to turn it into more of a race to see who was the quickest, recording their fastest speed for the day. Simon thought he was prepared to race too and went along with it.'

Oh no, Meg thought, *Simon, what have you done!*

'We all rushed back to the scene, where an air ambulance was on standby. As I got there, Simon was semi-conscious and touched my hand tightly. He quietly whispered to me something like, "Please tell Meg and the kids I love them very much."

"Of course," I said but I told him you would be able to tell them that yourself soon. I stayed with Simon at the side of the road, making him as comfortable as I could until help arrived. It looks like Simon may have misjudged the bend, which is the only reason this awful accident could have happened.'

'Let me get you a hot sweet cup of tea and I will stay with you until we get some news.'

'Thank you, Louis.'

Feeling his arm around her and his gentle talking voice, was giving her all the reassurance she needed. It must have seemed like hours and hours before they got to know anything. They both sat hoping for good news and everything crossed.

Eventually, a doctor arrived and a look of extreme sadness was upon him. Louis and Meg stood up and waited for the doctor to give them the news.

'Mrs Johnston, we did all we could to save him but we couldn't stop the bleeding and the head injury proved fatal.'

Meg stood in utter disbelief—this couldn't be happening but the reality is, it was. In her little world, she began staring through a cracked windowpane in the hospital hallway, not able to speak, just total silence. She was totally broken! All she could see was Louis in deep conversation with the doctor. She thought she had come to bring Simon home after being checked out, not thinking she would never have him back.

What was she going to tell the children and Mum and Dad? What was she going to do? Louis came over to comfort her and told her he would sort everything out for me. She just wanted to be with Simon.

'Can I see him?'

'Of course, Mrs Johnston. Just give us a few minutes and I will call you in.'

Louis was an absolute tower of strength; without him, she would never have got through this awful tragedy. The tears hadn't started flowing yet but she knew they would come at some point; it was only a matter of time. Her life without Simon was something she had never imagined.

Always together doing everything as a family. Living in France for a new life and wanting to do so much. They had such hopes and plans for the future and now they had lost the one person who was able to make this possible. Suddenly, she let go of her feelings and fell into Louis's arms and cried loudly.

Meg could hear a voice in the distance saying, 'Mrs Johnston; we are ready for you now.'

The doctor came along and ushered her into the side room where Simon was lying. Standing outside the cold and silent room, she was unsure of what she was about to see. Meg kept thinking to herself that he was only asleep but knew he would never wake up and her thoughts went straight to the children.

She knew she had to be strong for them as she was now the head of the family and that wouldn't be easy. Simon always made the crucial decisions and she knew that would now be left to her. As Meg entered the room, she looked back and saw Louis in the doorway.

'I'm here and will stay with you.'

Blurred with fast-running tears flowing down her cheeks, she couldn't speak but just nodded as if to say to Louis, please stay with me. Having Louis nearby comforted her as she walked slowly to where Simon was lying.

Bending over, said, 'I love you. The children love you. Sleep peacefully, darling.'

Meg took hold of his hand and sat quietly for a few moments before walking away. What else could she do or say? The love of her life was no more. She wanted to know the exact circumstances of what happened to Simon and she knew there would be an inquest and everything would be made known very soon.

Meg had been told that Simon hit a bend at quite a fast speed and crashed into a barrier at the side of the road but she was finding it extremely hard to imagine how this terrible accident had happened. After completing some forms, they gave Meg lots of paperwork, which she couldn't get her head around or even understand but Louis ensured he would help her all he could. They slowly walked out of the hospital and stood talking for a short while.

'Why don't you leave your car here and get it picked up another day?' he said.

'Thank you but I need to clear my head and the drive back home may do that. I will be careful, do not worry!'

Louis wanted her to know that whenever she needed his help, just call him and he would be there for the children and her. Meg was thinking about how she would cope with the language as this would be complicated with her not-so-good French but she needn't have worried because Louis told her everything would get sorted in good time.

She also heard that the cycling club were being driven back to Dinan by the coach and the tour had been cancelled. Arrangements would have to be made and that was something which needed to be organised shortly. Would Simon want to be buried, cremated in France or be taken back to the UK?

They never talked about this to each other as they didn't ever think they would need to at this early stage in their life. Meg supposed they should have discussed this but like everything else, you tend to put this to the back of your mind but now she wished they hadn't.

It would have been easier to know their intentions should anything like this happen! Simon didn't have a large family. His family was here in France; Meg, the children, Mum and Dad, so it did make sense to have him near them. Eventually, they decided to have him cremated and they would have his ashes scattered in their garden, which he loved so much and where he would want to complete his dream of moving to France.

It was a long and horrible couple of weeks sorting everything out, explaining to the family and not knowing when or what the next step would be. She didn't want Dad to get too upset after his health scare, so she had to be very careful about upsetting him too much.

The boys were helping the best way they could but Meg knew it had affected them dreadfully. They became reticent but at the same time, would make it clear that they would help to carry out Dad's wishes of being here in France, trying to accomplish the things he wanted for the family.

Katie, on the other hand, wouldn't leave her side. She was like her shadow. One day she would be sad, the next a little happier but still thought her Daddy would return home.

'He has gone with the angels and is looking down on us Katie, making sure we are doing everything he wants us to.'

Chapter 12

The day of Simon's funeral was upon them. As they walked into the church, Meg experienced tremendous grief and sadness and had to be held up either side by Dad and Louis whilst Mum and Danielle were looking after the children.

Meg started to shake uncontrollably and kept thinking that perhaps this was a horrible dream and she would wake up and everything would be alright. Sadly, she was wrong. There was so much they had planned together for the future.

'Why, Simon, why have you left us? It's not fair.'

Meg started to blame Simon for the accident and frowned upon the hurt he had caused them. She knew this wasn't true but couldn't help herself. She knew, in time, these awful thoughts would fade away. How was she going to carry on?

She could see that Danielle had been busy—the church looked very beautiful where she had placed flowers everywhere; at the side of the pews and the altar—everywhere she looked, there were flowers.

'My contribution from me to you, Meg. I know you wanted the best for Simon.'

Meg was speechless and didn't know what to say except to thank her graciously. It was a lovely ceremony in the local church; Mum, Dad and a few of Simon's colleagues at Wickham Junior School in Devon, came over just for his funeral to pay their respects.

They were all very shocked to hear of Simon's accident and said that he would always be remembered as a great teacher and the school were hoping to have a memorial seat made to put in the playground in his memory. Meg was overwhelmed and thanked them so much.

'I know Simon was incredibly proud to be part of the school and would often talk about his outstanding pupils and staff.'

She was also amazed by how many of the villagers turned out to pay their respects too. Henri Pascall tapped her on the shoulder and told her that if there was anything, he or the villagers could do to help her during this sad time, she only had to ask.

'Thank you, Henri; everyone is so very kind.'

Some of the schoolchildren formed a guard of honour and Phillipe led the boys into the church. Phillipe was very saddened by the death of his friend, as they had become great friends and would go running together when time allowed.

The local pretre (priest) was very kind to them and wanted to know all about the life of their beloved and dear Simon. Meg told him he was a devoted family man with a heart of gold and loved his new life in France. He looked down at her, held her hand tightly saying, 'We will pray for you and your family'

They were invited to church the following Sunday so that they could remember Simon. She was overwhelmed by everyone's kindness and support shown to the family. Danielle and Louis had also been a great help to them in every way possible. They had been her tower of strength for which to hold onto at this exceptionally upsetting time.

Meg could see that Mum and Dad didn't want to leave them after the funeral but they needed to go back because Dad had hospital appointments. She told them not to worry and that she just wanted Dad to get better but perhaps give some thought about moving to France and being all together as a family.

'I know Simon would have liked that.'

Mum said that she and Dad had been talking a lot about this and hopefully if all went to plan, they would like to sell their house and come over and be with them. Meg was delighted to hear this; for some reason, this made her feel so much better about herself and somehow, a little more secure for the future.

Meg was surprised at how the children had accepted Simon's death. They seemed to understand and acknowledge that Simon was not with them anymore, although Katie kept saying, 'I am not leaving you, Mummy. Daddy has gone to heaven with the angels who will look after him, so I am here now to look after you.'

The twins were still finding it quite hard to come to terms with their Dad's death but were trying their best to move on with their young lives, so as head of the household now, Meg had to be brave and be there for them all.

The following week, they all decided to go to church as the Vicar suggested and as they walked into the church, a feeling of warmth and calm leapt up and surrounded her. She felt that Simon was not far away and that he was urging her to sit quietly and remember all the good times they had together.

Meg was beginning to accept that he would be with them forever, although not in body but in soul and she didn't want that emotion to leave her. She noticed glances from some of the locals in the church, glimpsing across at them but could tell they were comforting glances.

She acknowledged them with an affectionate smile. Meg and the children decided to walk back home and hold the thoughts of a lovely husband and father. Not speaking much, just holding hands and remembering the good times and hopefully, as Simon would want, more good times to come.

After a short discussion with the children, they agreed to scatter Simon's ashes near the magnolia tree in the back garden, a place he loved and where Meg could sit and talk to him. They had their little ceremony and it was just her, the children and Reuben.

Meg couldn't believe how calm and still Reuben was. He sat quietly whilst they scattered Simon's ashes. You can always tell when a dog senses something isn't quite right; they have this acute sense of instinct. Meg had always been so intrigued by this, because when she was laid up with flu a few years ago, Reuben didn't leave her side until she was better.

Reuben knew in some strange way that Simon was not with them anymore. She patted him on the back saying, 'Will you look after us now?'

The evening was warm and a slight breeze was in the air, so Meg took Reuben for a short walk. Walking peacefully into the woodland, close to the house, there was the beauty of the late-night sun spilling light through the trees and onto the footpath.

Every so often, a grey squirrel would scurry across her path and ascend into the nearby tree until it was out of sight. It felt like she had entered a sanctuary. Everything she thought mattered did not seem to be significant anymore. Meg felt peace here and as she was strolling through the grassy woodland, she was thinking of Simon and how she was missing him so much.

They had so many plans together. As she walked back to the house, the stream at the bottom of the garden flowed softly where the boys played. She could see Simon in her thoughts, watching the children as they played with various stones and sticks but he wasn't there anymore. The memories were full of everything possible yet disappeared into a haze as her grief began to take control.

'Simon, why did you leave us?'

Some days, she feel like a fire was slowly burning in her stomach, a hollow pain which grew stronger. Meg began to get anxious and couldn't concentrate on the simple things. She was angry because Simon left her with so many unfinished ideas but in time, she believed the pain and anger would ease.

Having three children to care for was something to hold on to. They were now her life and world. Without them, she had nothing! Life would go on and she would make sure Simon could be proud of her for hopefully being able to continue with their dream.

Taking life day by day was a good way for them to cope. Danielle had become a great friend and popped in most days to check on them. They started running together and this helped immensely. Some days, they would run 5k and others 3k; it was all according to how the mood took them.

Meg thought Danielle was sad but she was too wrapped up in her thoughts to notice.

'Are you okay, Danielle?' Meg asked.

'Um, yes, of course. All I want is for me to help you with your hurting and help to bring you back to some normality. I know it will take time but I want you to know I will always be here for you.'

Meg didn't know what to say. She put her arms around her and they embraced each other for ages. She was such a good friend in so many ways. Louis was keeping a low profile and Meg couldn't understand it. He had been incredible in helping and ensuring they were all okay. Why hadn't he phoned?

Mum had phoned earlier in the day and said that she and Dad hoped to come over within the next week. Meg was delighted and told her excitedly that she was very much looking forward to seeing them both.

'By the way, how is Dad?'

'He is looking a lot better and feeling less tired. The tablets seem to be working,' she said with a softness in her voice.

Jokingly, Meg told her to tell him to keep taking the tablets as they say. Katie started having a few nightmares and Meg could hear her crying most nights. She would wander into her room, cuddle her and tell her everything would be alright.

Having Nan and Gramps coming to stay soon made her feel a little better. The boys were helping her through tough times and Meg knew she had to be strong for them, too; helping to cope with their emotions.

Together, they would get through this. Simon was their life and Meg knew she had to follow in his footsteps and not let go of the dream they all had of living in France.

She looked up at the sky and told Simon, 'We will follow the dream through, darling. I know you are with us all the way.' Her feelings took hold and she stood still, held her head in her hands and cried uncontrollably but as each day went by, she knew her Simon was still there with her.

Once Mum and Dad gave her a date when they would be coming over, her decision was made to start back to work at the surgery. It would help in so many ways, as she needed some substance in her life now that she was alone with just the children to hold on to.

Having Mum and Dad with them would make life easier to cope with; they always loved helping out with the children, although Meg knew she couldn't burden them too much because Dad was only getting back to somewhat better health and she also knew they were feeling the pain of Simon's death. They also needed her help and support.

Meg decided to drive over to the surgery and let them know she would return to work soon. They were all very kind and told her not to rush back until she was ready.

'I think I am; I need to focus on my new life without Simon and take control of many situations that will be put in front of me. I was always dependent on Simon because he was such a decision-maker but now that role is mine, I must do my best to achieve the ambitions we both made before moving to France.'

Meg sat down with a couple of the staff at the surgery and they talked over a cup of coffee and biscuits. She asked if Doctor Bernier was at the surgery today.

'No,' said one of the staff. 'He has been away on leave and will be working at the hospital on his return, possibly for another week.'

'Oh, I see. No doubt I will catch up with him soon.'

As Meg was driving into town to fetch bits and pieces for the arrival of Mum and Dad, she sensed great excitement at the thought of them coming over and staying for a lot longer. She couldn't wait to be with them. Since the funeral, Meg had seen little of Louis—she just wanted to thank him for all he had done for them and hoped he would remain their good friend.

Perhaps he had a hectic work schedule, what with working at the hospital too but somehow Meg knew she didn't want to lose their friendship. It was becoming very important to her. Meg saw Danielle waving out from the shop and beckoned her in.

'Are you coping okay?' Danielle asked.

'I'm okay, although I do find it difficult at times but I do believe we are slowly getting there.'

She told Danielle that her parents were visiting shortly and they could be staying for much longer this time. Meg wondered if Danielle had seen Louis recently, as it was strange she hadn't seen him since the funeral. Danielle replied she hadn't but he did try to make time for Alice as often as possible.

'Oh, I see; I just wanted to thank him for everything, because without either of your help, life would have been so very different, whilst I was suffering a dreadful grieving process.'

Danielle placed her arms around Meg and told her she would be there as a friend always and she must never forget that. Meg meandered back home with the shopping, thinking perhaps she should contact Louis—he may think she had forgotten to thank him for everything, although Meg knew he wouldn't look at it like that.

No sooner had she thought about possibly ringing Louis; her mobile was ringing out loudly in the kitchen. She ran over and could see it was Louis. Meg couldn't believe it. She picked up the phone and said, 'Louis, how are you?'

'Good, how are you?'

'Oh, I get good days and bad!'

'I am very sorry I haven't spoken since the funeral but I have been away on a follow-up training course in Chartres, near Paris and decided to book some extra time and take a short holiday.

'Simon's death was a shock and it has taken me all this time to ask myself why it happened to such a lovely family guy. In some ways, I felt it was my fault, as I introduced him to the Club. If I hadn't, he would be here today.'

In that moment, Meg said, 'Louis, nobody knew the accident would happen. Life can be very cruel as well as kind. You weren't to know. Please, please don't feel this way. I couldn't ask for more because you were there when I needed you. I cannot thank you enough. In fact Louis, you were the rock that got me through this awful time in my life.'

Her heart was now beating very fast and Meg began to ramble on the phone. She then went on to say, that she was thinking of coming back to work very soon.

'That's excellent news, Meg! I will be back myself next week so that we can have a chat and perhaps I could pop over and see you and the children.'

'Yes, I would like that.'

By the time they finished speaking on the phone, Louis seemed a lot more himself; they even had a little laugh together. Meg detected tenderness in his voice and his kind-heartedness made her feel good again. She couldn't wait to see him and tell him that the accident was, in no way, his fault. He really must not think like this.

She had also received a letter from the coroner who stated on the death certificate that Simon's death was accidental and that he died from some very long word she couldn't pronounce, translated to something like an injury to the brain.

It appeared that it was nothing more than an unavoidable accident due to the circumstances. This would mean that she was able to put Louis's mind at rest, too, when they met next time. A few days later, she could see that tents had been erected in the village sports field opposite the Town Hall and whilst she was out for a short run, a lovely little lady asked if they were going to the village Fete on Saturday.

I know the children would love it, Meg thought to herself.

'There are many stalls, a dog show and even a fair with swings and roundabouts,' she told me.

'Yes, of course, we would love to.'

This could be turning into a busy week ahead, because Meg also had to prepare for the arrival of Mum and Dad's forthcoming visit. Freddie and Charlie were out walking Reuben whilst Katie was helping me make chocolate brownies.

'Nan and Gramps love these, don't they, Mummy,' as she started to wipe the mixing bowl clean with her fingers, her hands covered with chocolate mixture and as usual, all down the front of her dress.

'What a messy pup,' Meg said.

They both looked at each other and just laughed out loudly; it was something none of them had done for some time. The boys walked back into the house and went to the fridge for their favourite drink. They looked hot, even Reuben was panting and looking for his drinking bowl.

'We went into the woodland and down the country lane.'

'Reuben started chasing a couple of rabbits and hiding behind a tree, sniffing and searching here and there.'

The sun was shining through the trees and it was so peaceful. Charlie said how much both he and Freddie missed their Dad and wished he was still with them!

'He is with us, Freddie; Dad is watching over us all; he will always be with us.'

The twins ran towards Meg, putting their arms firmly around her waist, both quietly sobbing after she tried hard to comfort her twin boys, telling them they must all stay strong for each other.

'We will, Mum, we will make Dad very proud of us.'

'I know you will!'

She couldn't ask for anything more from her children. She decided to take five minutes and sit under the magnolia tree with a chilled wine. She began talking to Simon, which had become quite a habit. It was helping with her grief, knowing that he was beside her in her thoughts.

She started by telling him all the news and how the children were coping at their school. She felt good or perhaps it could be the wine taking its effect. Her thoughts then quietly drifted away and she began to think about other things.

She casually looked around the garden and noticed some of the vegetables they had planted earlier, gradually popping up from the rich earthy soil. She was amazed at how everything in the garden was blooming. Even Katie's sunflowers were beginning to show signs of life.

She sat wondering how Esme and Olivia were coping back in England. It was so strange she hadn't heard anything from her. She doesn't even know about Simon's accident. Meg had tried ringing her several times but no answer—but she did think if Esme wanted to talk, then she knew where Meg was. She could ring her anytime.

Today was the Fete, so they decided they would go along and make an appearance. Katie decided to make an extra batch of her delicious brownies. Looking so proud of herself, she steadily carried the plate and perfectly displayed her homemade goodies. They also decided they would put Reuben in the dog show. Katie's idea, of course!

'He might be good enough to win, Mummy.'

'Well, you did bathe and brush him lovingly last night. He does look and smell lovely. Let's see if we can get him entered.'

As they arrived, Henri walked over and greeted them with open arms.

'Hello, what is that lovely aroma?'

Katie shouted, 'Chocolate brownies and I have also made some chocolate chip cookies, which are my favourite!'

Henri replied, 'I can see you like chocolate a lot. Don't forget to save some for me!'

'I will,' and then Katie unassumingly walked over, head held high, feeling extremely proud of herself.

The dog show was about to start. A lady in the booth gave them a ticket and told them to be back in 10 minutes before the show to ensure they understood all the rules.

'We will,' Katie shouted out with excitement.

After a casual walk around the Fete, the boys saw some friends from school, so they wandered off. I told them not to go too far away—hoping they would be around to see the dog show. A crowd was now gathering to watch the annual event of the very popular dog show. They quickly marched Reuben over and were given a few instructions.

Katie was asked to walk Reuben around the ring in front of the judges. All breeds of dogs had entered, beautiful Brittany Spaniels, all sizes of dogs, shorthaired, longhaired but not many cocker spaniels. Meg could see one or two of the judges keeping a constant eye on Reuben and he was behaving exceptionally well for a change, sitting when told, stopping when Katie asked him.

Katie proudly paraded Reuben in front of the large crowd, not even appearing nervous in any way. The judges took a shine to Katie and gave her second place. She was thrilled. First place went to a Brittany Spaniel, of course but all the same, a worthwhile winner.

They pinned a rosette around Reuben's neck and gave Katie a certificate. Afterwards, she walked Reuben around the Fete. It was lovely to see her so happy and cheerful. Looking back at her, Meg saw a very excited little girl. Not long afterwards, Katie started running towards her and said, 'Look, who is here?'

Meg could see Louis standing just behind her. Louis remarked and said, 'How lovely to see you. Are you okay?'

Meg replied, 'I think so.'

They were now beginning to move on and she told him how the children had been remarkable in coping with their grief and sorrow and helping to deal with the pain and anguish which was always evident at times like this. He looked straight into her eyes, showing great sympathy and compassion.

Meg could see Louis was unsure of what to say to her. She felt his compassion towards her, as if he wanted to hold her in his arms but then he quickly looked away. He changed the subject, looking down at Reuben and commenting on his second-place award.

Then, rather nervously, he asked if there had been any news about the cause of Simon's death!

'Louis, it was nothing more than an accident which could have happened to anyone. In life, accidents happen and nobody knows when or where but they do. When asking yourself the question, could I have stopped him? The answer is no. He knew the risks involved and died doing something he loved; we must all remember that.'

'You are a very strong lady, Meg.'

'I have to be; not for me but for everyone around us. We are a very close family who will always be there for each other and I intend to carry on where Simon left off.'

Whilst talking to Louis, she could sense such sympathy and empathy, which gave her the strength and motivation to resume a little more routine in their lives. Meg told him her Mum and Dad were coming over in the next few days and he said that was wonderful.

She wanted to convince her Mum and Dad to sell up in England and buy something smaller here.

'I know it is not an easy thing to do at their age but Dad's health has not been too good and I think it is best to have them close, not only for me but for the children too.

'I have now made up my mind that we shall be staying in France and not packing up and returning to England as I first thought shortly after Simon's death. What would be the point? We must fulfil Simon's dream and carry on. That is what we are going to do!'

Louis placed his hand on Meg's shoulder, saying they were being very brave and doing the right thing. Katie came running back after having her hair plaited at one of the stalls, looking very grown up.

'Dr Bernier, do you like my hair?'

'I certainly do.'

'What a shame Alice isn't with me.'

'How about I bring her over to meet you next weekend, Katie?'

Meg looked at her little girl jumping up and down excitedly and she quickly replied, 'That would be lovely.'

However, it had taken some time to sort out a meeting with the girls and Katie would love a new little friend. They all agreed to meet at eleven o'clock the following Saturday. Meg then suggested they could make some plans for a picnic if the weather were good.

'Is Dr Bernier joining us too, Mummy?'

Meg looked curiously at Katie and said, 'Um, I don't know; he is very busy. He could be working at the hospital.'

'You will have to find out, won't you?' Katie said with velocity in her voice.

Meg had to admit. She was thinking the same thing too. Before she could say anything, Katie asked Louis if he would like to join them at the picnic.

She whispered in her ear, saying, 'I can't wait for you to ask him, Mummy.'

A grin came across her face and Louis bent over her and said, 'I would be delighted.'

Chapter 13

After Mum and Dad's early arrival on Thursday morning, they just sat chatting for what seemed hours. They talked about Simon and emotions were high but felt that Meg was coming close to accepting the accident and so were the children.

They had to focus on their life ahead and with the help of their family and friends, they were succeeding.

Mum looked up and quietly said, 'I want to tell you something.'

Her voice was trembling slightly and Dad held her hand very tightly.

'What is it?' Meg asked.

'After a lengthy discussion, your father and I have decided that we shall move out to France to be near you and the children. We have already put our house on the market and we have somebody interested in buying it.'

Meg was beaming and said, 'I didn't think for one moment that you would go ahead with this, although I knew it had to be the right decision for you both.'

Meg was completely exhausted with happiness and couldn't wait for the day to come when they would be altogether once again.

'We have put everything in place back home in England and there is no need for us to go back until we sign the completion papers.' This was such great news for Meg. At the back of her mind, she knew Mum and Dad were worried about them.

Being close and nearby to keep an eye on them (as parents do) would help with Dad and his health problems and make him less worried about them. Meg rushed upstairs and flopped onto the bed, crying silently to herself. Mum was in the kitchen busying around and Meg mentioned that she would like to return to work part-time like before Simon's accident.

'What a good idea, Meg!' Mum said, 'You should have people around you, helping you regain some social life.'

Meg stepped outside and felt fresh. The temperature was feeling so much warmer and as she walked over to where Dad was tying up some rose bushes, she put her head on his shoulder.

'I love you Dad!'

'I love you too,' he replied.

As they walked down the garden towards the stream, they just stood there and stared at the landscape. Reuben followed and sat beside them.

'What a lovely place you have, Meg!'

'I know but I want you and Mum to make it yours too.'

Dad took hold of her hand, squeezed it very tightly and said, 'I think we will, my love. You and the children are all we have left and being being close to you is all we ever wanted.'

Meg kissed him and walked back to the house, feeling sheer joy.

Time to open a bottle of champagne! she thought.

Meg felt the knotted nerves in her stomach slowly unwinding and she knew it seemed strange but there was also a sense of warmth circling her. She knew it was Simon telling her he was happy that they had all made the right decision.

Saturday morning and it was turning out to be a beautiful day. They were expecting the arrival of Alice and Louis shortly and Katie and Mum were helping with the picnic basket. Dead on eleven o'clock, the doorbell rang.

'Bonjour,' Meg shouted out.

She couldn't remember how long it had been since she began to feel a little happier and more herself. Katie ran as fast as her little legs would carry her. She opened the door and greeted them with delight.

Meg called out, 'We are in the kitchen; come on in.'

Louis shook hands with Dad and kissed Mum on both cheeks. She, too, blushed when he kissed her. 'What a lovely man,' she said.

'Yes, he is very kind, extremely hard-working and an excellent friend.'

They all sat down and had a cup of coffee and Alice and Katie played like they had known each other forever. The boys were getting their fishing tackle up together, hoping to get a catch. Alice ran over to Louis and asked if Katie could come to her house one day and perhaps go to the zoo and show her the chimpanzees.

'They have many different animals and I would like to show Katie the penguins too.'

A delighted Alice and Katie skipped and ran once again into the garden. Dad was already packing the car with the food and drinks and it was looking to be a lovely day. Luckily, they could all fit into one car as Louis had a large seven-seater which just about got all of them in at a squeeze.

Eight, plus a dog but who cares, they managed! The drive was about forty minutes to Cap Frehel, which had beautiful views overlooking a glorious bay and was ideal for their picnic and a great beach for the children. The sea looked calm and very blue, with the waves crashing onto a sandy beach.

Mum and Dad seemed to enjoy Louis's company and talked to him endlessly. They did seem to get on well with each other and it was good to see them chatting and joking. Meg decided to take a walk along the water's edge, her long dark silken hair softly blowing in the early summer breeze, holding a pair of flip-flops in her hands as she walked bare footed, with the coolness of the sea splashing against her toes.

As she looked back, the children were playing happily altogether and laughing. A much welcoming voice was beckoning. She turned around and it was Louis asking if she was okay.

'Yes, I am fine, thank you.' Just having a quiet moment!

They walked together along the water's edge, sometimes looking at each other, sometimes just focusing on what was in front of them and it was then Meg felt his hand brush against her. She wanted to hold out her hand to him but knew it couldn't be.

Her life without Simon was still very painful and she was carrying a lot of pain. It was going to take time for her to even think of any new relationships but who knows, perhaps, one day! They returned to where Mum had laid out the blanket and carefully arranged the food. The sun was getting hot and Dad was showing signs of lovely, red rosy cheeks.

'You have caught the sun, Dad!'

He chuckled and said, 'I expect that is rust, after all the rain we have had back in England recently.'

They all laughed and sat down to some enjoyable and welcoming food. The fresh air was giving them all a tremendous appetite. The boys seemed to have vanished for ages but she could see them in the distance. Louis said, 'I have them in my sight.'

It seemed that Louis was taking over from Simon in so far as keeping an eye on them, which Meg thought was very reassuring. They were making the most of a lovely day rock pooling, searching for all different types of sea creatures. They couldn't wait to tell us what they had caught.

'Let me tell them, Charlie,' Freddie announced. 'We have detected shrimps, crabs, snails and even sea urchins.'

'Mum, I think we saw jellyfish too!'

Katie asked, 'Will they eat you?'

Freddie turned and said, 'Don't be silly, Katie. Of course not but they will give you a nasty sting if you try to touch them. Don't try nothing foolish.'

'I won't, promise,' Katie yelled out.

Alice and Katie were sitting on the wet sand, attempting to build sandcastles when Mum went over and joined them.

'Do you know something, girls?'

'What, Nan?' said Katie.

'I remember sitting on a beach in Cornwall with your Mummy when she was about your age, building sandcastles. It has brought back a lot of memories for me.'

Katie held her arms out and placed them around Nan's waist.

'Please stay with us forever. I don't want you to go back to England ever.'

'Well, we may have to visit for a short while but we will be back. France will be our home too very soon.'

Alice was looking slightly uncomfortable and unsure why Katie was talking to her Nan this way. Katie asked Alice if she had a Nan and Gramps.

'I don't think so.'

'Well, you can always borrow mine if you want!'

Nan overheard what she was saying and with a slight chuckle, went back to reading her book. The waves began to crash upon the uneven rocks, glistening in the late afternoon sunshine.

'Be careful,' Meg shouted out. 'The tide is beginning to turn and the rocks could become very slippery.'

Katie and Alice were still busy making sandcastles when Meg said it was now getting late and they would have to pack up and get ready to return home.

'Mummy, can't we stay longer?'

'We shall have to go very soon because Alice and Louis have to drive home too.'

'Alright but can we come here again?'

'Of course, we can,' Meg said, 'it has been such a lovely day.'

Meg then asked if everybody enjoyed themselves. In a harmonious tone, everyone shouted, yes! Mum was busy drying off the sand from the girl's feet. As she did, Meg remembered her doing this when she was a little girl. Sand gets everywhere—horrible stuff.

'Have you enjoyed yourself Mum?'

'Yes, very much. How about you?'

'I have loved every minute, Mum. It has been a great day and so pleased we were able to spend time altogether.'

Mum told Meg that life would get better but one step at a time. 'There is a long journey ahead of you, Meg but we are here for you and the children.'

Looking a bit dishevelled from the wind which was beginning to blow fiercely, they all agreed they must do it again sometime.

'Just what the doctor ordered,' Louis shouted out.

Meg gave a wry giggle as they all walked back towards the car. They said their goodbyes to Louis and Alice and thanked him for what was a truly wonderful day. Louis thanked Mum for a delicious picnic, waved out and said, until next time!

Meg was hoping there was going to be a next time. He then turned around once again saying, 'Don't forget work next week, Meg. I will be there and looking forward to seeing you all on Monday.'

Standing in the doorway and waving goodbye, they all agreed it had been a perfect day.

Chapter 14

Since returning to work, Meg had felt her confidence grow. All emotional aspects of her life were now taking a turn for the better. Louis brought Alice over to play with Katie regularly; the boys had been selected for the school football as team members. Danielle had been such a good friend and when the weather allowed, they tried to have a run together at least once a week.

Of course, she saw Louis at work, although recently, it would seem he had been spending a lot of time away from the surgery as he was working more shifts at the hospital. It had been almost eighteen months since Simon's accident (she didn't like to call it his death) but still felt exceptionally raw to her.

It had been quite hard getting back into the groove of work but she knew everything would get better and it wouldn't be too long before she could get involved with the day-to-day running of the surgery again. Patients and staff had spoken with her and held her hand, some tightly; saying they had all been thinking of her and that every day was a new day.

Meg thought how lovely the local community were towards her. She was sitting quietly alone in her office when there was a tap on the door. Looking around, she could see Louis standing in the doorway.

'Hi there, is everything alright?'

'Good so far.'

He walked across the room towards her and as they talked, she noticed his eyes were focusing straight on her. He pulled up a chair and sat beside her. They both felt awkward feelings at that moment. What was happening? Her heart was beating faster than a racing car. All she knew was that, she felt safe and protected when they were together.

They sat and chatted for a while before he told her he had to go and see a patient. As he left, he turned around and looked back and said, 'Take care, Meg, perhaps we could get together again soon.'

'That would be lovely,' Meg replied with elation.

Driving home, she couldn't think of anything other than Louis. Was she being silly? Was this right? He had been in her thoughts for much of the day.

Danielle rang her on the mobile. 'How are you, Meg? I was hoping to pop over this evening after work if that is okay with you.'

'Of course, I will get the wine chilled.'

'That sounds lovely, Meg. See you later.'

As Meg parked the car in the drive, she saw her Dad busy in the garden. She waved and said, 'Just popping inside for a quick shower.' Dad then got back to his pottering and weeding. It was so nice to have Mum and Dad with them. They were a family once again.

After her shower, she just slumped onto the bed. There were so many thoughts going on in her head. Did Louis really want to see her and have another day out with them or was he just being extremely friendly and supportive? She didn't know what to think! They all sat down to a lovely meal prepared and cooked by Mum.

'Eat up, everyone; there is more if you want it!'

The boys' couldn't wait to finish before they walked over for seconds.

'That was great, Nan!'

'It's been a long time since I have cooked for a family,' she said, 'and I have to admit I am getting used to it,' glancing at her grandchildren.

Danielle arrived with a bottle of something under her arm.

'Hi guys.'

'We are in the kitchen, Danielle,' Meg shouted.

Katie ran up to her, jumping in the air with sheer delight and gave her a loving kiss. Danielle returned the affection and handed the boys and Katie some sweets. Meg ushered everyone into the garden and everyone sat under the magnolia tree in the evening sun.

Meg carried out a tray of chilled wine, squash and some cheesy biscuits and they just sat chatting and laughing, which was now becoming a little more frequent for them all in recent weeks. It was getting dark and a little nippy, so Mum and Dad decided to go inside and make their usual hot drink before going up the wooden stairs to bed. It wasn't long afterwards the children followed.

Mum shouted, 'Shall I clear away the glasses?'

'No, Mum, I can do that; you go to bed and get a good night's rest.'

As Danielle was leaving, Meg began to wonder whether she should tell Danielle about these feelings she had for Louis or should she keep quiet? She had nobody else to talk to—she couldn't speak to Mum and Dad because they might think it was too soon.

Meg decided not to mention anything and they waved each other goodbye. A few weeks later, Mum and Dad had settled well into their new lives in France and the children loved having them around. Being busy at the surgery and Louis doing his extra shifts at the hospital, Meg hadn't seen too much of him.

The receptionist told her Louis was due back within the next couple of days. Once again, her heart was beating fast; she was beginning to feel quite excited but at the same time, very nervous at seeing him. Why? The next day, Meg strolled across to Reception, where she saw Louis fumbling through paperwork in the treatment room.

He summoned her over. Meg slowly but slightly eagerly walked over to him. He touched her shoulder and asked how the family were. She told him they were all looking forward to arranging a short holiday during the school holidays.

'Ah, where to?' He asked.

'Um, not too far away.'

Louis mentioned that he hoped Alice and Katie could meet again soon.

'Let's arrange something, Meg.' She could tell by the enthusiasm in his voice that he wanted to organise something soon.

'How about next Sunday?' She said with a hastening in her voice thinking sooner, rather than later.

He looked pleasantly relieved, as if that was what he wanted to hear. He then checked his diary and said that sounded good with him.

'It's a date then,' Meg said.

She couldn't wait to tell Katie they were meeting up with Louis and Alice again on Sunday. Mum, Dad and the boys had arranged a fishing trip on Sunday so that it would be just Katie and herself. Louis told Meg not to prepare a picnic, he was going to book a restaurant for lunch.

'All you need to do is turn up. I have planned everything else.'

Meg couldn't wait for Sunday to arrive. Katie was full of excitement and so too, were the boys about their fishing trip with Nan and Gramps. They were all bouncing around like rubber balls and it was a most fantastic feeling. Walking towards Mum, Meg asked, 'Are you both happy and enjoying living here?'

'Of course, we are dear, as you can see for yourself, Dad's health has improved, making me happy and less worried.'

'I am so pleased, Mum, because I have been thinking, instead of looking at the property in the village we recently chatted about, why not come and live with us? We have plenty of room, as you can see. Dad has everything he needs for the garden and we can go out on day trips to the shops and have quality time with the children. It makes complete sense!'

Mum looked up in amazement and didn't know what to say.

'Do you mean we live here permanently?'

'Yes, of course, I do. Why not? The money from selling your home in England will give you and Dad everything you want, including that new car Dad has his eye on!'

'I don't know what to say, Meg.'

'Don't say anything. Dad would love to stay here; he loves the garden and looks so happy when digging away, pruning the roses and watering the plants. We can all live together as one happy family. What do you say?'

Mum squeezed Meg's hand and told her she couldn't have wished for a loving, more thoughtful daughter.

'Ah, I must have got that from you, Mum.'

With a spring in her step, Mum hastily walked into the garden, about to give Dad the news. He noticed her silhouette on the ground, shining in the bright sunshine; he looked up with some difficulty straightening his back from planting the veggies. As Mum began to tell him about their little chat, the expression on his face was a picture.

Although Meg couldn't hear what they were saying, she could see the delight on their faces. Katie asked Meg if Nan and Gramps would live with them forever.

'Perhaps poppet; we will have to wait and see.'

Mum walked back into the kitchen and told Meg that Dad agreed with the decision to live here. Katie was overjoyed, cheering and jumping, clapping her hands together. The twins were delighted, too, because they could take Gramps fishing on the nearby lake. Sunday was rapidly approaching. Louis rang her to say that he thought the girls might like a visit to the zoo.

'Katie would love that,' Meg told him.

'Good. I have booked a restaurant near the zoo for lunch.'

'That sounds wonderful.'

Louis told her that he was going for a run beforehand and would pick her and Katie up around midday. She checked to ensure Mum had packed enough food for two ravenous boys and Reuben for their fishing trip. Katie was wearing her favourite dress—it was bright yellow with little white daisies and she looked lovely, with her long golden hair falling over her back.

Looking at Meg, she said, 'Daddy always loved me wearing this dress.'

'I know he did and you can always think of him when you wear it.'

'I will, Mummy, I will!'

She knew Simon would want them all to be happy. Meg looked out the window at the boys loading up the car with their fishing tackle into Dad's car. They appeared to be a functional family once again. They had to move forward. Life was changing, only slightly but enough to make adjustments for everyone.

The boys waved out as the car drove off for their day's fishing. Dad tooted his horn and they were all off. Reuben stood up, gazing out of the back window, looking forward to his day of adventure. Meg turned around and saw the clock. It was almost midday. They both sat waiting for Louis and Alice to arrive and lo and behold, at that moment, she heard the car drive up to the house.

Katie was showing signs of extreme excitement, Meg too. They both scrambled into the car, both Alice and Louis looking very smart indeed.

'Two gorgeous girls,' Louis called out.

'Thank you, Louis, always ready to impress,' Meg quietly remarked.

Alice and Katie sat in the back of the car and were chatting non-stop all the way. Meg could see that occasionally Louis would glance across at her, then quickly turn away. She also wanted to react in the same way, sensing a fondness between them. As they drove along the N176, in the distance they could see St Mont Michel with its famous monastery.

'After lunch, perhaps we could visit the zoo as promised. It is only a small zoo with very few animals but there is enough for the girls to admire. There are chimpanzees, wild deer and sea lions and penguins too but the funniest is the meerkats, a big attraction for the public. Alice loves them!'

Just before they arrived at St Mont Michael, they stopped at this lovely little French restaurant that Louis had visited before and where he booked them in for lunch. It was a beautiful day and the restaurant was bustling with lots of people enjoying the lovely weather.

The smell of seafood was terrific and Louis told them that this town was famous for its shellfish, especially oysters and mussels.

'Shall we sit inside or outside?'

'Outside,' was the general agreement from everyone.

They found a lovely table overlooking the river that ran through the town's centre. Meg thought to herself, *how Simon would have loved this.* Looking away for one moment, she felt a tear trickle down her cheek. She gently wiped it away and replaced her sunglasses.

Noticing Meg's poignant look, Louis loudly said, 'Let's order.'

They must have sat for at least an hour or two, chatting and laughing, before it was time to get up and take a short drive to St Mont Michael.

'Have we been here before, Mummy?'

Meg told Katie this was somewhere they had planned to visit with Daddy one day. Katie bent her head to the ground; she was weeping somewhat but it wasn't long before there was a happy look on her face when Alice said, 'We are now off to the zoo to see the animals.'

It was more like a wild park than a zoo and the enclosures didn't look secure to her. Nevertheless, it certainly was an experience. Nothing like their local zoo in Devon. The thing that mattered the most was that both the girls loved every minute and yes, Louis was right; the meerkats were very funny.

They both walked closely behind the girls and Louis looked up and said, 'Have you enjoyed your day?'

'Oh yes,' Meg replied.

She wanted to say to him that she didn't want it to end but she thought the expression on her face told him that. Louis turned to her and said, 'Making us happy made him happy too.'

She was beginning to feel some affection between them and wondered if Louis was feeling the same. In a split moment, she felt him looking at her and as she turned to him, he bent over and kissed her.

'I am sorry, Meg, I didn't mean to do that.'

'Louis, it's alright.'

As they leaned towards each other, they kissed again, this time more passionately.

'I know it hasn't been that long since Simon's death,' Louis remarked, 'but I have wanted to kiss you for a long time. Being with you, I feel such a different person. You make me feel loved and belonged, which is something I haven't felt for such a long time. Perhaps one day, Meg, I will explain it all to you.'

'In your own time, Louis.'

All Meg wanted to do was to hold and caress him in her arms. She kept thinking, is this too soon to start any relationship but her heart kept telling her differently. She had made the decision to move forward and start a new life and Louis could be part of that.

They stood talking to each other for ages and she felt there was more to his past. Would he be able to find the right time to explain if something was troubling him? Ah, well, no doubt in his own time. They gathered up the girls and slowly walked back to the car.

They didn't exchange many words on the trek back but she was feeling some affection which she hadn't felt for quite some time and felt the old Meg was coming back and she loved it. As they drove back home, there was some silence between them but there were also passing glances and she noticed Louis gave her an affectionate look, which she tenderly returned.

She looked back behind her and could see both the girls fast asleep. It wasn't long before they were turning into the driveway and as she stepped out of the car with Katie asleep in her arms, Louis said, 'I would very much like to see you again, Meg.'

They both wanted to embrace each other once again but didn't feel it appropriate in front of the children. He touched her hand, squeezed it tightly and said, 'Thank you for a beautiful day.'

Arriving back at the house, Mum, Dad and the boys were waiting for them.

'Have you had a lovely day?' Dad asked.

'We certainly have!'

Meg gingerly carried Katie upstairs to bed. One very tired and exhausted little girl who had a very exciting day! After tucking her in, Meg ran downstairs and was greeted by Reuben licking her legs and jumping up for a cuddle.

Dad mentioned that the boys were getting good at this fishing lark, chuckling to himself like he usually does. It was then Meg couldn't help looking over at the family and thinking how lucky she was to have these wonderful people in her life.

Chapter 15

The school holidays were quickly approaching and Meg needed to book some time off work for a short holiday with the children. Mum and Dad were heading back to England to finalise the sale of their house.

'I am going to miss you both! Hurry back, please!'

Dad told Meg that if everything goes to plan, they should be back in France within a couple of weeks. Now that Mum and Dad had returned to England, she was on her own but having Danielle popping in often, was wonderful and she was always delighted to see her.

Meg still hadn't said anything to her about Louis and her feelings but she would when the time was right. If there was a right time! It was a new day and a new week and as she looked out of her kitchen window, she looked out upon a world bursting with new life.

The pink-white flowers from the magnolia tree and the blossom from the cherry tree were blowing like confetti in the wind and onto the lawn. The wild cherry tree across the lane was spectacular, with a profusion of white bridal blossom. The fields are a patchwork of many shaded greens and the ploughed fields were all different shades of brown.

The trees that lined the woodland showed off their new coats of gentle green. If time allowed, it was time to get her paints and easel and start to draw some of the beautiful landscapes around this beautiful village. Sometimes, when she was standing in the kitchen, she could see deer come out of the woodland to the middle field to eat, sometimes twice, the hares leapt, the cock pheasants strutted and the nervous rabbits scurried along the way.

The blackbird and the nightingale competed in song, sparrows screeched at each other, then suddenly disappeared into the hedges and silence descended again. Meg sometimes felt that she was in a different world. She imagined this to be pure heaven and one of the reasons why they moved to France.

Work at the surgery was undoubtedly busy. So many people needed their aches and pains sorted out. The elderly would pop in for a chat and were indeed fascinating people. They would tell her about their lives during wartime and how they managed with little food.

Food was scarce and handing down clothes from family to family but they always remained positive and happy. They had to be, as they were unsure of their fate each day. Meg listened with great interest and held the hand of a dear little old lady who said she had lost her father and brother fighting in the war.

Meg couldn't imagine living through a war but could relate to losing someone close when she lost Simon. The little old lady left the room and gave Meg some wise words.

'Take care, my dear; you have been feeling great pain but your life will get better. Grief and pain go hand in hand but so do love and devotion. I don't have a crystal ball but there is much hope for your new life!'

Meg later learnt that the little old lady gave out words of wisdom to many in the village and helped them get through extremely difficult times. She certainly gave her words to cherish and cling on to. Saying goodbye and thanking the lady for giving her such wise and beautiful words; as she was about to close the treatment door, she suddenly heard chattering in the distance.

It was Louis and a strange lady talking quite loudly. Meg brushed past and gently nodded to him. He turned away briskly and continued talking to the lady who looked very smartly dressed, with gorgeous long black hair and a little better maintained than hers, Meg thought to herself.

She couldn't help wondering what was going on. He was in deep conversation and she could hear the name Alice mentioned. Meg walked casually towards the front door of the surgery and proceeded to her car. Thoughts were running through her head as she drove back home.

What did that lady want? Who was she? The boys had football after school and Katie was having tea with a friend so that Meg could have a little time to herself. She decided to go for a run which she hadn't had time for in such a long time. Changing her clothes and putting on her trainers, she set off towards the park in St Helene.

She was beginning to feel slightly out of breath and thinking to herself how out of condition she was. To Meg's surprise, she could see Louis sitting on the park bench, talking once again with this lady and they both appeared, to be in deep conversation.

Running past them both, Meg waved out to Louis but again, she could see he appeared to look very uneasy. She kept running, thinking, could this be someone new in his life? Had she been stupid and silly in thinking there could be anything between them?

Meg was beginning to feel more and more let down and very anxious. Was she overthinking it? She arrived home and ran straight upstairs to run a hot shower. What a fool she was! She kept thinking of Louis with that woman, lady, whatever. Who was she, for goodness sake?

Once the children were home and in bed, Meg sat in the kitchen and poured herself a drink. She had to admit that she seemed to be drinking a little more wine than usual but in some strange way, it was giving her the confidence and strength needed to put her life in some perspective.

Glancing out of the window, thinking hard and with her hands wrapped around her chin, Meg began to wonder whether this was an answer to all of this. It must have been about an hour or so later when the phone rang. It was Louis.

'Oh, hello,' she said. 'Is everything okay?'

'Yes but we need to speak!'

She answered quietly but there seemed to be some urgency in his voice. She asked, once more, 'Is everything alright?'

Louis did, however, reassure her there was no need to worry. 'Let me explain about the lady who you saw me talking to.'

A wave of relief comes over her, thinking perhaps all would be revealed and everything would be alright or could Louis be hiding a dark secret which could be troubling him? She didn't know what to think! The next day, Mum rang to say that they had been held up at the solicitors, so they wouldn't be able to get back to France as planned and could be at least another week or so.

'Is there a problem?' Meg said in a poignant voice.

'Nothing to worry about,' Mum said. 'The solicitor has just returned from holiday and everything has been delayed but everything is fine. I will let you know once everything is in place and we can come back, hopefully for the final time.'

Now that the children had started their school holidays, they needed a little holiday for them all, so she decided to book a few days away but she had to find out from Louis what he wanted to speak to her about, so they arranged to meet for a drink in the village.

Still, she must first ask Danielle if she could pop over and sit with the children.

'Of course, Meg, no problem.'

They met in a lovely little bar in the tree-lined square of St Helene, which is a preferred meeting place for the locals. Louis arrived first and rushed over and took Meg's hand and guided her to a seat in the window. He bent over and kissed her on the cheek, which she, too, responded with subtle fondness.

Louis ordered a chilled beer and Meg had a glass of Chardonnay.

'Meg, I wanted to enlighten you about the lady you saw me talking with. Her name is Nicole and she is my wife and the mother of Alice.'

Looking at Louis in sheer amazement, Meg didn't know what to say. She felt her knees shaking and her heart beating twenty to the dozen. She couldn't believe what she was hearing, her stomach started to churn over and she was experiencing a feeling of complete despair.

'We have been separated for almost four years but never divorced. Not yet, anyway. We met at University and got married quite soon after we graduated, about a year or so afterwards and both of us have possibly regretted it ever since.

'We both find we have different interests and living together as husband and wife did not work. The only good thing that has come out of our marriage was Alice. Alice was born and we were happy for a short time, enjoying parenthood like you do.

'After about a year, things got complicated; we argued whenever we were in each other's company and we knew this was not good for Alice. Nicole wanted more out of life than being at home and looking after a baby.

'I suppose she felt she fell pregnant far too soon after we married and had missed out on a lot of enjoyment in life as everyone else does. My main concern was for Alice and what would happen if I left. Would Nicole manage without me?

'Nicole was a medical student like me. After graduation, I continued with my career; Nicole on the other hand decided to give up everything she had studied and went down a different path, working as a make-up consultant in a large department store.

'A complete waste of her studies, time and money spent but then that is Nicole; she changes her mind like the weather! It was a tough decision for me but I knew there was no other way. We concluded that it would be best for both of us if we separated.

'I must admit that Nicole does care for Alice and loves her dearly. We still see each other two or three times every month and try our best to be courteous. I can positively say that there is nothing between us, Meg and you must believe me. If it hadn't been for Alice, we would have divorced long ago.'

She kept listening with interest and was hoping he was telling her everything, although feeling Louis was still hiding much more.

'We both agreed that Alice would remain with Nicole and I would be able to see her as often as possible between my working schedule at the surgery and the hospital. Thinking it could work, it was decided that Nicole would continue living in the flat and I would find somewhere to live close enough so that I could visit regularly.'

'You didn't have a sister that looked after Alice,' Meg remarked.

'I am so sorry but that was an untruth. I don't know why I lied to you. Perhaps it was because I hadn't told you the whole story, which would have complicated matters.'

Louis found himself babbling at this point, saying his heart kept telling him that he had found someone he had feelings for and believed that someone was Meg.

'I just knew I didn't want to lose that feeling.'

'Are you happy, Louis, with this arrangement or do you want to divorce?'

Meg couldn't believe she had just said this; the words just rolled out of her mouth. She couldn't stop herself and was now feeling very embarrassed at what she had just said.

Quickly, Louis answered her, 'A divorce is the right thing to do for everyone. I know that now. I can see Alice whenever I want to and I don't want the courts to limit my visits, so that is why we have not gone ahead with a divorce until now.'

'What do you mean?' Meg asked.

'Meg, I have very strong feelings for you and I hope you have the same feelings for me.'

Meg couldn't believe what she was about to say for one moment but it came out anyway. *Here we go again!* She thought to herself. She kept saying to herself, 'Say what you feel, Meg,' and so she did.

'Louis, I am getting my life back and I would like you to be part of that for both the children and me. Alice and Katie have become great friends. Mum and Dad enjoy your company; the boys are always excited when you visit. You have put substance back into our lives but as you know, Simon will always be with me and I cannot change that.'

'Yes, Meg. I know he will but when you are ready to take the next step, I will be there for you if that is what you want.'

They both leaned across the table and held out each other's hands. Suddenly, she felt a strong feeling of love and devotion. The little old lady in the surgery was right; she knew her life was going to change. Everything she told her was slowly happening.

Meg was now beginning to understand why it had been tough for Louis to divide his life between work, Alice and Nicole. He was trying his best to do the right thing but knew it would be complicated if he still had Nicole in his life. Louis had to make some crucial decisions and Meg was not going to stand in his way, although she knew she wanted him to choose, if he could, without too much hurt.

It was getting dark and the bar was empty, so they both left and strolled back to where they parked the cars. Holding her hand, he squeezed it tight like he had done so many times before. They stopped alongside Meg's car and standing motionless, he brushed away the hair from her face as they gazed into each other's eyes.

He placed a loving kiss on her lips and said, 'I will ring you tomorrow.'

'Am I falling in love all over again? Is it too soon?'

Driving back home, Meg couldn't help thinking about Nicole. Was he telling her everything? She wasn't quite sure and needed to know more before she made any important decisions about their relationship, because she had her family to think of who were the most important people in her life right now, although she knew her feelings for Louis were getting stronger all the time.

What should she do? She had decided to hold on to her feelings and Louis' secret for a while. Meg needed to make sure she was doing the right thing as she didn't want to hurt anyone just in case it was only infatuation. She didn't think it was but after all that had happened in her life recently, she needed to be sure she was making all the right decisions not just for her but for the family too.

As promised, Louis rang her the next day. They had a long chat and laughed a little but told him she was taking the children away for a few days. He thought it was a good idea and Meg told him that a few days away with the children may put everything in perspective.

Arranging a short holiday away would give her thinking time, although she knew there wasn't much to think about but needless to say, she wanted to be able to explain fully and truthfully to her family her feelings for Louis at the right time.

Excitement got the better of her and Louis was constantly on her mind. Having a break for a few days was going to be good but at the same time, she knew she was going to miss him. Strolling into the garden, she sat under the magnolia tree.

She could hear herself speaking to Simon and as she did, a leaf fell from the tree above and hovered above her head. It was surreal, somewhat bizarre. Could this be a sign that Simon was listening to me? Meg began talking out loud, asking for his blessing should things work out between her and Louis.

A sprinkling of blossom fell from the magnolia tree. She immediately knew that this was Simon answering her and giving his approval. In a very strange way, it was as if he was encouraging her to go ahead and make a new life with Louis.

As Meg looked up through the branches of the tree, she called out, 'I will never forget you, my darling and I know you would want me and the children to be happy.'

Excited children, suitcases packed, car loaded, Reuben making sure they did not leave him behind, they set off for a few days to the seaside. Meg just knew they had to make the most of this quality time together and that's what they were going to do.

They put so much into their short holiday break and were so lucky they had warm and sunny weather. The children ran in and out of the sea constantly every day. Reuben was walked and exercised more than usual, loving all the attention he so totally deserved.

Katie would sit on the floor giving him cuddles and playing with him but it didn't take him long to snuggling down in his bed for a long sleep at the end of a very busy day. After Simon's accident, Reuben would walk around the house and garden, looking lost, hoping to see Simon pop out from behind the fence or tree.

All you have on your mind at that awful time is your own feelings, not even thinking about how your faithful furry friend would be feeling. On reflection, she felt sorry because she knew he wasn't getting the attention he should have.

It didn't take long before he bounced back to the Reuben they all knew and loved and began to appreciate that they were always there for him, even though they had been dealing with a family crisis.

Chapter 16

Their holiday was almost coming to an end. Meg had done quite a lot of thinking, trying to sort her life out and making some crucial decisions hoping they were the right ones. They returned having spent some happy days together. Although tired, the children made this holiday very special for her, too.

She just loved the way they were so grown up and making her life a lot easier in what were still dark days. She now knew it wouldn't be long before she could let them in on her secret about Louis and hoped they would understand and be happy, not just for her but for all of them.

Mum and Dad had now returned to France and settled into their new French way of life. Time was flying by and winter was now drawing near once again with the days beginning to get shorter. Dad had been chopping up the logs for the wood burner as he always does and doing a good job, too.

The boys were helping but soon lost interest when a friend called and asked if they would like a game of floodlight football at the stadium. They rushed off and told Dad they would bring the logs in later. Dad turned around and sniggered slightly, which was all that was needed to see he was okay with that.

Mum ran out of the door and said, 'There is a phone call, Meg; I think it is Louis.'

'Oh, thanks, Mum; I am on my way.'

She handed me the phone with a strange grin on her face. They always say you can't keep anything away from your mother. Is she aware of anything between herself and Louis? Of course not. She had not said anything to suggest there was anything between them. Or had she?

'Hello Louis, how are you?'

'Good, thanks but I wanted to tell you that I am being sent to England for a short while to lecture students on the immune system at a hospital in London.'

'Wow, how interesting! How long?' Meg asked.

'Still waiting to hear but it could be for a month or two or even longer.'

There was a short pause before Meg said, 'What an opportunity, Louis. You must go for it.'

'I know and it is something that I have been working towards for such a long time.'

'Fantastic news! I am delighted for you.'

Louis asked if they could meet up on Saturday before he left for London.

'Are you going that soon?' Meg said in an unassuming voice.

'Yes, they need me for the first lectures next Monday. Everything has happened so quickly.' Feeling somewhat nervous, Louis just wanted to spend time with Meg before he departed to London, knowing he was going to miss her very much. 'Both Alice and you were my main concerns when I made this decision.'

'No, Louis, please don't give it a second thought and don't let us stop you from doing something you have wanted to do for such a long time.'

His voice changed on the phone and he said, 'Do you know something, Meg, whilst I was living with Nicole, she never once showed any interest in what I was doing. I began to fall into the trap of just working at the hospital and not achieving the goals in life that I had set for myself.

'I honestly wanted to raise my sights higher within the medical profession and I knew that if I wanted to do this, I must go ahead without Nicole in my life. I could see that if I didn't take the opportunities given to me, at some point my mental health would suffer and all that I had worked for so long, would have been for nothing.

'We talked at length about what we should do and I was pleased when Nicole decided we should go our separate ways. As I told you before, the agreement is that Alice remains with Nicole but I have access to her as often as possible.'

'Well, Louis, if what you have told me is true, then you are doing the right thing, not only for Alice, who is so important but for yourself too.'

'Are you still OK with Saturday, Meg?'

'Yes, that would be lovely.'

'I will book a table at the local restaurant Chez Hubert in St Helene for 7'oclock.'

In a softening voice, Meg said that she hoped everything would work out for him and was looking forward to Saturday. As she put the phone down, Mum walked across the kitchen.

'Are you ok, dear?'

'Yes, Mum that was Louis.'

'He appears to have become such a good friend to you, Meg and I am delighted that you have similar interests and like being in each other's company.'

'I am going to miss him a lot,' Meg remarked, in a somewhat matter-of-fact voice, trying hard not to blurt anything out.

She rushed out the kitchen door and walked back into the garden, where Dad was digging up the vegetable patch. Dad bent over on his spade and said in a quiet and modest voice.

'You look puzzled, Meg.'

'I have a lot on my mind Dad but everything will sort itself out.'

Meg then quickly changed the subject and said, 'Are you enjoying the gardening, Dad?'

He looked up, sensing something was troubling her and said, 'If you need to talk, I am a good listener,'

'I know you are Dad, what would I do without you?'

He then looked down at his watch and muttered, 'It must be time for a cuppa?'

'It's like the Gobi Desert here.'

Meg tapped him on the shoulder and gave him a cheeky smile. She wanted to tell her Dad about Louis, always knowing he would be there for her, no matter what the outcome. Would Dad find it hard to adjust to a new man in his daughter's life?

Dad and Simon were exceptionally close and Louis would have to take the place of someone very dear to Dad. All these questions kept circling around her head. The time had to be right before she told anyone! Meg was taking the children into town to get their hair cut but as they were leaving the salon de coiffure, Danielle was standing outside the florist.

She quickly walked over and told her the news about Louis and his work in London. Danielle put her arms around Meg, beckoning her into the shop for a quick catch up. They sat and talked for almost an hour between customers asking for flowers for their loved ones. The fragrance surrounding the shop was beautiful; the scent of freshly cut jasmine, lavender and lily of the valley was gorgeous.

As they were about to leave, Danielle wanted to know how long Louis would be away but Meg couldn't tell her because she didn't know exactly. Katie looked up and said she would miss Louis.

'Can we still see Alice, Mummy?' she asked.

'I hope so,' but at this point, Meg could see the boys begin to fidget as if to say they needed to get back home for tea.

'We will catch up again soon,' Danielle called out.

Mum had cooked Coq-au vin for tea and it smelt amazing. Meg was only sorry she wasn't able to eat with them but thrilled at the thought of meeting with Louis at the restaurant. She put on her jacket and told Mum and Dad she wouldn't be late home.

She drove to this little quaint restaurant in the centre of St Helene. Louis was waiting for her and handed her some beautiful flowers and as usual, his gentle mannerism just captivated her. They sat and constantly talked between a delicious meal and plenty of wine.

Meg was so happy that Louis had this fantastic opportunity to work on something he had been trying so hard for a long time to achieve. After many exams and hard work, he had made the grade of not only becoming a doctor but also an Immunologist if things worked out for him.

Meg felt extremely proud of him. He told her that he had packed a couple of bags and was on the early Monday morning flight to London. She couldn't stop thinking that it could be a long time before she would see him again but as usual, social media would play a large part in their frequent contact with each other.

A slight giggle from both of them and as he stretched out his hand to clasp with hers, they sat and quietly took a moment to look at each other. They left the restaurant, not saying too much and as they walked over to the car, he put his arms out and held her tightly; so tight, it hurt but she didn't care.

They kissed for ages and ages but she always felt that he was trying to protect her and keep her safe.

'Keep in touch Louis and I hope everything goes well for you.'

Driving back home, she couldn't help thinking about how much she had enjoyed an evening spent with Louis but most of all, hoping he and Nicole would sensibly work everything out for the best and their future.

Meg stepped out of the car and slowly walked to the house, the lights shone through the half-opened curtains and as she opened the door, Reuben came running to greet her. It was quiet and everyone had gone to bed, so she sat with Reuben, just staring into the glowing fire, thoughts running wild and her head spinning.

Her eyes were slowly closing and the warmth of the fire caused her to fall into a deep sleep. She must have been there most of the night because Dad came down and shook her gently.

'My dear, are you okay?'

'Oh yes, Dad, I must have fallen asleep.'

'Get a hot drink, go to bed and get some proper rest. Today is Sunday, so you can sleep all day if you wish.'

If only I could, Meg thought to herself.

Dad made a cup of tea for both of them and as she took it upstairs, turned and said, 'Thank you, Dad.'

'That's alright, dear; now you get some sleep, you look like you could do with it.'

Meg chuckled and she knew everything was going to be alright. It was midday when she woke. The children! She jumped out of bed, pulled back the curtains and could see them happily enjoying a day in the garden with Dad, who was always in his element when they were with him.

Meg casually walked downstairs, Reuben was happy in his basket chewing something or other and Mum was preparing lunch—Sunday roast smelt amazing!

'Morning,' she said.

Mum jokingly replied, 'I think it's good afternoon,' turning around looking at the clock.' Pouring a cup of coffee, she asked probing slightly, 'Did you enjoy your evening with Louis last night?'

Could this be a good time to explain her feelings for Louis? Meg resisted yet again. When would she know the right time?

Chapter 17

Monday morning at the surgery was extremely busy but not unusual—there was always the weekend aches and pains that needed attention but all Meg could focus on was her thoughts of Louis travelling to London and hoping he arrived safely.

Waiting in anticipation for him to ring, later that evening as she sat patiently by the phone, Louis rang. Meg didn't want to seem as though she was eagerly awaiting his call, so she let it ring a few times before calmly answering. Louis had booked into his hotel and so far, so good and was meeting up with another doctor for an evening meal at the hotel, who, too, was carrying out similar lectures.

Mum popped her head around and then quickly walked away. Was Mum doing a gentle bit of prying? After they finished their natter, Meg was feeling saddened as she put the phone down and could feel her heart beating fast. Could Louis be missing her like she was missing him?

Unceremoniously, she walked back into the living room; her face was beaming like a Cheshire cat.

'Decision made! I am going to do it! It is good to have you all together. I have something to tell you!'

Heads turned around in amazement.

'Are we going on holiday again?' Charlie asked.

'Nothing like that Charlie but it is something important that I believe needs your approval.'

As Meg began to tell them about how Louis and she had become good friends, she could see the sheer delight on the faces of both Mum and Dad. The children began teasing each other, giggling and poking each other. Meg told them that both she and Dr Bernier or perhaps she should say Louis, have now become very good friends outside of work.

'I expect you have all noticed that we both enjoy each other's company and I know you all have a lot of respect for him. We are seeing a lot more of each other and he makes Mummy very happy. You must also remember he will never replace your Dad and most importantly, I want you all to know that. I have felt over the past few months that it is now time for me to move on and make a life not only for myself but you also.'

Mum and Dad didn't ask her too many questions but said, 'As long as he made me happy, that's what mattered.'

Meg thanked them both for their understanding and told them that she would make sure she was doing the right thing not only for herself but for everyone.

'I know you will,' they both said.

Sensing the children's reactions gave her the answer she wanted to hear.

'We love you, Mum and want you to be happy. Dad would want you to be happy too.'

In the weeks that followed, their phone calls got longer and longer and sometimes they would FaceTime with Katie getting involved, asking all sorts of questions about London and how she had never been there, even though she lived a small part of her life in England.

Louis replied, 'Perhaps one day we can take you to see the many interesting sights.'

'Yes, please, I would like that.'

They would talk and laugh for ages, saying it wouldn't be long before he was back in France, perhaps another couple of weeks or so. Meg felt so happy at the thought of seeing him again. He had been gone for almost six weeks, which seemed a lifetime.

However, he did say that he wanted to talk about something with her but didn't want to discuss it over the phone. She wasn't sure if it filled her with delight or displeasure. She was hoping by the tone of his voice it wasn't the latter.

They said their goodbyes and he told her he would ring at the weekend. As she put the phone down, thoughts were running wild in her head. What was so important he needed to discuss? Days were now running into weeks and winter was well and truly upon them.

Frosty mornings, clear blue skies, crisp, clean and fresh. Meg just loved this time of year! A run before work, even a trip to the gym was something she now looked forward to very much and she was beginning to feel good about herself.

On a couple of occasions, Danielle was able to join her on a run.

'Not too sure about joining the gym though,' she remarked. 'A bit too much like hard!'

Meg was surprised to learn, however, that they had run over 10kms some days.

'Wow,' Danielle said. 'I didn't know I had that in me.'

They both stopped in their tracks, out of breath, with rosy cheeks and hot breath forming a small cloud in the cold air. Meg thought it over and over in her mind and now that Mum, Dad and the children were aware of her relationship with Louis, perhaps it would be best if Danielle knew too.

She quickly spoke, without stopping for a breath telling Danielle her fondness for Louis.

'Well, Meg, you kept that quiet, didn't you? I am not surprised though you both look so good together.'

Danielle seemed to be muttering with excitement, saying, 'I have known Louis for quite some time—he is a very kind man and extremely dedicated in his work but I have to tell you that he would never let anything come between him and Alice. He adores her and would do anything for her and is an extraordinarily stable and honest person. Tell me Meg, is Louis more than a friend?' she asked in a very pertinent voice.

'We are taking things slowly but yes, it is more than friendship.'

However, Meg did say that she too adored Alice like her own and would never let herself come between them.

'I know you wouldn't,' Danielle replied, 'but I had to say something not only for the sake of Louis and Alice but you too. Taking on another child in a relationship can be difficult but with so much trauma you have experienced over the past few years, I think you will cope admirably.'

Danielle went on to say that Louis had been very unhappy with Nicole for such a long time. Then Danielle had to admit to Meg that she did know about Nicole, as both she and Louis had been friends for quite some time; not in a romantic way, just a shoulder to cry on at times.

Louis would come into the shop and would confide to her about his life with Nicole but lately he had asked Danielle not to speak about Nicole to Meg. He wanted to find the right time to tell Meg himself.

One day he will find that someone he can be happy with, I think that could be you!

Danielle went on to say that she knew how much Simon's death significantly impacted Meg and the children. 'Simon would undoubtedly want you to be happy, wouldn't he?'

'Yes, he would but I didn't think anybody would come into my life so quickly. It doesn't seem that long since the accident and I keep thinking, should I wait? But something tells me I will know when the time is right and I think I have.'

'Time is a healer, Meg and it is almost three years since you lost Simon; I don't think you would be rushing into anything for one moment. I believe you have chosen the right time.'

Looking up at her, Meg gently gave a smile and nod of appreciation.

'Thank you for being my friend, Danielle!'

'My pleasure,' she said.

It seemed ages that they were standing chatting in the country lane, their legs getting redder from the cold air and the warmth of their bodies cooling down. It was getting twilight and the trees were blowing frantically in the wind. They were both looking forward to a hot shower.

As they jogged nearer the house, Danielle's car was parked in the driveway. Ice was beginning to form on the windows and they could see frost appearing on the ground.

'It is going to be a cold night,' Meg said.

'Yes, you are right.'

Danielle quickly thawed out the windscreen on her car and as she started up the engine, she waved out and said, 'I hope to see you again very soon.'

'Next time 20k,' Meg shouted.

Danielle answered, 'You must be joking,' speaking with a humorous tone.

Meg ran into the house, pushed by the children playing with Reuben and said, 'I am off to have a hot shower.'

Mum and Dad were sitting beside a roaring fire, nodding off with a snore here and there. She was now beginning to miss Louis a lot—it just seemed such a long time since she saw him last and although they kept in touch daily, it wasn't the same.

The village was getting ready for Christmas and the lights and trees looked festive in St Helene. The Maire had been invited to switch the lights on, so they all decided to pop down to the village for the annual illumination of the square.

The children were always excited this time of year and Meg wanted to make it memorable for both the children and Mum and Dad.

She did know, however, that Louis would be back very soon, making it even more special. She invited him and Alice for Christmas lunch and hoped he would accept the invite. The tree-lined streets looked beautiful, with the lights glimmering down from the branches and there were little miniature Christmas trees mounted on the balconies above the shops.

How beautiful. The villagers all helped to make it very festive and inspiring for everyone. They all strolled back home; the cold air was quite bracing. Reuben enjoyed sniffing the frozen ground and as they walked further, she could see the lake near the house frozen over—it was going to be a very cold night.

'Hot chocolate all around!'

'Oh yes, please!'

They sat and clutched the delicious hot chocolate with their hands wrapped around the mugs for extra warmth and they just gently stared into the burning fire. As Meg glanced across the room, she could see that Dad looked tired and pale. She hoped he wasn't coming down with something.

Since living in France, his asthma had been good and she put it down to the clean, fresh air. Meg ambled over to him, brushed his brow and said, 'Everything okay, Dad?'

'Just a little tired,' and as he quietly got out of his chair, he said, 'I am off up the wooden stairs to bed. Goodnight, everyone.'

The children gave him a gentle kiss and said their goodnights too. Meg mentioned to Mum that she thought Dad was looking tired.

'You know your Dad. He doesn't like to worry anyone but I thought the same. I know he is taking his tablets but he is due for a check-up at the doctor's next week.'

'Good but let's keep an eye on him!'

Everyone was up and about early the next day; it was school for the children and her day off at the surgery, so she was going to make the most of it. Charlie and Freddie were excited because they had been chosen for the school football team and were playing a match after school later that day.

The boys were making such a good impression at their new school and making lots of new friends. However, Katie was still somewhat shy and found it a little harder to involve herself in school life entirely but she was getting there.

She was loving her swimming, although perhaps not quite the same as she did back in England.

Only time will tell, Meg thought to herself.

Meg thought she was still missing Olivia quite a lot and often asked her if she was coming back here to live. She couldn't answer that, not knowing if her life had now changed for good back in England.

'You never know, Katie; she may come back for a visit; who knows?'

Meg decided to catch up on odds and ends around the house and perhaps pop into town to see Danielle and have a girlie chat and a cup of her yummy coffee. Dad was still looking a bit peaky and Meg was beginning to get slightly worried about him. Once he had visited the doctor, she would have peace of mind.

She kept busy with work and household chores and told Mum and Dad she was off to St Helene to chat with Danielle. As she strolled through the town, it looked very festive. It was early December, so she did a little Christmas shopping.

It was very different from shopping back home in England. You could browse the shops without being pushed here and there and fighting for car spaces. It was so much more relaxed and she liked it.

Chapter 18

The sky above was looking grey and as Meg walked precariously on the icy footpaths, a sprinkling of snow began to fall to the ground covering the cobbled pavements. It was starting to look so pretty with the sparkling snow pitching on the rooftops. It reminded her of a Christmas card.

It was beautiful! The market sellers were busy setting up their stalls, which would remain open until Christmas Day in the village. The smell of the crepes cooking was so inviting and delicious and she had to stop and buy one. Strolling across the square to the florist, she saw Danielle serving a customer.

She looked through the window and waved out at her and said, 'Come on over. I won't be long, Meg; I am just about to finish this bouquet and will be with you.'

'Don't rush,' Meg told her.

She loved being in the shop with the sweet-smelling fragrance of all the flowers filling the room with beautiful perfume. Christmas was a busy time for Danielle, as the tradition in France was to give plants or flowers as presents. Sitting quietly towards the back of the shop, it wasn't long before Danielle joined her. She was interested to know if Louis had rung and asked when he would be returning home.

Hopefully very soon, she said as it would be nice to have him back for Christmas. As usual, they sat and chatted for quite some time and a couple of cups of coffee later and in between customers, Meg got up and left, saying she would meet with her again soon.

Meg enjoyed their chats and they always seemed to be putting the world to rights. Danielle had become a very dear friend to her. Outside, the snow was falling heavily and the brisk wind allowed it to drift into the side of the road. When Meg got home, she saw a strange car in the drive. *Who is that calling at this time of the day,* Meg thought to herself.

As she walked into the kitchen, she could see Mum was looking extremely distressed and she rushed over to her and said, 'What is the matter, Mum?'

'It's your father! Dad is having trouble breathing and couldn't catch his breath. He also slumped into the chair, looking very grey, so thought it best to call the doctor. A doctor is with him now. I did try calling you but your phone went to voicemail.'

Feeling terrible, Meg reacted, 'Oh, I am so sorry, Mum. I was at the florist and sometimes there is a bad signal.'

She didn't know what to say.

'Don't worry my dear, you are here now.'

Meg cautiously walked over to where Dad and the doctor were and asked if he was okay. He told me that Dad needs to up his medication and take things easy for a while. He may have been overdoing things, which was the body's way of telling him to slow down.

Dad then looked at her and smiled as if to say, "Are you talking about me?"

Meg gazed at Dad and told him that he must listen to the doctor.

'I will,' he said with a cheeky grin.

Even the doctor gave a little smirk. 'You need to treat the older ones like children sometimes and tell them what to do.'

'I agree,' Meg said.

The doctor began writing out Dad's prescription and told them that he was in pretty good shape apart from taking a little more medication. That was a relief to them all, even Mum had colour back in her cheeks and they thanked the doctor who wished them all well.

Ushering the doctor out of the door, Meg casually asked him, 'Do you happen to know Dr Bernier?'

After some thought, he said, 'Oh yes! I remember I spent some time with him when we were junior doctors at Dinan General Hospital.'

'Do you know him well?' Meg asked.

'Not really.'

He did tell her however, they would go to this little bar near the hospital after a busy day for a bit of relaxation and he found him extremely hard working. His wife had given birth to a little girl at the time they were training together. He did appear to be going through a troublesome marriage at the time.

'Yes, I know,' Meg uttered.

'He also told me that one day he had always planned to specialise in Immunology, which was a path in his career he would like to follow. Louis was always adamant about that but it would mean more hard work for him and having such a volatile home life, he couldn't see any way of achieving this.'

Meg was feeling much sadness for Louis having to go through a difficult marriage at a time when he wanted to gain so much from what he loved doing. He had to put everything behind him and wait for the right time to proceed with the dream of becoming an Immunologist one day.

'I feel so proud that he is finally achieving what he set out to do.'

Snow was still falling with no sign of stopping and as Meg walked out to the garden with the doctor, she thanked him for taking care of Dad.

'No problem and if you need me anytime, ring this number should I need him urgently.'

Closing the front door, Meg could see Mum was fretting around Dad. She could see Dad didn't want any fuss but would get it anyway.

'Well, that was good news, wasn't it, Mum?'

'Yes but I did think he may have had to go to the hospital.'

'Don't worry, Elizabeth,' (and he only called her by her Christian name when he wanted to make a statement); usually, it is Liz or dearest. 'I am fine and can't wait to get back out in the garden and join the boys fishing.'

'Oh no, you're not,' Meg told him sharply. 'Rest well and get used to us all fussing around you.'

Dad sighed as if to say, "I don't do rest," but they were going to make sure he took it easy for a week or so. She didn't know what made her think it but she had it on her mind for some time now.

'Now that Mum and Dad are permanently living with us and Dad's health is not one hundred per cent, I can see the garden is quite large and needs a lot of upkeep, giving him a lot of work, so I have decided to pack up my job at the surgery and stay home with the family.

'I know when Simon died, it gave me something else to think about and for that, I was very grateful but now I have more important things to think about. I would be more help to the family by being here for them. There were still boxes in the garage that needed sorting through and there is always gardening, which I know Dad will have to put to one side for a time yet.'

Meg hastily told Mum and Dad and they said, 'Please don't do anything you will regret!'

Meg spoke to Mum quietly and said that Dad's health worried her sometimes and she wanted to be there to help her. She had been so annoyed with herself when Dad was poorly and nobody was able to reach her. That must never happen again.

Mum put her arms around her and they held each other quietly for a moment. It was like when Meg was a little girl and she came running over to Mum asking for a cuddle, wanting some love and attention. Meg always knew she would be there for her, no matter what.

'My mind is made up!' Meg declared. 'I will hand in my notice at the surgery on Monday.'

'Please make sure you are doing the right thing,' Mum said.

'I am; I know I am!'

Chapter 19

Meg's last day at the surgery was a happy one; chocolates and beautiful flowers were handed to her as a sign of their appreciation. The staff had been wonderful to her and had greatly supported her when she lost Simon, for which she would be truly thankful.

Who knows, one day, she could be back but at the present time, her heart lay at home. That evening, they were all sitting around the table eating dinner when the doorbell rang. She could see a dark shadow shining through the glass door. She gingerly opened the door and to her amazement, it was Louis. She couldn't hold back her excitement any longer.

Meg just rushed into his arms and they kissed and held each other close and very tight. She didn't want to let him go.

'I wanted to surprise you, that's why I didn't phone. Call it an early Christmas present,' he said with a slight giggle.

It was lovely to see him and she thought that he felt the same. Meg accompanied him into the kitchen, where the family sat together, finishing dinner. Mum got up and asked if he had eaten.

'Yes, I had something to eat at the airport.'

Realising that both Louis and Alice would be alone at Christmas, Meg decided to invite them to join their Christmas celebrations and said, 'How about joining us on Christmas Day for dinner?'

Louis looked very startled but said without any prompting and with the utmost pleasure, 'Thank you very much Meg, Alice will be over the moon!'

Katie ran over and put her arms around him—it reminded Meg when Katie would hug Simon. She immediately turned her head to one side and once again, tears began rolling down her cheek.

With a slight tremble in her voice, Meg said, 'That's settled, everyone here for Christmas lunch.'

Then Dad interrupted, saying, 'The more, the merrier.'

Louis walked over to where Dad was sitting in his favourite chair and said, 'I hear you haven't been too well, Mr Thomas.'

'Oh, you can call me Mike. With the excellent care of the wife and daughter, I will be digging that garden again in no time,' he chuckled.

Louis looked across and gave a wry smile.

'Take it steady, young man,' he said. 'You had us all very worried!' Dad gave Louis a friendly wink.

As they walked to his car, the path was very slippery and where the snow was beginning to thaw, the coldness of the night air was making it very icy. Just as they were saying goodbye, Meg decided to tell him she was thinking about giving up her job at the surgery. He looked very surprised but he could understand her reasoning.

Meg was feeling awful because it was Louis who had arranged the job for her and probably thought, at the time, it would help to get her through a challenging time in her life. She then said that she became distraught when her Dad was taken ill.

'I now feel that both Mum and Dad are my responsibility because living in France, must be a such a big change for them, far away from what they have been used to and without any help or support. Without any help from me, they could find it difficult to tolerate a new life at their age. I began to realise I need to be around them as much as possible.'

'Meg, you are incredibly kind, putting others first before yourself. You are the opposite of Nicole and this is what attracted me to you. Your gentleness and kindness is overwhelming.'

Meg started blushing and Louis could see that she didn't take compliments well.

'Changing the subject,' Meg said, 'I have told Danielle about our developing friendship,' and then together laughing at how she used the word "developing".

'Do you mean our everlasting friendship or romantic relationship?' he said.

In a hushed but exact tone, Meg said, 'You know what I mean, Louis.'

Glancing down at her, he said, 'Of course, I do.'

As Louis got into the car, Meg could see cases of wine and numerous bottles of whisky on the back seat.

'Getting ready for a party,' she called out.

'Just a little bit of Christmas shopping.'

Closing the front door, Meg shouted, 'Goodbye and give my love to Alice.'

'I will and we shall be looking forward to spending Christmas Day with you and your family.'

Feeling exceptionally happy, Meg walked back into the house. Excitement was growing, knowing that Christmas Day was going to be very special with everyone they knew and loved, enjoying the festivities with them. Dad was taking it easy, trying to read a French newspaper with great difficulty, so Meg gave him a couple of English gardening magazines she had bought in the town.

Suddenly, she looked out the window and saw a little red car slowly manoeuvring up the drive, tooting its horn. A very smart man stepped out of the car and she could see it was Phillipe. Meg ran over to him and they greeted each other with a kiss on both cheeks, just as they do in France.

'Hello, stranger,' Meg said.

'Bonjour, Meg.'

Phillipe had the most striking auburn hair and radiant blue eyes. He was always impeccably dressed, whatever the occasion. Meg could never understand why he hadn't been married or had a girlfriend because he had a great personality, was funny and exceptionally kind.

'Firstly, let me apologise,' he said, clasping his hands together. 'I didn't mean to lose touch with you over the last few months but you know how it is, life gets in the way and before you know it, days fall into months.'

With a comical grin, Meg uttered, 'I forgive you, Phillippe.'

He always appeared to be very good-humoured and was always making jokes.

'I can't believe we haven't seen you around St Helene.'

'I have been back in England for the last four months, teaching year 11. I even went back to Wickham Junior School to see the memorial seat presented in Simon's memory. Meg, it took my breath away—a lovely man who will never to be forgotten.'

Phillipe touched Meg's shoulder and she told him she would like to visit the school one day and pay her respects too.

'Would you like to step inside for a cup of coffee?' she asked.

'Perhaps we could take a rain check, Meg? I am off to chair a school meeting but I thought we could catch up after Christmas.'

'I would like that a lot,' she said.

Meg could see Simon's death had affected him in some kind of way as he did look saddened when they discussed him. She could tell Phillipe wanted to make sure that they were alright and had no worries. Losing a good friend takes a very long time to overcome. She hadn't thought much about Phillipe because her life seemed to be progressing in all different directions but knew that Simon would have wanted her to make sure she didn't lose contact with his friend.

"I must endeavour to remain friends with Phillipe, possibly for Simon's sake."

As Phillipe walked to his car, Meg shouted, 'Keep in touch, Phillipe.'

Phillipe acknowledged her and said, 'Perhaps we can go for a run sometime.'

Meg gave a thumbs up as if to say she would like that. Christmas Day had arrived and excitement was in abundance. They were all enjoying the most wonderful Christmas, having far too much wine and food but so good in many ways. The laughter of the children, playing games, Mum and Dad listening to the Queen on the television.

They still had English TV and catching up with all the news from back home in the UK was undoubtedly something Mum and Dad loved and would have missed and of course, they had to listen to the Queen's Christmas message at 3 o'clock!

As usual, Dad slowly dropped his head to his chest in a relaxed sleep. Bless him!

'Does anyone want a cuppa?' Mum asked.

She has this motherly way of always fussing around, which was something Meg loved about her. She had been her strength throughout and Meg couldn't begin to thank both Mum and Dad for being there for them and getting them through a very tough time in their lives.

She glanced over at Louis, playing a game with the boys and noticed that he appeared to be drinking heavily. Feeling somewhat concerned, Meg kept her thoughts to herself. As it was now getting quite late, she did say that if he and Alice wanted to stay the night, she could make up extra beds, knowing how much alcohol he had consumed.

'Thanks Meg, if it's not too much trouble.'

Meg hastily got some bedding together and Katie asked if she and Alice could sleep together.

Alice looked up and said, 'Please, please,' with a very excited tone.

'Louis can have the futon in the lounge. That's settled, then!'

Louis and Alice returned home after lunch the next day but not before expressing their extreme gratitude for such a lovely Christmas Day.

Standing in the doorway, Louis gave Meg a loving kiss and said, 'Can I ring you in a day or so?'

'Yes, of course and maybe take Reuben for a walk alongside the river.'

'That would be lovely!'

Tidying up after a busy Christmas was always a chore but with many helpers, it didn't take too long to get the house back in order.

Mum called her and said, 'Is this Katie's scarf?'

Taking a quick look, she said, 'I don't think so but it could be Alice's. Louis should be phoning me this evening so I can mention it then.'

That evening, they decided to settle down and watch some TV, longing for the phone to ring but it didn't. Why hadn't Louis phoned when he promised he would? Although he had some time off, perhaps there was an emergency at the hospital, so decided not to bother him.

It was a couple of days later and Meg still hadn't heard from him. She did try his mobile but it went straight to voicemail so having slightly an enquiring mind, her next move was to drive over and deliver the scarf in person, a little method in her madness, as they say.

She had no reason to think anything was wrong, so she called out to Mum and said, 'I am driving over to see Louis; I won't be long.'

Meg had never visited Louis at home, so this would be a first. They had always met at the Bistro or he would come to the house and pick her up when having a day out altogether.

She knew where he lived because they drove past many times on different occasions and he told her that he was hoping to buy something a little bigger one day, something which would accommodate him and Alice more comfortably.

Driving through St Helene and on the road out of the village, Meg approached this small but lovely cottage. It was tucked away off the road, surrounded by trees and woodland. She casually walked up to the front door and rang the bell. It was all very quiet and she stood there for quite some time but got no answer.

Taking a peek through the small-paned windows, to her horror, Meg could see several empty bottles lying on the table. The room looked untidy and she was surprised to see how a doctor could live like this.

Have I knocked on the right door? Meg thought to herself. *Is this where Louis lived? It must be the wrong house.*

Eventually, she could hear footsteps trundling down the stairs, the front door opened and Louis appeared looking unshaven and very dishevelled. He looked shocked to see me.

'Is everything okay?' he asked in a somewhat shaky voice.

'I am but how about you,' Meg said curiously.

'I would ask you to come in but the house is messy.'

'No worries,' Meg said. 'I just popped over to give you Alice's scarf.'

'Ah yes, thank you, Meg.'

Whilst she was standing outside in the cold December air and feeling somewhat uneasy in his presence, he attempted to reach out for the scarf but appeared extremely wobbly on his feet. As he leaned forward, to her horror, she could detect a smell of alcohol apparent on his breath.

Meg was completely shocked and didn't know what to do or say. Louis spoke with such a shameful look, saying he didn't want her to see him in this condition.

'Whatever has happened to you, Louis?'

'You had better come inside out of the cold.'

They stood in the doorway but he didn't ask her to venture too far into the living area. The cottage hadn't seen a sweeping brush or vacuum cleaner in days. Louis started to tell her what had happened since he left us at Christmas.

'Firstly, I have to say that Alice and I had a wonderful Christmas with you and will never forget your kindness. Christmas was very special for both Alice and myself.'

'Oh, Louis, we are still talking about how much we laughed and joked. We all had a fantastic time too.'

Louis then went on to say that as they drove back home and started to light the fire, settling in for the evening, there was a knock at the door. It was Nicole. She came rushing over, saying she wanted to take Alice back home with her— she had no reason because it was decided before Christmas that Alice could stay until the New Year.

Nicole was appearing very agitated and displayed a chaotic and extremely unusual manner and this was beginning to worry him. He asked her why she had made this decision.

She asked, 'Is it true you are seeing someone?'

'Yes that is correct but what does this have to do with you?'

He wasn't going to enlighten her too much and left it at that.

'Oh, I see,' she said. 'Why didn't you say anything?'

'I don't think it is any of your business, we have been apart now for quite some time and I think that the time has come for us to go ahead, make new lives for ourselves and move forward, possibly down the divorce route.'

Her voice faltered and as she lowered her head, said, 'What about Alice?'

He was now beginning to get annoyed and upset by her attitude. Nicole always knew that one day they would end their marriage and that Alice would be the main priority in her upbringing.

Having gone over and over this many times, he could tell that because he was trying to make something of his life and make new friends, this wasn't going to suit her and she was going to make his life hell and become difficult.

'I didn't want to burden you, Meg with my problems because you have had enough of your own over the past couple of years.'

'That's all very well, Louis but someone must be there for you and I will, if you let me.'

At this point, Nicole was then beginning to get very vindictive and her voice had a strong bitterness.

'I will certainly make sure you only see her when I say so,' speaking in an outraged voice. Nicole called out to Alice and asked her to get her coat. Alice came running to the door, revealing a sorrowful look.

'I don't want to go, Daddy. I want to stay with you.'

Bending over and holding her hand, saying it was best if she went with Mummy and that Daddy would see her soon. Mummy and Daddy needed to have a long talk and then they hoped everything would be alright and that they would be together again.

It was becoming tough for Louis to explain what had happened; his eyes were bubbling up with tears but Meg was determined to listen to everything he said.

'It was awful, Meg! Alice was standing in the doorway, looking at both of us, crying loudly. "I don't like you shouting at each other," she said.'

Louis picked her up, cuddled her and told her it would be best to go with Mummy. They could have a day out together and do whatever she wanted, perhaps visit the zoo once again.

'Yes, please, Daddy,' and as she walked away, she turned back and waved, saying, 'see you soon, Daddy.'

He felt heartbroken and didn't know if Nicole would even agree to let him see her again, judging by her spiteful and malicious manner. He was hurting so much inside, he just sat in front of the fire and began drowning his sorrows with plenty of wine and whisky.

'Come on, let's get started,' Meg said. 'We will attempt to get your house ship-shape and looking tidy when Alice comes back to see you.'

A feeble grin emerged on his face and he said, 'My wonderful Meg.'

There were just a few wine bottles on the rack but nothing else. Louis promised her that it was just a mad moment and that he would never allow himself to drink like this again. He was a professional treating sick people and needed to control every eventuality and be the excellent doctor everyone loved and respected.

He also had to be a father to Alice. He didn't know what came over him but it would never happen again. Meg believed him and they both decided that taking Reuben for a walk along the river would help clear both their heads and so they arranged to meet the next day and do just that.

'Look at the time,' Meg gasped. 'I must rush and pick the boys up from football practice. Are you sure you will be alright?'

'Yes, of course, I will. Don't worry about me.'

'Make sure you have something to eat and try and get some sleep. Oh and don't forget to shave. It's not nice kissing men with stubbly beards,' she said laughingly.

'Has there been plenty of men then?' Louis said with a grin.

Meg could see he was getting a little bit of himself back and said, 'There may have been one or two in the past.' Meg turned around to Louis, saying, 'Tomorrow is another day and we will get through it together.'

Thanking Meg, he agreed to meet with her tomorrow. As she was driving back to pick up the boys, she was hoping Louis would be okay. It must be dreadful not knowing when or if he would be seeing Alice again. Meg could tell Nicole was going to difficult and had to be fully prepared for what she might say and do to get custody of Alice.

After explaining everything to Mum and Dad, as usual, Mum was ready to listen; Dad didn't seem too bothered, although he had taken quite a liking to little Alice because she would sit with him, Katie on one knee, Alice on the other, whilst he would read them a story. Dad was an excellent listener when talking about other people's troubles but would never interfere in other people's problems, only there to give a guiding hand when required.

However, he told Meg not to get involved with their argument, especially when it concerned Alice.

'It would be best if you weren't dragged into it.'

'I know, Dad but he needs some support.'

Having been there for her when Simon died, her heart was telling her that she must be there for him too.

'That's my girl—always helping others.'

'I must have got that from you, Dad!'

As promised, Louis rang and he appeared to be much more himself and very cheery.

'Do you still want to take Reuben for a walk?'

'Oh yes, he would certainly enjoy that.'

'Let's say 2 o'clock then! I will pick you up and then we can drive into Dinan and walk along the river. I know a little café on the riverbank where we can stop for a coffee.'

Meg was waiting anxiously for Louis to arrive; even Reuben was pacing up and down in anticipation of a walk looking at the lead hung on a hook in the hallway. No sooner than she could say, "He won't be long," his car appeared up the drive.

'How are you today?'

'Much better and have you noticed, the beard has gone,' as he softly stroked the side of his face.

Meg laughed out loud and was so happy to see a different Louis. He had the old self back and she liked it.

Chapter 20

The crisp late December sun shone through the somewhat hazy clear skies, their breath steaming in the cold air as they talked and strolled along the riverbank. It seemed to do them a world of good. Reuben was excited, running up and down the bank, enjoying the fresh air and checking out the other dogs too, feeling somewhat amorous with a young Labrador bitch.

'Reuben, this way,' Meg shouted, feeling slightly embarrassed at his actions.

They both carried on walking and talking, occasionally thinking hard of how Louis could make the situation easy for both him and Alice, even more so, surprised to hear that Louis was now making plans for a divorce. He told her he knew the time had come for him to try and go forward and make a new life for himself.

Alice would, of course, be the main priority in all of this and told her that he would do everything in his power to have his little girl back with him permanently and he went on to say this would be a new start Meg, for all of them! Feeling relieved that Louis had finally made a decision, she knew this was right for himself and Alice.

Walking slowly and taking in the beautiful view of the river, Louis shouted, 'Ah, there is the café I was telling you about. Shall we pop in for coffee and cake?'

'That would be lovely,' she had to admit she was feeling a little tired after the long walk. 'They do delicious crepes here too!'

'Oh well, let's go for it, we deserve a treat,' Louis said. 'Chocolate crepe and café latte it is, then.'

Meg asked, 'Do you know when you are seeing Alice again?'

'Not sure but soon, I hope. I must admit that I am looking forward to spending weekends with her when work allows and I hope Nicole doesn't spoil that for me. As you know, work sometimes gets in the way, so that is why time spending time with Alice is important.'

They sat for a while, enjoying their delicious chocolate crepe and watching families with their children laughing and playing. Kites were flying high in the milky blue sky and there was the sound of a band playing Breton music in the distance. Children were jumping in and out of the river and then, suddenly, Louis bent over and gently kissed her cheek.

Meg reacted the same way and they both felt such a loving bond between them. Reuben was sitting chilling in the winter sunshine, looking calm and peaceful, clutching a stick he found along the way, wondering whether he should give it a good chew.

They began their walk back to the car. They were chatting away about nothing specifically, when he said, he had been thinking of getting a puppy for Alice.

'She would love that Louis; she is always talking about Reuben and how adorable he is. Perhaps for her birthday,' Meg softly muttered.

Louis said, 'Yes, maybe!'

Arriving home, Meg didn't want the afternoon to end. She asked Louis to come inside and have a meal but he told her he was busy during the coming week. He was travelling to Bordeaux to tutor another seminar for young medical students.

'I will have to do some swatting up myself first,' he said with a slight grin.

'Of course, I understand!'

'I will certainly call you in a day or so. I should only be gone a few days.'

After a loving hug and a somewhat passionate kiss, they said goodbye. She was going to miss him so much but she did believe everything would have a way of working out for both him and Nicole. She did, however, feel very uneasy at that thought Nicole could become very difficult about the whole divorce.

From what Louis had said, they certainly needed to come to some compromise and mutual agreement over Alice, which appeared to be the most important thing of all. That evening, feeling very tired, Meg decided to have an early night. She thought everything was catching up to her and Mum whispered, 'You are looking a little pale, Meg.'

'I will be alright; I just need some sleep!'

She walked wearily up the stairs to her awaiting bed, hoping everything would work out for Louis. He was permanently on her mind and she wouldn't have any peace until the telephone rang and they could talk. Meg didn't remember anything until she woke up the following day.

Feeling a little less tired and with a gentle yawn, Meg opened her eyes, had a little stretch, walked and stood at the window gazing at the beautiful countryside surrounding their lovely home. A couple of riders on horseback went past, a tractor from the nearby farm transporting fertilisers and several pheasants hopping across the freshly sewn fields.

The peace and serenity here was second to none. The sound of birds gently tweeting as they left their nests looking for food for their young. Raindrops began to fall and gently cascaded down the windowpanes and in between the tall trees, she could see dark skies-possibly a stormy day ahead.

She could stay here for hours but alas, there were chores to carry out and she could hear the children running up and down the stairs. It was always a mad panic in the mornings before school, the boys giving each other verbal abuse about where they had left their football boots and whether they were clean or dirty.

She hurriedly walked downstairs to ask the boys to be more polite to each other. Once breakfast was off the menu, they happily raced outside to catch the school bus. That left Katie to sort out but as usual, she was much more organised than the boys. Katie met up which a friend at the school gates and shouted, 'Goodbye, Mummy.'

Meg watched her slowly walk up the steps into the school. When Simon died, he may not have left her lots of money but he left her something so very special that money could never buy and that was Freddie, Charlie and Katie. The three beautiful children they had together was something that could never be taken from her.

She just sat in the car, watching Katie walk out of sight into the school before she drove off back home. Perhaps she could sort out the garage when she got back! Mum and Dad had gone to the coast for a few days, so she had plenty of time to herself, so decided to get on with it and sort out the junk and boxes stored there.

After a quick chat with Danielle on the phone and a cup of coffee, it was now time to tackle this mammoth task in the garage. Walking outside into the frosty morning air, Meg could see blue lights flashing in the distance and the sound of sirens.

Whatever is happening, she thought!

Meg quickly walked over to the gate and saw at least two police cars speedily pass by. Perhaps there had been a nasty accident up ahead. Not something you hear too much in the village. It was usually very quiet, not like back home where you heard sirens all day. It was very unusual. She went back into the garage and began sorting out the many boxes and clearing away junk.

Looking through a big blue box, Meg came across some photos of Simon. How lucky she was to have had him in her life? There were photos from when he graduated from University, after receiving his diploma. Some of their wedding and what a lovely day that was.

The photos were bringing everything back to her and she knew it was going to be a very long road, trying to control the grief and once more she was becoming a tearful wreck. Meg stood holding the photos close against her chest and not letting them go.

After a few hours, the garage was looking so much better and the boy's snooker table was properly assembled and ready for use. The boys would be so pleased because it was a present from Simon the last Christmas before his accident.

Meg carefully pulled it out and gave it a dusting and positioned it right in the middle of the garage where the boys could come out and play with each other. Meg was hoping the boys would be happy to see their table ready for a competitive game with each other. Reuben was jumping up and down as if he was telling her it was time for his walk.

Walking back into the house, she fetched his lead and they headed for a walk. They decided to cross over the fields, instead of walking down the lane and Reuben was ahead of her as usual, sniffing and quartering as he went. In the distance, she could see blue flashing lights.

They seemed to brighten the skyline and she wondered what it could be. Was it the same flashing lights she saw earlier in the day? Suddenly, a police officer appeared and asked where she was going.

'Just taking the dog for some exercise over the fields,' was her reply.

'You should turn back!'

'Why, what has happened?' Meg said in a frightened voice.

'We have been searching for a young girl missing from her home since early this morning.'

Meg held her breath. She couldn't believe what she was hearing. She glanced back behind her, not knowing what to say or do. Her body had now turned to jelly and she was speechless. All she could think of was her Katie and how she would feel if it was her child. What must her parents be thinking?

Meg quickly attached Reuben's lead and they returned to the country lane. They finished the walk in no time and she was glad they finally got back home. She put some logs on the fire, poured herself a cup of coffee, before putting Reuben in the car to pick up Katie from school.

They drove back home in complete silence as she didn't want to worry Katie by telling her about the missing girl. However, she did see the police cars and asked her what was going on.

'I don't know darling.'

Meg didn't want to frighten her by saying someone was missing so she quickly changed the subject. The boys were home later than usual, telling me there was a lot of police presence in the village. The police were diverting traffic and making everyone drive a different way out of town.

Meg kept hoping and praying they would find the missing girl and that no harm would come to her. There wasn't too much crime here in the quiet villages around St Helene and because it was so rare, the whole town seemed to be talking about it.

Saturday couldn't come quickly enough and Meg was thankful they were together. In some strange way, it had been a funny old week and she was beginning to miss Mum and Dad but luckily, they were due back home from the coast shortly. Katie asked if she could do some baking.

'What a lovely idea but first we must go to the shops.'

They drove into St Helene and she saw Danielle busy arranging flowers in buckets outside the shop.

'Hey Danielle,' Meg shouted as she was waving frantically out of the car window.

She saw her and walked over.

'Hi, you guys, are you all okay?'

Meg had to admit her English was much better than her French.

Danielle said, 'News has got around that a little girl has gone missing.'

Katie looked up at Meg with dismay.

'What has happened, Mummy?'

Meg began telling Katie that a little girl had gone missing and the police were out in the fields searching for her. Katie kept asking questions and wanting to know more but Meg could only tell her what she knew. Meg told Danielle that she had an encounter with a police officer yesterday who had told her they were searching for a young girl.

'How terrible for the parents! Do you know if they have found her?' Danielle asked.

'I haven't heard anything so far but let's hope she is found safe and well.'

During the conversation, Danielle told Meg that she saw Esme buying some bread a few days ago.

'What! Where! When! I have been trying to contact her for ages and it just went to her voicemail,' Meg remarked.

'Well, I think it was her. She was wearing a grey hoodie pulled right over her head. She looked like she needed a good meal, so skinny.'

'Thanks for telling me, Danielle.'

'By the way Meg, are you up for a run sometime?'

Meg was always ready to burn off those extra calories.

'Certainly. I will ring you.'

They quickly toured the supermarket for some shopping and thought perhaps she should pop around to see Esme.

'Where are we going?' Katie asked.

'Just taking a slight detour, Katie.'

As they drove past Esme's house, Meg could see a police officer standing in the doorway.

'Oh my God, whatever has happened?'

Meg decided to stop the car and told Katie not to leave the vehicle.

'Is this where Olivia lives, Mummy?'

'Yes but stay where you are, I won't be long.'

As Meg walked up the shingly pathway, a police officer approached her and asked what she was doing.

'Esme is a good friend and would it be possible to speak with her?'

The door was ajar and Meg could see a very shaken and distressed Esme inside. She had been crying. Calling out to Meg, she ran towards her.

'Oh, Meg, I am so pleased you are here.'

Esme put her arms around Meg, not wanting to let go and began to tell her what was happening.

'Greg has taken Olivia,' she frantically replied.

As Meg looked up at her, she noticed her face was covered in bruises and her eyes were bloodshot and slightly closed.

'Has he done this to you?' Meg asked.

Esme said she tried hard to stop him taking her but he started hitting and kicking her. He grabbed Olivia and just took her. She didn't know what to do! The police are now looking for them and she was waiting for news.

In complete shock, Meg was dumbstruck and didn't know what to say. This had to be the little girl the police are looking for! Her thoughts were for Esme and finding Olivia. She told me they all returned to England and hoped to start a new life but things didn't work out.

The friends he thought he had didn't want to know him and his parents had moved away and he didn't know where they were. They decided to rent a small flat but knew that without a job; they wouldn't survive for long.

'I tried ringing you many times, Esme but you didn't reply.'

'No, he took my phone away from me and I couldn't have contact with anyone. Not long afterwards, he started hitting and pushing me around and at one point, he kept me locked in the bedroom like a prisoner. I became frightened, not for me but for the safety of Olivia.

'She would stand outside the door and talk to me. I would say, "Mummy is alright, don't worry; everything will be okay soon." I could hear Olivia sobbing and I could do absolutely nothing. His personality would change by the hour. One minute, he would be the Greg I used to know and then, without reason, he would explode with rage and become very violent.

'He was never violent towards Olivia, just me. It was as if he needed somebody to release his anger on. He had so many trigger points and I could not identify them quickly enough before it was too late.'

Esme looked so frail and thin; touching her, Meg could even feel the bones beneath her skin. She was so frail and Meg wanted to help her in any way she could. Standing together, they just held each other tight, not wanting to let of each other. What a nightmare!

Meg told Esme that she would be back tomorrow but to please ring her if there was any update on the situation or if she could help.

'I will, Meg, I will.'

It was very difficult to explain to Katie what had happened and that her little friend Olivia had gone missing. Katie kept pestering, saying, 'Has he taken her again, Mummy just like before at the school?'

What could she tell her! How she drove back home, she didn't know. Katie was silent and quiet but Meg told her everything was being done to find Olivia and that she would be home safe and sound with her Mummy very soon. Meg didn't know that for sure but she had to tell her something. The boys were at the bottom of the garden with Reuben and as she walked down to speak with them, she started to update them on the disappearance of Olivia.

'Do you think they will find her?' Charlie said.

'We have got everything crossed and we can only hope so. The police are doing everything they can.'

However, it had crossed her mind that they may have left the country. What a day! Her phone didn't leave her side just in case Esme had some news.

No news is good news, Meg thought.

She had to tell Danielle because she was worried, just like her. Meg told her that Esme was covered in bruises and was hoping she would seek medical attention to see if she had any broken bones, because Meg noticed she was holding her sides when she spoke with her.

'She could have fractured ribs or even worse, internal injuries,' Danielle replied. 'That's it. I have just closed the florist and I am going over to see if I can do anything.'

'Oh, that is so kind of you, Danielle. I could not leave the children and I wondered how we could get help for her.'

'No worries, I am on my way. I will ring you when there is any more news.'

'Thanks, Danielle; I will stay near the phone.'

The thought of her alone in that house and not knowing where her child was had been haunting me. What kind of person can do this to someone like little Esme, who was very helpless and highly vulnerable? Meg hoped he went to prison for what he had done to her!

She did have one thought—she wondered if he had taken Olivia to the caravan where she had visited the other day and where the strange lady was staying. Should she tell the police to investigate this? He could be holding her there against her will and because the caravan was in an isolated area out of sight, it could be very hard to find.

'Yes, I think I will let the police know!'

Esme didn't know that Meg had made it her business to find out where Greg was staying a little while back when she had suspicions about him. She spoke with a desk sergeant, explaining what she knew about the caravan she had visited. He didn't speak English too well but Meg understood most of what he said.

He was very thankful for this information and said they would be looking into it. In a very concerned voice, Meg mentioned that some of the dog walkers from the village, were trekking the fields and country lanes, helping the police to find Olivia.

'We appreciate the help of the village,' the Sergeant replied, 'we have our best team out there working day and night in the hope she will be found.'

There was never a dull moment here in St Helene. Meg always thought the bustling village of Hampton Deverell was chaotic but now she was not quite so sure. Was she now beginning to become a Miss Marple too as well as an Agony Aunt? Not quite sure this was what she had in mind when they decided to move to France.

Chapter 21

How Meg got any sleep that night, she didn't know. She remembered waking up with a bolt in the middle of the night. She must have been dreaming but everything seemed so real. She dreamed the police had found Olivia and she was back with her Mummy.

Half awake, she casually walked downstairs to the kitchen and nibbled on a piece of cheese left over from last night's supper. She was pleased that it was Sunday and they didn't have to rush around with school runs. She left the children in bed while she sat and gazed out the window, drinking a very lukewarm coffee, staring into space and waiting for the phone to ring with any news about Olivia.

With all the drama of Olivia, she forgot to call Louis. She sat at the table, picked up her phone and sent him a message. The message read, "I'm sorry I didn't ring you last night. Please ring me when you get this message or when it is convenient. I cannot wait to see you. All my love, Meg," with some loving emojis.

She didn't want to tell Louis about Esme and Olivia as it would only worry him and with the divorce going ahead, he could do without this upsetting news. However, Louis was due back home at the end of the week. Looking down at her phone, she could see a text from the desk sergeant at the police station.

Staring at the message, Meg couldn't believe it. They had found Olivia at the caravan with Greg and his so-called lady friend. She felt a wave of relief pass all over her body. She couldn't wait to contact Esme. Her phone was ringing for ages but no reply, it went straight to voicemail.

Whatever is happening, where is everyone? Meg felt very restless and uneasy because she couldn't contact anyone. What should she do? She couldn't leave the children alone, so her only hope was to get hold of Danielle. She rushed upstairs to change out of her pyjamas when she heard the doorbell ring.

Running down the stairs in Olympic style, Meg rushed to open the door. It was the police.

'Bonjour, je Suis Insp. Jean Dubois.'

(Good day I am Inspector Jean Dubois)

'Parlez vous anglais?'

(Do you speak English?)

'A little,' said the Inspector.

There was an update and he told me that Olivia had been found! Meg stood in complete amazement but also very happy at the news.

'Is she okay?' Meg asked.

'She is unharmed, back home and safe with her mother.'

'I am so pleased Olivia is safe and well. Everyone has been so worried.'

The Inspector told her they are holding her father in custody and would most likely charge him for grievous bodily harm with intent towards Esme. Meg wanted the Inspector to know that if she could help further with their enquiries, just let her know.

'Thank you, Madam Johnston. That is all for now but we may contact you again.'

He thanked her for the information which helped immensely in the search for Olivia. She watched as he walked down the path to the police car and suddenly, she noticed Mum and Dad turning into the drive. Returning from their short holiday, Meg could see the anxious look on their faces.

Mum called out, 'Is everything okay?'

'It is now. Let me put the kettle on and we can sit around, have a cup of tea and I will tell you all the news.'

Never a dull moment in St Helene! Putting down her hot cup of tea, she could hear her mobile ringing and as she hurried to answer, she could see it was Danielle.

'Hi, have you heard the news?' Danielle said in a very excited voice.

'Yes, the police called around earlier and told me they had found Olivia. Terrific news!'

Danielle went on to say she was with them both having just got back from the hospital with Esme. 'I made her see a doctor because I could see the acute pain she was in and after a couple of x-rays, they found two broken ribs and a fractured collarbone. That man is horrible,' Danielle said with such repulsion.

Meg replied in a voice of outrage saying, 'I would like to hurt him, the way he has hurt Esme.'

Esme was now resting at home and Danielle mentioned that she would stay with them tonight and ensure they have something to eat. Meg couldn't thank Danielle enough for all her help and she replied, 'That's what friends do.'

The following day, Meg rushed over to see Esme. Meg could see a dark figure through the window and gently tapped the windowpane to catch her attention. Danielle was just leaving as she arrived. They stood on the doorstep where Meg thanked her so much for her help and kindness.

'I am now off to open the shop but please get in touch if you need me at all.'

'You are a star,' and Meg thanked her once again for all she had done.

Olivia came running to the door and threw her arms around Meg. She picked her up, cuddled her and kissed her on the cheek.

'Are you alright, sweetheart?' Meg asked.

'Yes but Mummy is all bandaged up.'

Meg walked through the dark hallway into the living room, where a fire was glowing, looking very comforting and warm.

'Hello Esme, how are you feeling today?'

'A little sore but I will survive.'

'Would you like me to take Olivia back home with me so you can get some rest?'

She quickly reacted and said, 'No,' in a firm voice but then her voice softened. 'That's a lovely idea, Meg but having her with me gives me the strength to carry on.'

Meg certainly knew how that felt. The hesitancy in her voice made her think that she never wanted Olivia to leave her side again.

'Of course, Esme, I quite understand. I had the same feeling within me when I lost Simon, all I wanted was my children by my side, helping me through the most challenging time. Well, if you do change your mind, just let me know.'

Esme looked up with kindness on her face showing so much gratitude towards her. They sat and chatted for ages and she welcomed the cooked lasagne which she had gladly made for them. Carefully placing the meal in the oven, Meg laid the table. Katie had picked some flowers from the garden and arranged them carefully into a vase on the kitchen table.

'They are beautiful, please thank Katie for me,' Esme replied. 'You are so very kind, Meg, I don't know what I would have done without you and Danielle supporting us and when I feel better and more robust, we must start running together again.'

'Of course, we will but you must get your strength back first. We don't want any more broken ribs!'

'Don't make me laugh, Meg; my ribs can't stand the pain.'

Meg gave her a loving smile and a reassuring tap on her shoulder. Esme told her that they were holding Greg for questioning and keeping him in custody until his court appearance. The Inspector had already told her but hearing it from Esme gave her some hope that they would make sure he couldn't hurt either of them again; they would assess his mental state too.

'Let's hope they punish him the way he has punished you,' Meg said in a very harsh voice. 'He can't get away with all this abusive behaviour towards you.'

'I know and I want nothing more to do with that man again. Greg has ruined my life and he will not destroy Olivia's. It would be best if we both moved away for good and didn't come back here!'

'One thing at a time, Esme; we can sort this out—let's see what happens.'

'There is something else I must tell you, Meg! He has also owned up to handling and supplying drugs.'

'What!' Meg was looking horror-struck.

Esme went on to say she had a hunch there was more to all the anger than he was showing. There had to be other reasons he acted this way. His temper was unpredictable, causing him to fly into outrage.

'I think his lady friend has been in possession too!'

'That doesn't surprise me,' Meg replied.

'The police said that the charge will now increase from grievous bodily harm, physical abuse and false imprisonment, with the addition of drug supply and use.'

'They very well may throw the book at him,' Meg told her.

After seeing Esme and Olivia, Meg felt less stressed but still needed Esme to ring her to ensure they were both alright. Walking down the drive towards the car, she casually turned around, wondering why this nasty man could be so cruel and cause so much hurt and pain to such a kind and loving person.

It was only now that everything about Esme and Olivia began to hit her. She found it impossible to walk without tears. When would all this end? It seemed to be one thing after another but then she remembered someone saying that when life hits you the way it has, it's only the ones who cope that get through the barrier of pain.

That was true but she had to admit her coping strategies were getting weaker and weaker by the day. She could then feel Simon's presence within her, guiding her through a dark tunnel but hoping there would be light at the end for everyone. He was there; she knew he was.

Chapter 22

Meg was feeling slightly excited at the thought of Louis returning home. There was so much to talk about and sometimes so little time when they were together; however, she did want to make Louis's homecoming special. Dad was doing his usual thing in the garden, making the ground ready for early planting of the veggies and now beginning to wonder how he manages to carry on.

What would life be without him? He was my rock, best friend and the best Dad anyone could wish for. Meg had to admit they did come to France for a quieter lifestyle—not too sure about that now. Since arriving here, they have had so much turbulence and sadness, she was now wondering if they did the right thing.

'Snap out of it, Meg, of course it was the right decision.'

Her only regret was that they didn't have Simon with them anymore but she knew he loved them and was looking down to make sure they were managing the way he would have wanted them too. Being a strong family means they can support and be with each other, whatever the outcome.

Meg slowly wandered back to the house, wondering whether she would get a call from Louis and lo and behold, just as she pushed the door open, her mobile started ringing.

'Hi you, it's me.'

Of course, she knew who it was. Louis liked to joke with her at times and she found it quite amusing, especially today when she was feeling slightly sad after leaving Esme and Olivia.

Louis shouted out in a loud voice, 'I am on my way home tomorrow, so I should be with you all around early afternoon.'

This was the news she wanted to hear, after the most turbulent week she had encountered.

'I will get Mum to make one of your favourite casseroles.'

'Yes please. I haven't had a home-cooked meal for ages!'

Mum overheard the conversation. Meg quietly called out, 'Is that okay, Mum?'

'Tell him Hunter's Chicken is on the menu!'

The next day was beginning to unfold nicely—everything was in place for Louis's homecoming and Meg's excitement had taken hold of her. Even Katie and the boys were asking when Louis would be arriving. Hopefully, it would be early afternoon.

Charlie and Freddie were taking Reuben for a walk and Katie was helping Mum prepare dinner in the kitchen, so Meg thought she would drive over to see Esme and Olivia. She walked towards the house and tapped on the window. She could see a man and lady standing next to Esme talking.

"Do I stay or should I come back?" No, Meg thought she would knock on the door and within no time, the door opened. Esme was standing there.

'Meg, I have two police officers with me who have told me that Greg is going to make a court appearance next week. Due to my injuries and not being the first time Greg has caused me harm, together with the other charge of handling drugs, there is every chance he could be looking at a prison sentence. Nothing is certain but that's the way it looks. It could be that I may have to give evidence in Court.'

Esme was beginning to look anxious and slightly worried.

'Don't worry, Esme,' Meg told her. 'If you need me to come along to support you, then, of course, I will.'

Meg put her arms around Esme, telling her that was good news and that everyone must stay optimistic and keep everything crossed. The two police officers walked out the door and told Esme they would be in touch with any latest news. Esme thanked them for letting her know. Looking up, Esme rested her head on Meg's shoulders, crying uncontrollably.

'Let it out Esme, everything has been bottling up and now is the time to let go.'

Meg didn't want to leave her whilst she was in this state but told her she had been a courageous lady and should be proud of how she tackled the situation. Esme gently wiped away the many tears and began telling Meg how grateful she was for the kindness shown to her and Olivia.

Holding Esme in her arms, Meg wanted her to know both she and Olivia were safe and that's how it would stay. Rushing back home, Meg quickly hurried indoors, grabbed a glass of her favourite bottle of white wine, ran a hot bath and sunk into never-ending bubbles.

She was looking forward to seeing Louis and again, her heart fluttered in total anticipation. It must have been almost four o'clock when the doorbell rang. Meg rushed downstairs, hair still looking bedraggled, having not had time to comb it but who cares? She just wanted to see Louis and looking this way, had to take her as he finds her.

She gave a little chuckle at the thought but as she opened the front door, he was standing there with two large bouquet of flowers, one for her and the other for Mum. Mum came to the door to greet Louis who handed her the most beautiful bouquet. Mum gazed at his kindness and told him he shouldn't have.

'Of course, I should; I believe you are making my favourite meal, so it is the least I could do.'

Mum blushed with some slight awkwardness, thanking him in a somewhat softened voice. Did Meg detect a lump in her Mum's throat as she thanked him? The evening was exceptional and of course, the news about Esme and Olivia was dominating the evening.

He was so pleased they were all there for her.

Louis said, 'Perhaps I should pop over and see her tomorrow to ensure her bruising is healing satisfactorily. She does amaze me with her strength seeing she is only a tiny petite young lady.'

'She is a fighter Louis but all I want now is for her to get a new life and who knows, she may meet somebody one day who will look after them both.'

Little did Meg know how true this was going to be. 'She deserves some happiness in her life.'

'Agreed,' Louis replied.

A couple of weeks passed and still, there was no news about Greg's sentencing. They were all living in hope but as time passed, they couldn't help thinking whether Esme would receive the news they all wanted to hear. They had both started running again and Meg could see such a massive change in her progress.

She appeared much more outgoing, they even laughed a lot more together and Meg could see a much stronger Esme. She had changed so much; let's hope for the better. Once Esme knew the verdict on Greg's sentencing, she and Olivia could move on.

A short jog around the town was a good tonic for them. Suddenly, Esme's mobile rang as they approached the village church in St Helene.

'Hold on, Meg, I think I should take this.'

Trying hard to reach the phone in the back pocket of her running tights, she could hear the phone ringing loudly. Esme answered rather anxiously but in a quiet voice. There was total silence for a moment and then her face began to beam. She sunk to the ground, hands touching knees and Meg had difficulty holding her up at this point but seeing the delight on her face, it appeared to be good news.

'The Court has given Greg an eight-year tariff but it could be longer as they will also assess his mental condition.'

'Oh, Esme, I am so pleased for you. Both you and Olivia can now get on with a new life together. What a result,' Meg commented.

'There is no need for me to give any evidence because he told the Court he was guilty and that he also admitted to a further six offences of physical abuse towards me together with owning up to the drugs offence. Greg was told never to get in touch with either myself or Olivia again because he could go back to prison for breaching the terms of his licence which has now been implemented from the date of his sentence.'

They both stood there in total shock but so very thankful there was final closure for Esme and Olivia.

'I think this justifies a drink or two to celebrate.'

'Yes, I think so too,' shouted Esme loudly.

'Let's hope this is the end to all the heartache he has caused you and tonight we will celebrate new beginnings. No more suffering, no more worry; as I said, you can now move on and focus on the future ahead.'

Esme just jumped into the air and put her arms around Meg. They both stood embracing each other. Meg couldn't even imagine how she had endured such pain and suffering from someone she thought would look after them but even now, she could tell Esme still had strong feelings for him even though he had put her through so much pain and anguish.

Letting go would be the hardest thing for her but with friends around her, she would get through and receive all the support she needed. Esme's motto is: *forget the past and look to the future.*

When Meg got home, she put a couple of bottles of bubbly in the fridge, ready for a night of celebration. They celebrated with Esme and it was great to see so many happy faces, neighbours and a couple of her friends from the village pop around.

Everyone who cared and loved Esme and Olivia was delighted with the outcome and wished them well for the future ahead.

I wish I hadn't drunk so much last night, Meg thought to herself! *I can hardly see straight.*

Luckily, Mum was downstairs organising the children for school. Good old Mum!

'Not so much of the old,' she shouted out.

Katie was waiting by the door for me to drive her to school but Dad came to the rescue and said, 'I will take her. I don't think you are capable of driving.'

'Thanks, Dad; you are a star!' Meg decided to do a brisk walk rather than a run to clear my head. As Meg ventured outside, there was a real nip in the air. In that instance, Meg heard someone call her name.

'Meg, Bonjour.'

'Ah, Henri, Bonjour.'

He was unlocking the office at the Mairie.

'I haven't seen you for a while, is everything okay?'

'Yes, Henri, all good now.'

She told him the news about Esme but he, too, had heard the news.

'If Esme needs anything, she must come along and speak with me.'

'That is very kind, thank you Henri.'

Saying goodbye, Meg then continued with her walk. She decided to pop in and see Danielle on her way back home. As usual, the floral display in the front of the window was stunning.

'Danielle is so talented; she makes flower arranging look so easy. I wish I could make up bouquets and arrangements like that! Hi Danielle, how are you?'

'Very well,' but Meg could see that she was a little bothered about something and the expression on her face wasn't giving her good vibes.

'Are you sure you are okay, Danielle?'

'Um, well, I think so. I am getting swamped with orders, wondering whether I can cope with everything at the shop. Not only do I have to order all the flowers, arrange and then deliver them but there is the books to do and with just myself working here and the shop getting much busier, I am beginning to find it very stressful. When I finish at the end of the day and eventually get home, all I want to do is go straight to bed; I am so tired, Meg!'

'Is there anything I can do to help?' Meg asked.

'Not really; I will have to see if I can get some extra help!'

Meg was thinking hard at this point since she had now given up her job at the surgery, allowing more time with the family, especially Mum and Dad. Dad's health did worry her greatly but she supposed she could help Danielle out in her hour of need, even if it were only to help with the odd delivery, even make up bouquets. She was looking exhausted and she had been an absolute star looking after Esme and such a fantastic friend to her-it was now her turn to repay her.

'Count me in, Danielle; I'm your girl!'

'Are you sure?' Danielle said in an excited voice.

Meg told her that she always enjoyed popping in for a chat and not only that, she absolutely loved the aroma and fragrance of the beautiful flowers.

'You will have to show me how to hand-tie bouquets, I can even help with the deliveries. I am a quick learner. If I can strap up someone's arm or leg, I can learn how to tie up bouquets!'

They both laughed loudly and she could see that the stress on Danielle's face was diminishing. She wondered why Danielle hadn't told her before about how the pressure of the florist shop was affecting her but help wasn't on Danielle's agenda.

Being a strong person with exceptional willpower, she found it hard to ask for help. She had found time to help with Esme; she even stayed with her overnight to be close to her. Also an excellent and true friend who supported both her family and herself through one of the saddest times of their lives.

She was kind-hearted, warm and loving, so Meg was pleased to be there for her.

'Mum and Dad told me they were very grateful that I could help. I told them that my hours were flexible and that I would be there for any emergencies at home. I know I gave up my job at the surgery to spend more time with you both but this is much more flexible because should there be a problem, I can be with you within minutes.'

'This will be good for you Meg, it will give you an interest other than looking after your old Mum and Dad!'

Mum said if there was any cleaning or even making the odd cups of tea, she would be willing to help also.

'When do you want me to start?' Meg said enthusiastically.

'It's up to you, Meg.'

Meg thought and said, 'Is tomorrow okay?'

'Meg that would be excellent. The shop opens at nine o'clock and I shut for two hours at midday, giving me time to catch up on paperwork and tidy up everywhere.'

'You can now have a proper lunch break because I will be here to help.'

Danielle turned to Meg and said, 'Thank you isn't enough words.'

Meg knew what she meant, saying, 'Don't give it another thought, I will be here at nine o'clock sharp!'

Chapter 23

Meg had worked with Danielle for a couple of months now and loved every minute. Mum sometimes popped in to tidy around and brush the floors where leaves, pollen, cut-off stems and ribbon pieces had fallen. They were a small team and Danielle was the happiest Meg had seen her in ages.

Danielle had even made plans for them to go into town together and see a film with a meal afterwards. That had never happened before! Danielle now had time for herself and who knows, she may one day meet the man who would love and care for her the way she cared for others.

Life couldn't be better. Katie was just loving the experience of travelling on the school bus. It made her feel very grown-up but with her went the twins who looked after her. Less running around for Meg which had made her life at the florist a lot easier.

Esme was getting back to normal with her mobile hairdressing; every time they met up, her confidence grew from strength to strength. A complete change from the nervous, frightened and unhappy little Esme they all sadly knew six months ago.

Danielle and she worked well together, although Meg only went into the shop on a flexible basis. Business was blooming (sorry for the pun!), just like all the beautiful flowers surrounding them. As Meg put down a half-drunk cup of coffee, she gazed out of the shop window, sunlight streaming into the room, which was semi-blinding her.

Out of the corner of her eye, she could see Louis strutting around, looking somewhat anxious. She beckoned him to come over but he seemed to ignore her. Meg stood in the doorway of the shop and shouted, 'Louis, are you okay?'

He turned around with a wry smile and said he was but something told her he had something on his mind. She couldn't leave the shop because Danielle was out delivering flowers, so she began shouting louder and eventually, Louis ambled over.

He held her hand tightly and said he had just visited Nicole to pick up Alice for the weekend. 'She told me I would have to look after Alice for a little longer than the weekend.'

'Why?' Meg asked.

'She told me she had to go to hospital because they want to carry out blood tests and scans, after she had been feeling rather tired and run down.'

'Perhaps it could be worry and anxiety surrounding the divorce proceedings and the future of Alice,' Meg remarked.

She could tell that Louis was not taking this news very well. Her symptoms told him it might be nothing but it could be something more serious.

'What are you going to do?' Meg asked gently.

'Alice is staying with me for the foreseeable future until we know the outcome and results of the tests.'

'You must let me know if there is anything I do to help.'

'I am so pleased I have you by my side,' Louis said.

'Think nothing of it.'

What else could she say?

'I must go now and collect Alice after school club but I will let you know how everything develops.'

He gently placed a kiss on both her cheeks and held her tightly.

'Everything is going to be okay, Louis; I know it will.'

One crisis after another. Again, the same thought kept reappearing all the time-move to France, they say! Springtime was just around the corner and wildflowers were popping up here, there and everywhere. Birds were singing to their heart's content and what was grey skies yesterday were now azure blue with hardly a cloud in the sky.

Mum had gone into town to do some shopping and it was herself and Dad putting the world to rights. They were all anxious to hear the news of how Nicole was progressing and no news was good news, so they had to be patient and wait, without burdening Louis with loads of questions.

Not long afterwards, Louis rang to say that Nicole was back home and the test results showed she had a very low blood count, causing anaemia which was controllable with iron supplements and injections. Although Meg was sorry to learn this, she also knew it could be treated and that her life was not necessarily in danger.

Louis told her she had a friend staying with her until everything was under control, possibly a male friend but she still wanted him to take care of Alice. Ah well, another crisis sorted! With Nicole continuing to recover, the latest news was that Nicole wanted Louis to have total custody of Alice when the paperwork for the divorce goes through.

She now felt that although she loved Alice with all her heart, it was evident that Alice was the happiest when she was in her daddy's care. Meg couldn't believe what she was hearing! Thankfully, the biggest hurdle for Louis was almost over and with the divorce papers almost finalised, they were all keeping everything crossed that there would be no setbacks.

Once the divorce had gone through, they had heard that Nicole would be moving away permanently and going south to stay with a male friend, who they think was possibly more than a friend. Perhaps Nicole had found someone who could give her what she wanted—always in the limelight without giving a thought to others.

What Nicole wanted Nicole got! Louis remarked by saying, he wished him all the luck in the world! He will certainly need it with her moody and lavish ways! Meg couldn't help thinking that Nicole was never the right person for Louis. Things happen in life for a reason and there was possibly no sense in them continuing with their marriage.

Although you could work together to correct any wrong, divorce may be the only answer. Louis and Alice would have a better life together, they were just oozing so much love and happiness for each other. A couple of weeks rolled by and with the divorce well and truly out of the way and the settlement between Louis and Nicole finally agreed, Louis was in a good place, moving on with his life.

His work at the surgery and hospital was now quite demanding, especially with his new role as an Immunologist. Meg was feeling so proud of what he had achieved and so wholeheartedly with him every step of the way. The warmer weather was upon them, which meant Meg could now take a break and sit under the magnolia tree, which was blossoming pink buds.

She could even smell their fragrance as she wandered past. The once-bare trees slowly blossomed as the sun shone through the glossy leaves after their long winter hibernation. Lighter evenings, warmer days ahead. How beautiful! She began to reflect on the past here in St Helene.

Such an awful time in more ways than one but at least some happiness had come out of it all, with Esme and Olivia moving on with their lives and Louis's divorce finalised at long last. She would begin quietly talking to herself, hoping Simon would hear her.

Yes, the guiding hand was once again beside her. Sitting for a moment, she began to collect her many thoughts. Eventually, she slowly got up, whispered goodbye, sweetheart, sleep tight and gradually lifted herself from the seat. Strolling back to the house, began wiping away the many tears.

Why did she still feel so saddened by the loss of Simon? Why was it so difficult to let go? Was it because, as they said, true love never died? It had to be the latter?

The day had arrived and it was puppy day for Alice. A fluffy white and grey puppy was handed to Alice at the front door from a local spaniel breeder just outside of Dinan.

'Do you have a name for him, Alice?' she asked.

'I do, meet Oscar.'

He was just a ball of fluff and only nine weeks old. Katie and the boys just rushed over and wanted to pick him up but Alice was very reluctant to let go, although it wasn't long before Oscar was running around and playing in the garden with Reuben. The two dogs played happily together and it was lovely to see how they interacted with each other.

An early birthday present for Alice, everyone could see how happy she was at the thought of caring and loving something meaningful and so essential in her young life. Everyone was joyfully playing in the back garden; there was a sound of a car approaching outside.

It was the postal van and Meg excitedly ran down to fetch the post. Sorting through, Meg could see a letter addressed to her. Eagerly opening the letter, she could see it was from Jennie, a friend back in the UK asking if she could come over and stay for a few days on her way down to Avignon, where she was arranging to meet up with a couple of friends.

It thrilled Meg at the thought of seeing her once again. It had been such a long time since they had seen each other. *Oh,* Meg thought, *where is she going to sleep? Oh well, she will have to bunk up with me. Let's hope she doesn't mind!*

Jennie had been a friend of Meg and Simon's for many years. Having known her through the Running Club, she never married but was always on the lookout, as they say and always had an eye for a handsome and wealthy man! They have had some good times and she looked forward to a catch-up.

There was so much she wanted to tell her! After reading her letter, Meg decided to ring her. After a long conversation over the phone, said, 'Well, if we don't hang up now, we won't have anything to talk about when we meet.'

They both laughed and it was just like old times. Jennie was catching a ferry that evening and hoped to be with them the following day, possibly later in the afternoon. Everything was getting prepared for Jennie's arrival and even the children were excited at seeing someone new from back home.

Mum was preparing to welcome Jennie with one of her delicious creations in the kitchen. Beef bourguignon was on the menu. Later the following afternoon, Meg could see a car turning into their driveway. A small red sports car and Jennie was waving out to them.

'Hi everyone, I found it! I got lost a couple of times but driving through the country lanes is relaxing, nothing like the traffic back home. What a peaceful place you live!'

As Jennie stepped out of the car, she looked incredible. Not a hair was out of place and her clothes were immaculate. She looked gorgeous! They stood and hugged each other and slowly ushered her into the house.

Chapter 24

Jennie and Meg spent a lot of time catching up on the past and she wanted to know all about Simon's accident and how they were all coping. Meg told her they were still struggling to come to terms with what happened and although they hadn't been in France very long when the accident happened, the love shown to them by the villagers was unbelievable.

Because he was a young man with a family and with everything to live for, made it even harder to bear. Life for them was better and after a lot of soul-searching, she had met someone who had been extremely supportive and kind to her and the family.

They had become good friends, which had helped considerably with the drama and heartache involved at this awful time in her life. They were taking small steps but their friendship had developed and as she said before, they were taking each day at a time and enjoying just being with each other.

In so many ways, this would be what Simon would want for her.

'So his name is?'

Speaking quietly, Meg said, 'Louis.'

'He sounds like a nice guy.'

'He is, Jen. He is an Immunologist at the local hospital and works at our local GP surgery in St Helene.'

'Wow, a doctor,' Jen uttered.

Meg began to tell Jen about Dad's poor health and the decision to move Mum and Dad to France.

'What a good idea, Meg, at least you have them near you!'

'Yes and they love it here, which is a godsend.'

'Will I be meeting this new chap of yours, Meg?'

'Of course, I thought I could invite him for a drink this evening.'

'That would be great! I had better put my best clobber on then and tidy myself up.'

'No need for that, Jen! We all dress casually out here and that is one of the nicest things about living here. Even going to a restaurant doesn't require you to overdress. Smart casual is all that is needed.'

'Well, I am going to put my best clobber on anyway,' Jen said with a certain attitude.

Not long afterwards, Meg could see Jennie chatting with Dad in the garden, who was busy planting whatever he planted this time of year. Reuben was sniffing and running around the garden when Jen started playfully throwing a ball to him. Reuben was certainly enjoying his new companion.

Meg could see that Dad was trying to protect his lettuce plants, which he had carefully nurtured in the hope that Reuben and the puppy didn't decide to have their own little picnic and chew every plant. Mum made them all tea and cakes and as Meg walked towards the house, she could see Jen sitting on the seat under the magnolia tree, chatting on her phone.

'Everything alright?' She asked.

'Yes, no problem; just checking up on a couple of things,' but her face told differently. She looked very strained and a little uptight.

Meg didn't want to ask too many questions and hoped she might decide to talk it through with her later. Oh, heck, she nearly forgot. She hastily ran to her phone resting on the kitchen table and rang Louis. Perhaps he was busy and wouldn't appreciate her call but he picked up quickly.

'Is everything alright?' He asked.

'Nothing important but I wanted to know whether you would like to come over this evening for a drink and meet my friend Jennie who is staying with me for a few days, before travelling south.'

'I think that would be okay; if anything crops up, I will let you know. Put the wine in the fridge and hopefully will see you around seven this evening.'

'Great, see you later.'

They were all waiting for Louis to join them in the garden for drinks when Meg heard his car coming up the drive. Louis briskly stepped out of the car and walked up to where she introduced him to Jen.

'Hello, pleased to meet you,' he said.

Jen responded towards him very strangely. She was gazing straight into his eyes and brushing herself close to him.

'Are all the doctors good-looking, just like you,' she cheekily said with a sly grin on her face.

Meg could see him blushing up and feeling somewhat embarrassed and very awkward. She couldn't believe what she was hearing, so she jumped in quickly and changed the subject. Meg fetched a tray of ice-cold Prosecco and handed them out. She could see Louis feeling rather uncomfortable but as she caught his eye, he winked softly to her.

As they sat chatting in the garden, Jen pushed herself to sit closer to Louis. What is she doing? Meg had already told her that they were now moving forward into a relationship. She didn't seem to take any notice and perhaps she wasn't even bothered. Meg just wanted this evening to end and speak to Louis alone.

Jen was telling Louis all about how she was travelling through France and hoping to meet some friends in Avignon if she got that far, she said, looking into his eyes and speaking in an exceptionally soft and sexy voice. She asked him what his interests were and whether he, too, liked travelling.

Jen was beginning to get a little bit too close and personal in what she was saying. Not once did she make any casual chat with her. Just Louis. At this point, he told her he had a daughter. Jen just looked at him in amazement. Children certainly wasn't on Jen's itinerary. They were trouble as far as she was concerned.

Jen sat back on the seat and quietly remarked, 'Oh, I see.'

He told her that he was married once but it didn't work out, so it was just him and Alice and they were very happy, especially now that they had Meg in their lives.

'We couldn't be happier.'

That made Jen look up with a somewhat bizarre look.

'So it's true then Meg, you are in a relationship?'

Both Meg and Louis glanced at each other at the same time and without a word said, 'Yes, we are.'

It was the first time they could say they were a couple. They believed Jen made the final decision for them, as she could see Jen's face beginning to redden. Having been full of apologies, not knowing how much Jen had put her foot into it, with regards to making eyes at Louis, they all sat back, laughed a little and drank a lot.

The evening ended better than it started and feeling slightly embarrassed, they soon realised Jen's remarks meant nothing. Jen was always at the forefront of any situation but they knew her actions intended no harm.

Walking down the garden path, Louis put his hand around her waist and said, 'Well, I didn't expect that. There is only one for me; you, Meg.'

Meg told Louis that Jen had always been flirtatious and could sometimes make a complete fool of herself in certain situations.

'I can see that,' Louis replied in a flippant voice.

Jen couldn't be more apologetic about her behaviour earlier concerning Louis and said, 'I am so sorry. I don't know what came over me. I am not in a good place, so please don't be angry.'

'I'm not angry, Jen; let's forget it ever happened. We both understand and Louis has no bad feelings against you.'

'What a lovely man he is, Meg; you are so lucky to have met someone who cares for you and the family. I wish you lots of good luck in the future.'

However, she looked a little edgy earlier when talking on the phone, Meg asked if anything was troubling her. Was her personal life bothering her?

She quickly replied, 'It's Matt!'

'Matt, who,' Meg remarked in amazement.

'We have lived together for the past four years and I thought life was just fantastic but I was wrong. Eventually, I found out he was seeing a friend behind my back and that it had been going on for some time. I also discovered that he had been gambling away lots of the hard-earned money we had saved.

'He would frequently visit betting shops and put large amounts of money on the horses. He would even bet online too. He was not the man I thought he was. I couldn't believe it and it has left me not trusting men; although I can see you have found some happiness, I hope it stays that way, Meg.

'The money we saved was a deposit for our dream home. I had found out nearly all the money had gone and to be perfectly honest, I am almost broke. However, I do have some personal savings which were locked away, so I thought with what was left, I am going to do some travelling on a budget and when the money runs out, well who knows!

'I will have to see what happens. Possibly, find work somewhere. I need to get away and make a new life for myself.'

What could she say, except Meg hoped that everything went well for her and that one day she found the right person.

'Thanks, Meg; start a new life with somebody new, somewhere.'

'You will always have me as your friend, Jen; I am just a phone call away.'

A couple of days later, after lots of talking and putting the world to rights, Jen left St Helene, thanking Meg for the kind hospitality, saying she would keep in touch. It was good to see a more cheerful and optimistic Jen than she noticed a day or so earlier. She finally told me that the happiness Meg had found was what she hoped for too.

'Settle down and be happy, that's all I want,' Jen said. 'I have changed over the years, Meg; I am not the person I used to be, although the other night, I think that was the drink talking and my underlying problems were surfacing, which were uncontrollable.'

After saying goodbye to the family and her, she got into her little sports car and sped away. Meg hoped she was okay but couldn't help worrying about her. Although she seemed bright and bouncy, a break-up like that always lingers on for a long time but perhaps a change in lifestyle will help her.

Let's hope so, anyway. Here she went again, Agony Aunt talking! A couple of weeks have passed and life has been more leisurely. Everyone has settled down to a quieter life, with the summer holidays nearly upon them, although Katie reminded her it is her birthday next week.

'Mummy, it is a special birthday.'

'When you get to my age Katie, birthdays are not so important.'

'Oh yes, they are. We shall have a party!'

Katie was right; it was her 40th birthday and honestly, she wasn't too worried about whether they celebrated. She knew she shouldn't feel this way. Perhaps she was getting too old for parties? Meg thought to herself. Was she getting boring in her old age? She should have known better.

Party invites were sent out; Mum was busy baking a cake and Katie was buzzing excitedly. Dad was mowing the lawn and tidying the garden and the boys were happy as long as there was food and drink. It was the day before her birthday and preparations were well underway. It was unusual for her not to be involved in the organisation.

Katie was adamant that Meg had to stay away and leave it to everyone else. Who was she to argue with this little girl? At times, she thought she was much older than her years. Since Simon's death, the children had grown up in so many ways and in a good way! With that in mind, Meg decided to go for a run.

On returning home, she was astonished to see a large tent erected in the back garden with bench seating and tables; balloons were flying everywhere, some stating her age! With a wonderful aroma of food. Meg thought about how lucky she was to have such a caring and loving family.

Mum told her they all wanted to do something because she was always helping others. It was a poignant moment and Meg was exceptionally thankful to them. What could she say except thank you all very much? She was 40 today! She couldn't believe what a beautiful day it was.

The family gathered around the kitchen table, where she opened presents and many cards. Katie had made her own very special card but that's Katie, always imaginative. Of course, Meg had the usual statement from Mum and Dad saying, 'I can remember the day when you were born.'

'Really! You can remember back that far,' Meg cheekily replied.

They all sat around laughing and reminiscing. It was lunchtime and as she looked out the window, she could see Danielle walking up the path. She was very surprised to see her holding the most beautiful bouquet.

'Happy birthday Meg but I am only here for the food,' she jokingly shouted out loudly. Mum overheard in the distance and gave a loving smile towards her.

'It was because of your kindness and help I was able to shut the shop up for the afternoon, so here I am.'

'Champagne, Danielle?' Dad asked.

'Oh yes, please, I never refuse champagne.'

Meg began to wonder if Louis would be coming. It would make her day if he did but she wasn't sure if he was working. Without another thought, a car drove up the drive and to her lovely surprise, it was Louis and Alice.

'Happy birthday, my darling Meg.'

'Thank you. I am so pleased you could both make it.'

'Miss your birthday, no way. Katie would never have forgiven us!'

Meg was overjoyed to see so many of her friends and loved ones enjoying her birthday celebrations. How lucky was she? Her day was complete. She had the most important people with her and couldn't ask for more. She did have a quiet moment where she thought of Simon but then that would never go away.

They all sat around drinking and music was playing in the background, not Mum and Dad's choice but music anyway. Louis pulled her to one side, telling her he had arranged a romantic few days in Paris with a hotel overlooking the River Seine. Meg was shaking with sheer delight.

'I don't know what to say!'

'You deserve to be spoilt, which I intend to do.'

She asked Mum and Dad if it was okay to look after the children, including Alice and the new puppy but without hesitation they said, 'Enjoy your birthday present with Louis, although we already knew about his plan to take you away. He had been planning this for some time now.'

The day ended with the most wonderful memories she would never forget. She had everyone and anyone who meant everything with her celebrating. She was extremely thankful to those who put time and effort into arranging her birthday party but she was beginning to feel slightly drunk, perhaps more than slightly. Too much champagne! Well, that's what happens at parties, isn't it?

They had arranged that when Louis was away from home, Alice would stay with them, as she doesn't need more upset in her young life being pushed from pillar to post and Louis knew that they were able to offer her love and support without question.

Alice had now become part of their family and Katie just loved having her around. Even Oscar had his own bed beside Reuben in the kitchen.

It seemed ages before the day finally arrived for them to enjoy her special birthday weekend away together. It was going to be magical and wonderful. With bags packed and goodbyes said, they were on their way.

Arriving in Paris was certainly a different world than the small village of St Helene. Traffic was causing standstills everywhere, due to the volume of vehicles. Restaurants galore and so many beautiful shops and boutiques. Meg could see she was going to have a great time. Louis had ordered a taxi to the hotel.

As they arrived, they walked up the concrete steps where there was a man dressed in a maroon uniform with gold buttons and wearing a top hat, shaking their hands showed them the way to Reception.

'My name is Alain, your concierge and will be looking after you during your stay here.'

Meg had never been to a hotel like this before. It was huge and very luxurious. As she looked up, she noticed the most spectacular chandeliers hanging from a spectacular ornate ceiling, displaying the most beautiful entrance to any building she had ever seen. She couldn't believe her eyes.

Just like in the films, Meg thought.

Never had she experienced anything quite like this before. Is this the feeling all have when money can buy anything? They quickly unpacked their weekend cases and after freshening up, went to a lovely little restaurant overlooking the Basilica of Sacré Coeur de Montmartre, which Louis had pre-booked.

She had been to Paris once or twice but it seemed so much different this time. Could it be she was falling in love once again? They say, Paris is the romantic capital of the world. It was indeed working on her. They walked the tree-lined streets, of The Avenue des Champs-Élysées. Wow!

They both stood in awe at its beauty and in the distance, they could see the Arc De Triomph and Eiffel Tower, all spectacularly lit up with coloured lighting. Exceptional architecture! The coolness of the night air swept around them and they could hear the street musicians in the distance. Plenty of artists were on the sidewalks begging to let them do caricatures of them.

'Two people in love,' one of the artists remarked.

'Did he just say that to us?' Louis softly said.

'I think so but how could he tell?'

'Because when two people fall in love, you want the whole world to know and if I could, I would get up on that podium over there and shout out my love for you, Meg Johnston.'

It wasn't the drink talking because they only had a couple of glasses of wine, so perhaps it could be inner feelings within, which he had held back for such a long time and are now being released in a relaxed and calm atmosphere. Standing beside him, clenching his hand very tightly Meg told him he had come into her life just at the right time and she didn't want him to leave her, ever.

'I love you with all my heart, Louis!'

They stood and kissed passionately and a little old lady passed by looking up and muttering to herself. She gave them a loving smile and hurriedly walked by. Meg knew at that moment she had found the man she wanted to be with for the rest of her life.

Now that they had made this official statement of their love to each other, they casually ambled through the vast nightlife of Paris, occasionally looking up at each other when their eyes met. Louis would give her a gentle squeeze around her waist now and again, assuring her that he would always be there for her.

Feeling tired after a long day, they returned to the hotel, where they had a nightcap in the lounge before heading to their room. The lift took them to their floor, where they quietly entered their room. They both slowly walked to the window which overlooked the Eiffel Tower, the beautiful sights of Paris were unbelievable; the lights of the city were twinkling everywhere and at that moment, they just fell into each other's arms.

Her nerves were fading and she was feeling in control of her emotions. The affection bestowed by Louis made her feel excited and his complete tenderness put her at ease. They had declared their love to each other and she wanted that to remain forever.

As they strolled over to the decorative four-poster bed, they both knew this would be a special moment for them as they lay cradled together and almost instantly, it was absolute magic; they made love.

It was beautiful and perfect. Louis had made her feel like a woman in love again. Suddenly, for no apparent reason, Meg had this overpowering thought of guilt descend upon her. She knew it was what she wanted but in her heart, she kept thinking, was this wrong? Would she always feel this way? She knew it wasn't wrong because she now loved Louis.

Early morning, there was a knock at the door.

'Bonjour Monsieur-le petit déjeuner est servi.'

(Good day, Breakfast.)

Louis said it would be nice to have breakfast in their room overlooking the enormous city. The waiter walked over to where they were sitting and uncovered Eggs Benedict.

'I hope you like them,' Louis asked.

'I will try anything,' after yesterday's walk around Paris, her hunger was still raging; a rack of delicious toast, jam and honey, strawberries and a bottle of chilled champagne. Never had she drank champagne for breakfast. She did feel like she had won the lottery!

The weekend went quickly and they managed to see as much of Paris as possible. They spent the last evening enjoying a boat trip down the River Seine, where Louis had arranged a romantic meal for two on board a glass boat cruiser.

They had so much fun, laughing and enjoying each other's company we didn't want it to end but of course, it did and they were soon back home to reality.

Chapter 25

The florist shop had been bustling lately with weddings and sadly, quite a few funerals. Danielle asked her how the Paris weekend went during their morning coffee break.

'Oh, Danielle, it was absolute heaven. Louis booked the most beautiful hotel and spoilt me from the day we arrived until the morning we left.'

'Any sign of a ring?' Danielle asked.

'No, it wasn't that sort of weekend. We just needed more time to get to know each other.'

'Could it happen one day?'

'Who knows, maybe! I want to wait a little longer before I make that very important decision.'

Danielle had such a cheeky look on her face when she was being inquisitive. Something Meg had to admit she loved about her. She reminded her of herself at times.

Danielle suddenly said, 'I too, have some news.'

'Oh, Danielle, what is it?'

'You may have already guessed but I will tell you anyway. Both I and Phillipe have been out running together. He is a lovely man and we get on very well together. We like being with each other and have become a little more than friends.'

Meg was blown away by what she was hearing, shouting loud enough for all of France to hear. She didn't know what to say.

'He makes me laugh and is fun to be with and well, I like him a lot, in fact, very much.'

'Didn't I tell you, you would meet a tall, dark, handsome man one day?'

The only difference was Phillipe had auburn hair and blue eyes but not quite six foot tall. They both stared at each other and gave out the most horrendous giggle.

Joking aside, Meg told her that she had found someone special in Phillipe and couldn't be happier for her!

'I am inviting him over for a meal at the weekend. I hope he likes my cooking, Meg.'

'Of course, he will!'

Phillipe had always been easy-going and a great friend of both herself and Simon. Phillipe introduced them to France and the beautiful people here and as known, got Simon his teaching post at the school.

'Do you sometimes think Meg, if Simon hadn't taken the post here, things would have been so different? Do you ever regret moving here?'

Knowing what she meant filled her with some sadness and as they stood talking, Meg could see her eyes looking into hers and felt some anger edging inside her.

'Yes, perhaps,' she said in quite a distinctive stern voice, 'but it was the right thing for them all at the time and it was always their dream. The dream eventually came true and we were very happy for a couple of years but the accident happened and as you know, it took some time to pull us all back together but here we are and being a powerful family, we coped and got through it.'

Danielle touched her shoulder as she always did in moments like this and kissed her cheeks.

'What can I say, you are one brave lady, Meg and I am proud to call you my friend.'

'Thanks, Danielle that means a lot to me.'

Meg quickly came out of her trance of deep thought and gave Danielle a deserved loving hug.

'Let's get back to work and arrange the flowers for Madam Dupont and her family, as she is popping into the shop in about an hour to collect her order.'

Meg couldn't help noticing Danielle's look; she appeared so happy and contented; she just hoped things would work out for them both. Time flew by and there needed to be more hours in a day. The boys were eagerly awaiting exam results and she had to admit there was some tension within the household; this kind of stress was always the case when results loomed.

Hoping it would be good news as both boys had put so much hard work into these exams, especially when the language had been complex. She shouldn't have worried too much. Both the boys did well, which meant they were on course for their final exams, with the results allowing them a university place, here or even back in the UK.

They would have to wait and see! She couldn't help thinking Dad was looking a little weary.

'Are you ok?' Meg asked.

'Yes, just a bit tired but I will be fine.'

Mum had told her that she thought he was overdoing it in the garden and he hadn't been sleeping too well.

'Why didn't you say anything before?'

'You know what your Dad is like. Stubborn to the end! He will not say anything until it is too late.'

'He can't and mustn't overexert himself, Mum.'

Having given it some thought, Meg had asked around the village if anyone would give Dad a hand in the garden. Some villagers jumped at the idea, much to Dad's displeasure.

'You're not as young as you were and we all worry about you.'

'I know, dear but I am ok, really I am.'

'Nothing more to be said, Dad! I have spoken to a neighbour willing to help with the digging, heavy work and even mowing the lawns, leaving you to do some less energetic planting of the veggies and flowers.'

'Is planting the only thing left for me to do, then?' Dad looked a little displeased but then thought about it and said, 'Yes, you are right, I still think I am 30 going on 80.'

They looked at each other and grinned slightly. Also, Mum was getting worried and didn't want him overdoing it. Dad knew that all meant well and thank you for caring but please don't take the garden away from me completely. I love it!

'Of course not, Dad,' It is and always will be, your little bit of France.

His cheeky smile spread across his face and she left him to do what he loved best. Maybe she should speak to Louis about Dad and ask if he needed any check-ups to be on the safe side.

The sky above, which was once a greyish colour but now turning a lovely azure blue and the sun was glowing brightly, so she decided to take the dogs out for their daily walk. She decided to go a different way than she usually walked, take the car and stop off by the coastal path.

It was somewhere she hadn't been before and something inside told her she had to explore more of beautiful Brittany. She rushed over and told Mum and Dad she was going for a drive with the dogs. I had my phone with me, should you want me for anything!

'Have a lovely time, Meg and be careful driving.'

Going out alone, Mum would always say those three words, *Be Careful Driving*.

It's what Mums do and she expected that when her children are old enough to drive, she would say the same. She put the dogs into the back of the car and steadily drove off. The sun shone through the windscreen, the leaves glistening bright green and the road so quiet.

It was tranquillity in abundance. She was feeling great. It was almost a 30kms drive but well worth it when we arrived. The view was outstanding, overlooking a calm and bright blue sea.

Little sailing boats were hovering around the bay, people were bouncing up and down in the waves of the sea, children were playing happily on the beach and sunbathers were taking advantage of the beautiful weather. Why hadn't she been here before?

Reuben and Oscar eagerly jumped out of the car and they began their coastal walk. The fresh air filled her lungs and she couldn't believe that she hadn't been there before. It was amazing! She began to take some photos on her iPhone to show everyone back home what a lovely place this is and well worth another visit.

As she steadily but carefully wandered on, she could hear her name being called in the distance.

'Meg, Meg.' She turned around and it was Esme. Meg was stunned to see her. How wonderful.

'How are you, Esme?' she asked.

'Olivia is staying with her grandparents in Paris and I am getting things sorted out.'

'What do you mean?'

'Let's walk over to the café and have a coffee.'

Meg started to drag Reuben alongside her but not before he had made friends with another little dog and wouldn't walk away.

'Reuben, come on,' Meg shouted in a snappy voice.

It didn't take long before they headed towards the little café on the cliffside.

'I will get the coffee Esme but could you hold on to Reuben for me?'

It wasn't long before Meg returned with coffee and eclairs.

'The fresh air gives you such an appetite,' she said jokingly. 'Anyway, Esme, what is your news?'

'Well, I was going to pop over and see you but everything has happened so quickly, I didn't know where to start.'

'No worries,' Meg said, 'I am here now.'

'Now that Greg was no longer a part of their lives and hopefully never would be, she had spoken with her parents and decided to move back to Paris with them and sell her property here in St Helene. They have a big house outside Paris where they run a Bed and Breakfast.

'Should I decide to move back with them, I will have my own annex, where I can look after myself and Olivia separately, away from Mum and Dad should I wish. Also, they have asked if I would like to help run the B & B with them as they are now getting older and would like more help. I could even run my mobile hairdressing from the annex too.'

'This is great news Esme; this could be a new start for both of you.'

Esme agreed and said she thought it would be good for Olivia to be near her grandparents. She hasn't had much time with them over the years and always asks her about them.

'There is no decision to make,' Meg told her, 'go for it Esme. This could change yours and Olivia's life forever.'

'I have also purchased a little car to get around and although I don't have much money, with the little amount I do have, I am just managing. There isn't much furniture so I will sell furniture with the house. I don't suppose I will get much for the house as it needs a lot of work inside and out but someone may look upon it as an investment or something, even bring it back to its original state.'

'You will be surprised at what you can get for it,' Meg told her.

She told Meg that she has now put everything in the hands of the Agent and waiting for news on the sale. Meg was pleased that Esme had made some important decisions, putting herself and Olivia first. She had to do it and she has! She knew Katie would be sad to see Olivia leave, telling Esme that both girls must keep in touch.

They are such good friends and it would be a pity to see their friendship fade away.

'I will make sure they do Meg; believe me, I will.'

Meg had to admit she was saddened at her news because she had become such a good friend but at the same time she wanted to make sure she and Olivia were safe after the frightful ordeal they had recently experienced in their young lives. Living back with her parents was possibly the safest place for them both, making her much happier.

'When do you think you will be leaving?'

'Possibly, within the next month.'

'That soon,' she said.

'Well, I think we should have a little leaving party for you,' Meg said excitedly. 'I will arrange something at my house and get in touch with you.'

'Oh, Meg, that is so very kind of you. Are you sure?'

'I am very sure, I am not having my friend leaving without saying goodbye and I know Katie would want to say goodbye too. I also know everyone in the village will want to give you a good send-off and wish you luck for your future.'

She wanted to give Esme and Olivia a party to remember, so she invited as many people from the village as possible. She was surprised at how many of them wanted to say their goodbyes. The weather was proving sunny and dry, so she decided to hold the party in the garden.

It was a Sunday afternoon and many villagers were returning from church and heading their way. Meg had put a sign on the driveway saying, 'Welcome to Esme and Olivia's leaving party.'

To her surprise, around fifty people turned up and she was hoping there would be enough food for everyone. Still, as usual, Mum came into her own, lavishly displaying all varieties of salads, pastries and bowls of hot chilli, having been consumed almost immediately.

She did us all proud! Katie even contributed by making some cookies. Another surprise. Danielle and Phillipe came strolling up the drive, arm in arm. Their faces were beaming and they were both looking so very happy. They hugged her and she ushered them to where Esme talked to Mum and Dad.

Danielle was holding a bouquet. Beckoning Esme over, she wished her and Olivia all the best with the move to Paris. As she handed Esme the flowers, her eyes filled with tears gently rolling down her blushed cheeks.

'Thank you so much and thanks to you Meg also. You have been my guardian angels over the last 12 months and I don't know what I would have done without you both.'

Katie, Alice and Olivia were happily playing together in the tree house and all could hear children laughing throughout the garden. The afternoon and evening went well; even Louis could get some time off to say goodbye.

Esme called them both over and said, 'Louis, make Meg happy like she has made me happy.'

'I will, I promise,' looking into her eyes affectionately, Meg knew he meant every word.

'It is not goodbye forever, just for now.'

However, Esme did say she probably wouldn't be back as it held too many bad memories.

'We all understand, Esme,' Meg softly replied.

As Esme and Olivia left the party, they stood and watched them walk away. Katie was tugging at her skirt, struggling to hold back the tears. Meg also felt exceptionally emotional but Louis placed his hand on hers and she knew everything would be alright.

Phillipe was taking care of Danielle, who, too, was wiping away tears with a cream lace hanky. What a day!

'We have given them both the send-off they deserve,' said Meg happily.

With most of the guests leaving around eight o'clock and Louis going to take an urgent call, they managed to clear up very quickly. Tables were down, chairs put away and rubbish cleared, so all that was left was to put their feet up, watch TV and go straight to bed.

Meg lay in bed thinking she must speak with Louis about Dad. She just wanted reassurance that Dad was alright. It had been playing on her mind since Mum thought Dad could be doing too much. It was the next day that she decided to give him a call.

Louis said he would pop over later that day but also told her that it would help if you remember, Meg; he is getting older now and he won't be able to do things he did ten years ago.

'I know Louis, I have told him that but you know what he is like, stubborn as a mule.'

'Like father, like daughter,' he said very light heartedly.

After Louis had a chat with Dad and persuaded him to take some tests, Louis wanted to take a look at some of his medication to make sure he was taking the right dosage and it could even mean different tablets or increase his tablets once again.

'Please, Mr Thomas, take it easy. Everyone worries about you!'

'I will,' Dad said very reluctantly.

Louis looked over at her and grinned as if to say, 'I'm not too sure about that.'

Chapter 26

Esme and Olivia had now returned to Paris and she texted her to say they had arrived safely and Olivia was enjoying her new school. She was exceptionally busy helping her parents run the B & B and had enjoyed meeting new people. They were waiting for the house to sell and then she and Olivia could move forward with their new lives.

Meg was delighted to hear she was happy and looking forward to a more secure and contented future. Fast approaching was the autumnal months and there was a definite chill in the air. She was helping the boys saw up logs with the chain saw for the burner.

There were plenty of chores to do in the garden and with the help of their neighbour, they were making good progress. The boys also helped to load the wheelbarrow and placed the logs into the log shed. It was teamwork but they managed.

Mum seemed to be carrying out endless cups of tea, which was very welcome. It was getting dark and the children were watching TV. Mum was ironing in the kitchen and she was thinking about taking Reuben for a walk before it got too dark.

Meg called out to Mum and asked, 'Where is Dad? Have you seen him?'

'No, Meg, I thought he was still outside in the garden.'

'OK, I will go and quickly have a look.'

As she wandered quickly down the garden, she shouted out to Dad but there was no response. She shouted for a second time but still nothing. Absolute silence. Suddenly, she could see a figure lying on the ground.

Oh no, she thought, *Oh no.*

It was Dad! She ran over as quickly as she could. He was lying motionless on the ground, looking grey and not responding. She felt a faint pulse and immediately went into nursing mode and started CPR on him.

'Dad, speak to me, please, Dad.'

She tried very hard with compression after compression; she told him, 'We can do this. You are my Dad; you can't leave us. You can't die. I won't let you!'

Looking down at his lifeless body, she knew he had gone. She stood, looking down at him; her body motionless. She couldn't imagine their lives without him anymore. Luckily, she had her phone with her so that she could ring for an ambulance.

There was no way she was going to leave him. She just stayed and worked on him for what seemed forever and she wasn't going to give up. She started talking to him in the hope he would respond. His unresponsive body just lay there.

Her Dad had gone! She carefully laid his garden jacket over him and returned to the house. Mum was humming like she does when she tackles the ironing.

'Mum, stop!'

'What do you mean, Meg?'

Meg gently walked her over to the chair and sat her down. She also gathered the children because they had to know too. As she broke the news to them, there was total silence.

Mum uttered very softly, 'Where is your Dad?'

Meg told her he was resting in his beautiful place and that she had rung an ambulance. She also rang Louis, who rushed over immediately. Louis arrived just as the ambulance drew up the drive.

'It's alright, Meg, I am here. Take yourself, Mum and the children into the kitchen.'

But Mum shouted, 'I want to see him. Please let me see him.'

The children were crying relentlessly. Meg couldn't believe this was happening. It seemed to be one tragedy after another! She took Mum over to where he was lying and she held his hand for the last time, leaning over and placing her body on his.

Goodnight, darling!

As she looked down at Mum saying goodbye, she couldn't believe what had just happened. He was only laughing and joking with them about an hour ago. Life is so cruel and unfair. They had now lost two husbands, two dads and a Grandfather.

It was then that she became inconsolable. The tears flowed and she became hysterical. Louis accompanied Mum to her bedroom, where he prescribed a sedative for both of them. Mum laid on her bed where she quickly fell asleep. He told Meg to do the same but she wasn't having any of it.

She just wanted to be with her Dad for the last time before they took him away in the ambulance to the Mortuary. They later learnt that Dad had a fatal heart attack and nothing would have saved him. He died in his favourite place, doing what he loved best. His spade lay beside him.

Meg began to wonder how, as a family, they were going to get through this second tragedy. It was happening all over again! Once Danielle heard the news, she was over and offered any help she could. Meg told Danielle that she would not be able to work at the shop until after the funeral because Mum would want her by her side.

'I entirely understand and you must not worry about a thing. When you are ready, just come into the shop, chat and have a coffee. Talking works wonders!'

'Thanks, Danielle; I will.'

The post-mortem report came back just as they thought. Dad's heart was weak and any exertion could have triggered a heart attack. Everybody told him he had to take things easy but her Dad did not have any of it. He would live the rest of his life the way he wanted by not giving up for whatever reason.

He died doing what he loved and with the people he loved and that gave comfort, not only to her but to Mum also. Dad had his funeral at the local church in St Helene and Henri Pascall, the Mairie, came to represent the village. Mum and Meg shook hands with many people but she felt like everything was a dream and they were both unaware of what was happening.

Still in shock, they held onto each other and didn't let go. Mum's wish was to have Dad's ashes remain with her, so after the cremation, they were put in a casket and given to her. Simon's was scattered around the magnolia tree because that was her wish.

They started with the dream of living in France with a family of five. Then it was seven when Mum and Dad moved over. Now they were back to five. Was moving to France the right decision? She really hoped it was. In five years, she had lost two of her nearest and dearest.

Life was so unfair, why them?

'What are we going to do, Meg?' Mum asked.

'Look, let's take each day as it comes.'

Mum held out her hand, saying 'What would I do without you?'

They stood crying and holding each other.

'We have beautiful memories, Mum, of two wonderful people.'

Louis had been a tower of strength towards them all and at times, wouldn't leave them. Meg told him they would be alright and that he had his work to consider but he wanted to make sure they were all coping as a family.

'We are Louis, we will get through this but it will take time.'

It had been four months since the death of Dad and things were gradually getting back to some normality but it would never be the same. They had his picture on the sideboard and as they walk by, they always say:

'Hello, Dad.'

Before the death of Simon, it could be said he was the one person who held their family together. Dad then became that person when he moved here but now they were both gone and so they had to be strong and they couldn't and wouldn't let them both down.

They discussed Dad a lot more now; even the children would laugh at some of the jokes and things he would say and do. Mum was now regaining some of her lost confidence but living in a strange country without her soulmate must be difficult.

Meg was delighted she had decided to join the local knitting club, where she met many people from all walks of life. Meg was now back at the shop working but Danielle ensures Meg only work when it suits her. Meg then told her she needed to work to get through a difficult part of her life.

'OK, if you are sure but you know I am always here for you, your Mum and the children.' Her gratitude towards Danielle was beyond belief. The kindness she had shown them was more than any long-standing friend could give. She was a truly remarkable lady!

Alice appeared to be missing Dad a lot. In her own way, she had also looked upon him as a grandad. She would often sit on his knee with Katie and he would tell them stories and sometimes the odd joke or two. They were going to miss him a lot.

The boys had certainly had sorrowful moments, taking to their rooms and lying on their beds, remembering their fishing trips together. He had certainly left them with memories which would stay with them forever, alongside the wonderful memories they had for Simon.

Christmas this year was a little different for them; losing Dad was quite upsetting, especially when families tend to unite during the festive period.

However, they would always remember his cheerful and happy ways and how he would dress up for the children as Father Christmas.

They all sat down with a glass of mulled wine, remembering those exceptional times, crying out with laughter but crying out with tears too. They all raised a glass, possibly two, at this remarkable and loving Husband, Father and Grandpa.

Louis, Alice and the puppy came over and there was fun and laughter filling the house. Even Mum was happy to sit around the log fire, singing carols and reminiscing about the good old days.

'Are you alright, Mum?' Meg asked as she caught her gazing at Dad's photo.

'He is with us and always will be,' placing Simon's photo alongside, she felt like they had never left them.

'What a silly pair we are, Meg,' Mum said.

'Not at all, we loved them so much and there will always be a place in their hearts for these two exceptional people.'

New Year quickly arrived and they got through Christmas better than she thought. Mum had made some lovely friends at the knitting club and understand she was making cakes for the next session, which appeared to be taking place at their house.

Their neighbour, who once was a landscape gardener and helped Dad before he died, had agreed to continue assisting where he could and spend a few hours per week, so the garden would hopefully reach Dad's standards. Meg hoped it would, anyway!

They should have veggies growing from what Dad planted and they had planted a tree down the bottom of the garden, near the stream, in remembrance of him and named it "Grandpa's special place". It was mid-morning when she decided to drive to the village, thinking she could detour to Esme's house.

Meg could see that there was a sign outside saying sold. Wow! In France, properties took a long time to sell. However, she was surprised Esme's house sold in less than six months. She was curious to know who bought it. Is it anyone they know? It was a lovely, quaint old house but much work was needed.

The property had a large back garden with enough room to stable a couple of horses, two apple trees, fruit bushes and possibly even space to build a swimming pool. Indeed, a project was waiting for the right person with the time and money.

Meg didn't realise how big Esme's house was. It was huge! She had only been inside the kitchen area and never outside, only catching a glimpse of the garden from the roadside. She could now see why Esme had found it hard to look after the property, especially during the last couple of troubled years when life was so tough.

Driving quickly by, she parked the car in the village and walked over to see Danielle. It was her day off but working in the shop helped her immensely relieve the stress over the past few months. She started to bunch up bouquets, sweep the leaves on the floor and even had time to make a hot drink.

'You don't have to do that, Meg. I can do that!'

She replied by saying that 'I need to do this. I think my mental health has been suffering over the past 12 months in many ways and working here has given me the strength to get through.'

'Very well but please let me know if I can help to make it easier for you and the family.'

Meg told her that Mum had joined a knitting club and made friends.

'Well, that is excellent news!'

She then asked, 'How's the romance, Danielle?'

Ah, 'I was waiting for you to ask me that. Well, all is good. We recently spent the weekend not too far away at a beautiful little fishing village in Southern Brittany. It was lovely, the weather was good and the company was excellent.'

'Are you more than good friends?' Meg asked.

'Yes, we are,' Danielle said elatedly.

Danielle told her that she had known Phillipe for many years. She had been living here briefly when she was introduced to Phillipe by a friend in the village. They were not attracted to each other instantly but recently when meeting up by chance, she changed her mind considerably. He appeared to be very kind, honest and a pleasure to be around.

'These are some of the qualities I had been looking for, Meg,' she said with clarity and meaning. 'I have to admit that we have both grown older and wiser and we both need companionship. There could even be a future for us one day; who knows!'

Meg was over the moon at Danielle's news and curiosity was getting to her, so she texted Phillipe and invited him to the house for coffee when he was free. She didn't expect a quick answer back and didn't get one. She knew Phillipe had a busy schedule.

He may have worked out her intentions by asking about his relationship with Danielle, as she was now becoming inquisitive and longing to know the strength of their relationship. Unquestionably, he would be right! She didn't want to pry or perhaps she did!

Mum thought her intentions were childish and told her to let things gradually happen naturally between them. Meg saw Phillipe cycling past as she entered the churchyard to place some flowers in the remembrance garden. He waved out and said he had received my text and that perhaps they could meet as a foursome soon.

'That would be very nice,' she told him!

'I expect you know that Danielle and myself have been dating each other!'

'Yes, Danielle did say something,' Meg said in a curious tone.

She told Phillipe they looked good together and hoped their relationship would progress. Danielle certainly needed someone in her life treating her the way she treats others with kindness and thoughtfulness and Meg believed the time was now and he could be the right person for her!

He placed his arm on hers and then said he was very sorry to learn about her father's death. Well, he hadn't been well for some time but Dad, being Dad, didn't want to alarm any of them, so he didn't say much about how he was feeling.

If Simon were here now, he would be devastated by Dad's sudden death. They were like father and son when they were together and knowing they are finally together now was helping her find peace and closure. Phillipe asked if she could arrange a dinner date as he was busy organising the winter ski trip.

'Of course, Phillipe, leave it with me.'

Meg made the necessary arrangements for this coming Saturday. It was Louis's weekend off, so it worked out perfectly. After Mum returned from her knitting club, she told her the group were talking about the house which was up for sale.

'You don't see many houses go up for sale in the village very often,' so this was a topic high on the gossip list.

'Oh, you mean Esme's old house.'

'Yes, that's the one,' Mum replied.

There was a sold sign in the garden; the latest news was that the buyer wanted everything demolished and a complete rebuild.

That's quite drastic, Meg thought.

It would help to forget the traumatic times that have happened there. A new house, a new beginning!

Chapter 27

Louis was on time and picked her up for the dinner date with Danielle and Phillipe.

Louis asked, 'Do you think this is a good idea?'

'Of course, I do! They are both friends, not strangers and I think the evening will go exceptionally well.'

'You are not prying, are you Meg?' Louis commented in a cynical tone.

'What me! Not at all.'

They all sat in a quiet part of the restaurant, overlooking a somewhat busy street. Seeing so many cars and people meandering around the square was unusual in this quiet little village. In the distance, they could see people dancing, singing with much hilarity.

Louis told her it was a wedding party celebrating. Dancing was a popular pastime at French weddings. In Brittany, the traditional dance was the Rond where people joined hands and danced in a circle.

The bride and groom usually celebrated in a restaurant, hotel or marquee where they had a cake called a croquembouche, which had always been the traditional French wedding cake—choux pastry puffs piled into a cone and bound with threads of caramel. So yummy!

'I don't suppose there aren't any weddings on the horizon that we know of,' Meg said out loud with a nosey tone to her voice.

'You never know,' Louis and Phillipe both said instantly together.

They all looked at each other and gently fell back into their chairs. Suddenly, she felt Louis's hand touching hers. Looking across at Danielle and Phillipe, they too were expressing the same feeling to each other. She didn't want to question them on their relationship in any way.

Their facial expressions told her everything, appearing blissfully happy together. As they left the restaurant, she suggested they do this again sometime.

Walking casually down the street, they could see the wedding guests still enjoying the celebrations.

Shouting out they congratulated them as they passed by. Children waving silk ribbons everywhere, another Breton tradition when a couple marries. Never had she seen St Helene so full of activity. It brought the village to life; everyone joining in, including the villagers.

Danielle took hold of her hand and Meg could tell she was eager to speak with her. Being a curious individual, something many people had told her many times, she couldn't hold back anymore and asked her if there was anything on her mind that she wanted to say to her.

'Not really but you can see I am so happy being with Phillipe.'

'Yes, I can certainly see that, Danielle!'

She went on to say that he had become very special to her.

'Thank you for listening to me, Meg; I wasn't sure if I was doing the right thing but now I do.'

Having listened to Danielle, Meg had no worries about their relationship because she knew that Phillipe would, one day, look after her and make her very happy. Returning to the car together, Louis politely opened the door. Turning slowly towards him was such a magical moment as she looked into his eyes.

Her body was like jelly as he held her close against his warm body. Please don't let go! Such crazy thoughts but heartfelt nevertheless! Their fabulous weekend trip to Paris appeared to have reinforced their relationship. Still, they needed more quality time if the relationship was to go forward, focusing on valuable time together.

A week later, whilst driving back from the village, she passed the demolition site, as the villagers called it. Stopping the car for a good look, she noticed Louis driving past. They flashed their lights and Louis waved but didn't stop.

How unusual! Perhaps he was on call and didn't have time. Yes, that was it! Feeling somewhat puzzled, she drove back home. She hurriedly got out of the car, glanced through the kitchen window and saw Mum sitting in the chair, looking at her diary as she always does each day.

'Are you okay, Mum?' she asked.

'Yes, just looking at some dates in the diary.'

'Are you planning something?' she said jokingly.

'I was thinking of taking a trip back to England to see Aunty Gabriel.'

Gabby, as they call her, is Mum's sister and since Dad had passed away, they could tell Mum had been missing friends and family back home.

'Are you ready to travel yet, Mum?'

'It might do me good! The only issue is that I don't drive and it is a long way.'

'I will drive you as long as you return,' Meg said light-heartedly.

Mum laughed and said, 'Of course I will; this is my home now.'

They made the arrangements and booked a ferry.

Who is going to look after the children? Meg thought!

They couldn't come with us because of school. She would also have to talk with Danielle about work at the shop, but she shouldn't have worried, Danielle was on hand, as usual.

'Please don't be silly, Meg; I will look after the children and Reuben.'

Meg told her it would only be for a few days until she settled Mum.

'No problem. I will look after everything!'

'You are a star; thanks, Danielle!'

Meg phoned Louis and told him what the plans were and he, too, was delighted.

'Just make sure you bring me back some of that tasty English Cheddar cheese.'

'I will do my best,' Meg answered.

She was beginning to get quite excited about returning home for a few days, she thought it was talking about Cheddar Cheese, something wonderful which would remind her of home. She could see quite a change in Mum. She had regained lots more confidence, which was a good thing.

They continually talked about Dad, helping them all deal with the terrible grief Mum, she and the children endured. They would laugh at the silly things he said and did. Walking around the garden and where Dad was always pottering, was now becoming so much easier for them to cope with, knowing this was a favourite place for him to spend his most precious time.

All plans were now taking place for the trip back to England. Danielle had moved in for a few days and Louis came by to wish them a safe journey.

'I am going to miss you,' she said, 'but I should be back by the end of the week.'

Then Louis shouted, 'By the way, Meg, don't forget the cheese!'

Louis kissed Mum and told her not to worry about anything but enjoy the time with her sister and friends.

'Oh, I certainly will, Louis!'

Waving goodbye was hard but knowing they were safe and in good hands made it much easier. As was often the case, the journey took about ten hours, including the ferry and when we arrived at Aunt Gabby's, we were exhausted.

It was the first time she had driven this journey on her own; Simon was always the driver and she was the navigator who would permanently correct the SatNav if she felt it wasn't taking us the quickest route, much to Simon's annoyance.

They often joked about these minor annoyances of hers. He always said to her, 'I suppose you know better.'

She couldn't help thinking if everything was OK back in France, so decided to check. She rang Danielle's mobile and she quickly replied.

'Oh, hi, Meg. Is everything OK?'

'Yep, I arrived about an hour ago, feeling exhausted but otherwise, all good. Are the children behaving?'

'Of course, they are, you mustn't worry. Phillipe is popping over tonight and having a meal with me.'

'Give him my love and please say goodnight to the children and the dogs for me.'

'Certainly Meg!'

'Speak soon. Love to you all.'

She felt much better after speaking with Danielle; it put her mind to rest immediately. She could hear Mum talking loudly in the kitchen with Aunt Gabby. She popped around the door and was offered a glass of wine.

'Thanks but I will shower quickly and go to bed.'

Aunty Gabby remarked, 'Treat the house as if it's yours.'

Meg gave her a loving smile and went upstairs to get some much-needed sleep. She must have quickly fallen asleep when she suddenly awoke hearing loud noises from downstairs. Looking down at her watch, she saw it was gone at midnight.

She wiped her tired eyes, stretched a little and slowly walked downstairs. She entered the room where Mum and Aunt Gabby were still talking.

'Oh, I hope we didn't disturb you, Meg.'

What could she say?

'Oh no, I have just come down for a glass of water!'

She could see Mum crying; were they sad or happy tears? She wasn't sure.

'Everything alright, Mum,' she asked.

'All good.'

She later learnt they were happy tears and both were reminiscing about family, talking about Dad and Simon. This journey would bring back many memories for Mum, hoping she could handle the past. Up to now, they had been cautious with Mum not to overcrowd her with too many memories but there comes a time when she must let go.

After a couple of days of taking Mum around to see family and friends, it was time for Meg to leave. She would have lots to keep her occupied during her stay and keep up to date with all the news back in England.

'Thank you, Meg, for bringing me back to England but I have decided to stay with Aunt Gabby for a little longer than planned.'

'That's OK,' she said. 'Let me know your travel plans and I can sort everything out for you.'

'What would I do without you?'

They kissed on the doorstep and Meg quietly told Aunt Gabby to look after her. She sometimes felt that Mum wasn't quite over Dad's death yet.

'I will look after her, Meg, you know I will.'

Caring and kindness ran in the family, as you well know.

'Simon was your tower of strength like your Dad was to my sister. Grief takes its toll but as you know, Meg, you fight it and remember the good times, which will always remain with you.'

'You are quite right, Aunt; I see so much of Mum in you.'

'We are sisters, after all,' answering back in such good humour.

Meg had to admit she felt a little sad leaving Mum behind because she knew she would miss her terribly but it was her decision and something she had to let her do. Everyone was pleased to have her home and Danielle was very welcoming.

'Has everything been alright, with no problems?'

''Of course,' Danielle replied in a very courteous voice. 'The boys have been very busy with school football matches. Alice has been staying too, bringing Oscar with her. Reuben and Oscar seem to be getting on very well together and Phillipe, I and the children have taken them on long walks along the river and the woodland.'

'It seems you have really spoilt them.'

'It was a pleasure and if you ever need me again, please always ask.'

Louis popped in a couple of times to check on Alice, as he had been working long shifts and was looking extremely exhausted. He worried her at times, but it seemed that most doctors appeared to work all day and all night!

'How are you getting on with Phillipe?' Meg asked in a polite but enquiring voice.

'He has asked me to go skiing. The school is organising a trip in February to the French Alps and I am thinking about it.'

'You must go, Danielle! I can look after the shop and anyway, you need a holiday.'

'I would love to go but it has been a long time since I skied.'

Meg said, 'Once you get those skies on, it will all come back to you. Go for it Danielle!'

'That's settled then.'

'Tell Phillipe your decision and don't worry about anything.'

'Awesome! Thanks Meg.'

Meg had a few missed calls on her phone and she could see they were from Louis. She immediately returned the calls. He appeared to be stressed and a little anxious on the phone.

'Problems?' She asked.

'Just a little tired but all the better for hearing your voice!'

'I have only been away a few days, Louis!'

Louis's voice was getting a little restless, saying it seemed ages since they last saw each other disclosing, 'I didn't think I would miss you this much, Meg.'

'Me too,' she said. 'I can't wait to see you either, Louis!'

Although they spoke on the phone for hours, nothing appeared relevant except how much they had missed each other. However, they spoke about the weather and what they had for dinner like all do when the conversation begins to fade slightly.

They eventually put the phone down and agreed to see each other the following day. Meg started to think back to when she first met Louis and the help bestowed upon her through the loss of Simon. He showed empathy and most of all, the encouragement needed to carry on.

At the time of Simon's accident, it could be said that Louis was a stranger because they hadn't known each other that long. Still, sometimes it is so much easier to talk to someone you don't know that well rather than with a member of your own family.

You don't need to hide the truth or the hurt when speaking to a so-called stranger. Nobody knows the heartache caused by losing a loved one unless they have been in that situation themselves.

She could hold on to the one person who could understand her feelings; Louis.

Chapter 28

It seemed such a long time since Mum left France to visit her sister. Talking with her regularly on the phone and via FaceTime, she appeared to be very happy. However, 'Come home soon, Mum; we all miss you.'

Almost two months was far too long without seeing her but she shouldn't have worried; Mum didn't want her to drive back to England again, saying it was a very long drive. After some discussion, Mum booked a flight back to France, making the return trip easier for her.

Mum's flight was on time. She was looking happy and refreshed after her visit. Her cheeks were rosy and Meg just couldn't wait to be with her. They walked slowly to the car and although she was beginning to look a little tired, Meg knew the trip had been good for her.

Meg decided to drive back through the little villages, not the dual carriageway, passing by the building plot with its renovation and she was surprised to see such a transformation. The roof on the house was nearly complete and windows were about to be installed. How could they get that far in such a short time?

So different, so modern. Wow, it looked great! She pulled the car into a small lay-by and just sat with her thoughts. The country lane was still and quiet, with the birds singing and with hardly any traffic passing by. She noticed a little red robin bouncing on a half-broken twig, balancing on a swaying tree. The little bird looked very tame, so she rolled down the car window and to her surprise, it didn't even fly away.

So tiny, yet so beautiful. The little robin red breast wasn't eager to go anywhere. Maybe he was waiting for some food—or just perhaps a friendly face. It was very apparent he wanted to stay with her. A walker passing by nodded to her and with that the little robin bounced off the twig and flew away.

'Goodbye, Mr Robin,' she called out.

She glanced over at Mum and could see she had fallen fast asleep. Travelling must have tired her out. She must have sat there for ages, thinking of the past and Esme's troubles when living at the house—remembering their running days, coffee mornings and lunch dates.

How could Greg inflict so much pain on Esme? She was someone who didn't deserve what life threw at her. Always gentle and loving. The only person she cared about was making Olivia happy and ensuring she looked after her the best way possible.

It was Esme who he physically abused and she took the pain and bruises for them both. Meg was pleased she was now making a new life for them both. She was safe now and that was all that mattered. It was late February and Danielle and Phillipe had left for their skiing holiday.

She was somewhat envious but also very happy for them both. They had been together for almost ten months and everything had turned into a beautiful and loving relationship. Being busy in the shop meant that she couldn't do her running as much but she was hoping for a quick run after work to burn off those Christmas calories, which were taking some time to disappear.

As she closed the shop and stepped outside, she saw Louis passing by in the car.

'Just the person,' he called out.

'What, me?' She said in a witty voice.

'Yes, you! I have just finished at the hospital and hoped I could see you.'

They arranged to meet at the restaurant for a quick drink that evening, so she had to put her run on hold and start counting the calories once again, anything to meet her wonderful man. What could be better? She rushed home, took a quick shower and asked Mum if she would kindly put Katie to bed.

Slightly out of breath, she rushed into the restaurant where Louis was sitting. He walked over and pulled out a seat. They tenderly kissed each other before the waiter arrived with a bottle of their favourite red.

Impetuously, Meg said, 'It has been at least a month since we spent time alone, perhaps longer.'

'I know and that is what I would like to talk to you about, Meg. I have been thinking.'

'What again,' Meg said light-heartedly.

As they sat close together, Louis mentioned the trip to Paris. Meg looked up as he told her it was unforgettable and sensational and he would never forget the day they both lovingly sank into each other's arms, announcing their love for each other. Meg noticed Louis was wiping away a tear from his eye.

'Sorry, Meg, I cannot begin to think how much my life has changed since meeting you. I am beginning to become an emotional wreck! I can't even think straight at work. I think of nothing else. You are on my mind 24/7.'

'Don't forget Louis; I am also beginning to think you aren't too bad, either!'

Louis beckoned the waiter over for yet another bottle of wine.

'No, wait a moment, let's celebrate! Champagne, please, waiter and make it a bottle of your very best.'

'Are you trying to get me drunk?' Meg uttered.

'Not at all. We are here making up for some lost time.'

She had to second that. She felt she didn't have a care in the world when she was with him.

'I am thinking of planning a holiday down South for a couple of weeks. Having mentioned it to Alice, she got all excited and wants you all to join us.'

'Do you need an answer straight away?' Meg asked.

'No, not now! Just think about it and if you agree, I can make the necessary arrangements.'

It did sound lovely. Louis said that he saw a stunning villa in the mountains overlooking Nice. There was an infinity pool, everything you would want for a relaxing holiday.

'Sounds marvellous and I am sure the children would love it.'

'Do you think your Mum would like to come along too?'

'I can ask her but I can't guarantee anything. She is still having bad days as well as good days.'

'I know what you mean, Meg. Just think about it!'

'When are you planning to go?'

'I was thinking sometime during school holidays in August.'

Meg was excited about spending a couple of weeks with Louis and the children. A change would do them all good. They hadn't had an actual family holiday since before Simon's accident and when she discussed it with Mum and the children, they were delighted at the thought of a holiday. Infinity pool, hot sunshine, superb French cuisine. Meg was there already!

'There is something else I need to tell you. Please don't be shocked when I tell you but I have bought Esme's old house. You may have noticed, when driving past that it has been knocked down and is being rebuilt to make it a family home one day. When we passed each other in the country lane, I was on my way urgently to see the builder and sort out some concerns that needed my attention.'

'Louis, I did not know,' Meg whispered.

'All I need now is someone to share it with.'

Meg was trembling at the thought. Could he mean her, them? Was she right to think this way? They left the restaurant and she told Louis she would let him know when she had an answer from the gang back home about the holiday!

'Remember Meg; this holiday would be an excellent time for our families to get to know each other and a perfect way of spending the quality time we all need.'

She couldn't agree more and left the restaurant one very excited lady. They said goodnight and she promised to ring him with an answer as soon as possible. It was dark when she got home and all she could see was the red light on the cooker timer shining through the kitchen window.

She hurriedly got out her key, opened the door and closed it with a bang. Oh no! She hoped she hadn't woken anyone. Reuben jumped to greet her and she sat with him by the half-glowing log fire for a few moments.

Reuben was snuggled up in bed, so she sat beside him and stroked his delicate soft fur coat. She must have fallen asleep beside him—the warmth of the fire must have made her sleepy and the wine and champagne were beginning to take effect.

She was beginning to make a habit of falling asleep in front of the fire. The next thing she knew, Mum was shaking her to wake up.

'Do you want a cup of tea?' she asked. 'What are you doing sleeping on the kitchen floor?'

'Oh, I must have fallen asleep with Reuben.'

'I can see that!'

'What time is it?'

'Six o'clock.'

'Oh no, I better get ready for work!'

Mum asked if she wanted breakfast before saying, 'You can't go to work on an empty stomach.'

'Thanks, Mum—poached eggs on toast would be lovely.'

Meg quickly rushed and got changed—shouted at the children to get up and get ready for school. The household yet again was buzzing—showers running, Reuben running in the garden for his morning wee, Mum cooking breakfast, boys searching for their football kit and her wanting to talk about a holiday Louis was planning.

All this before she went to work! She didn't think so! Perhaps the best time would be this evening when everyone was altogether and less rushing around. She arrived early to open the shop. Danielle still had a few days of her skiing holiday left and she wanted the shop to look clean and tidy on her return.

It wasn't a busy time for the shop so she could window dress with a spring collection of roses and ferns. She began to think to herself that looks pretty good, considering she was not a professional florist. A selection of flowers, pansies, small budded chrysanthemums and tightly budded roses, balancing on long stems, all gleaming in the almost spring sunshine, filled the panoramic window.

Today was a quiet day, so after lunch and early closing, she decided to go for her long-awaited run. It felt good to blow away the cobwebs, as they say and she needed this run to get her head around the excitement of a holiday with Louis and his purchase of Esme's house.

She was beginning more and more to want to say yes to his suggestion of a holiday altogether. Although she was a little nervous about what reaction she would receive, she was hoping everyone would agree to Louis' kind offer. Oh well, she would have to wait and see.

Arriving back home, Mum sat alone in the kitchen, pondering over a magazine. Should she wait until later to tell them Louis' news? On second thoughts, she decided to tell them over dinner. That evening, it was only a short time before they were all together and food was on the dinner table.

They sat talking like they do every night at dinner. Towards the end of the meal, she quietly said, 'There is something I want to ask you all.'

Charlie looked at Freddie with slight apprehension. Katie was finishing her pudding and didn't look interested, as fruit pie and custard was much more enjoyable! She decided to come out with it and tell them about the holiday, leaving the news about the plan for Louis's house purchase until later. One thing at a time!

'Louis has asked if we would all like to join him and Alice on holiday in the South of France during the summer holidays in August.'

Katie then immediately looked up from her pudding, saying, 'Mummy, please, can we go?'

There was a look of complete surprise on the boy's faces but sheer delight too. Mum appeared a little unsure.

'Are you OK with this, Mum?'

She replied in a hushed tone, 'I would like you all to go but please tell Louis that I was flattered that he had even considered me but I would rather stay here.'

'Are you sure because it would do you good? A change of surroundings, plenty of hot sunshine?'

'I know, dear but I am happy to stay here with the dogs. Please don't worry about me; I will be fine.'

She knew there were friends at the knitting club who would pop around and visit and of course, Danielle was on hand if anything urgent cropped up but Meg was still unsure about her Mum's decision to stay alone for a couple of weeks. It had been difficult for her the last few months and perhaps she wasn't quite ready for new horizons yet.

The children were excited, so she decided to ring Louis and tell him they would be coming on holiday. He was delighted that they all said yes but she had to tell him Mum would stay home. She could tell he was slightly disappointed because she believed he was doing this for Mum too.

It would have given her a break. Anyway, her decision was final, so Louis said he would go and finalise the plans for the forthcoming holiday. The villa looks fantastic, Meg and there is so much for the children to do. She asked him how the house was progressing and he told her it was all going well and that he would soon get a completion date.

'Once everything is signed, I will put my house on the market for sale or I may even rent it out to a local in the village.'

Everything was falling into place. The holiday arrangements had been finalised and the house was well on the way to completion. Let's hope nothing will go wrong to spoil anything. Mum took her to one side and said she was so happy Louis was taking us away on holiday and that she need not worry about her.

'But I do, Mum! I need to make sure you will be ok.'

'I am a grown woman, Meg and anyway, one thought has come to mind; to spend some time with Aunt Gabby whilst you are away.'

'That's a great idea, Mum. I hadn't thought of that.'

'I will ring Aunt Gabby to arrange something,' Mum said.

Feeling much better at the thought of Mum having company whilst they were away, she knew asking Danielle to look after Reuben and Oscar, wouldn't present any problems. She loved them passionately, so was anticipating a yes from her.

Arrangements in hand; Mum was staying with Aunt Gabby and to her astonishment, Mum had booked an airline ticket from Nantes airport to Exeter. She was getting good at arranging flights, especially with Aunt Gabby, who lived only 10 miles from the airport and had offered to meet her there.

She knew it was only February but there was so much excitement about this holiday, which was almost six months away. Could they all wait that long? She asked.

Chapter 29

The arrival back home of Danielle and Phillipe was warm and welcoming but as Meg glanced down, she could see Danielle limping slightly.

'Oh no, Danielle, have you been in the wars?'

'My wretched ankle but it's nothing. Just a nasty sprain. You know what these professional skiers are like,' she said, laughing out loud. 'I wanted to show everyone I could ski but that was a big mistake. Not having skied for several years certainly took its toll and on the last day, I took a nasty tumble and sprained my ankle.

'Fortunately, Phillipe was on hand and he took me to the First Aid Office on the side of the slopes, where they had all the necessary X-ray equipment without having to go to the hospital. Doctors were on hand because it was a school trip and exceptionally well organised.

'They could see that it was only a sprain and nothing broken but told me to keep it tightly bandaged for the time being and try not to walk on it too much. Of course, I knew I had my friend Meg waiting back home to take care of me with a knowledge of Physio!'

They stood in the hallway giggling and told her she needed to take care of her ankle. Handing Danielle a pair of crutches, which Meg always kept nearby in case of an emergency like this, especially having two boys who loved their football and the injuries at times this sport could cause.

'No, Meg, I can manage.'

'Oh no, you don't. Take them as it will help with your balance.'

Meg began to sound somewhat harsh but knew she needed much more support than bandages. Firstly, Meg told her that she would arrange some exercises for her which would help with getting more movement back into the ankle joint.

Resting was the best cure and not overdoing the walking too much. Secondly, there was no need to worry about the shop, because she was there.

'I won't hear of it,' she said.

'Danielle, you must rest your ankle and as your Physio, I order you to do just that.'

'Ok, Nurse Johnston!'

Rest was crucial with any leg and ankle injuries, together with gentle exercise. Once she could make Danielle understand, she could see she had a busy time ahead. Louis has flown over to a seminar in Germany for seven days and had asked Meg to pop around at the site where the build was progressing, should she have enough time.

She was hoping they didn't ask her too many technical questions having not been familiar with building terms. She was beginning to feel quite proud of herself. The shop was running fantastically, the builders were on time with everything and the house was not far off from finishing, hopefully when Louis returned from Germany.

The kitchen was almost completed and the wet room was finished. It looked magnificent. Louis must have spent an absolute fortune on the inside décor. The value of the property must have trebled. What an investment! With spring just around the corner, they were all thinking about their family holiday in August.

Meg could tell everyone was buzzing with excitement. Katie and the boys' couldn't stop talking about it. Their first real holiday since they lost Simon and she wanted to make sure it was a holiday for them to remember. Looking back, Simon's fatal accident just turned their lives upside down.

It couldn't have happened at a worse time for us all. Meg was overjoyed at the way they had now coped altogether and moved forward. Simon undoubtedly would be proud of them. All the arrangements were in place for Mum to fly back to the UK and stay with her sister and Danielle was thrilled at the thought of caring for the two little hounds, Reuben and Oscar.

Phillipe had been spending quite a great deal of time with Danielle. He wanted to be near her whilst her ankle was recovering. He blamed himself for her accident. I don't know why! It probably wouldn't have happened had he been with her that morning and not rushed over to get a couple of hot chocolates from the café on the slopes.

Meg told him that was a silly remark. It was an accident and he must not blame himself. He profoundly cared for Danielle and would do anything for her. Meg couldn't help thinking she had said these words before somewhere. She remembered it was when she told Louis that Simon's accident wasn't his fault. These words are now beginning to haunt her!

A couple of weeks later, Danielle could get around, be more accessible and not hobble anymore. Crutches aside, she took easy steps and could now help at the shop. It was good for her because Meg saw her getting bored at home. She had always been a workaholic and keeping still was not her forte.

The injury to her ankle was healing and the swelling had almost disappeared. Meg told her the exercises had done their work. Although the Physio worked on her ankle, she still looked rather pale.

'Are you ok, Danielle?' Meg asked.

'A little tired and slightly dizzy sometimes but I have put that down to the painkillers I am taking.'

'What painkillers?' Meg asked anxiously.

'Only paracetamol which the doctor gave me.'

'That's ok.'

'Nothing too strong, Meg but they do make me sleepy.'

The next day as Meg opened the shop, the post was still on the floor.

That's unusual, she thought to herself.

Danielle did say she would be in early today. Meg walked to the back of the shop, turned off the alarm, put her coat on the hook and opened up the shop as usual. She then decided to ring her at home. After a couple of rings, Danielle answered.

'Are you alright?' Meg asked.

Danielle remarked that she would be in a little later, due to a tummy upset and not feeling too great.

'If you are feeling unwell, stay home—I can cope on my own.'

'Thanks, Meg. I will see how I feel later today.'

Poor Danielle. She was never poorly and so unlike her to have time off. It was midday and Meg was just about to shut the shop up for lunch when he saw Danielle walking into the Pharmacy. As Meg locked up the shop, she casually walked towards the Pharmacy but she didn't notice her peering through the window.

What Meg saw, she couldn't believe her eyes! She was utterly flummoxed. The pharmacist was handing Danielle a pregnancy kit. Perhaps she had better walk away quickly before she saw her. Racing to her car, she grabbed a bottle of water to have with her lunch before returning to the shop.

Meg sat quietly in the back room with her sandwich and bottle of water, wondering whether the kit was for her or maybe someone else. She didn't know what to think! Surely, it wouldn't be for Danielle or was it? Were her recent symptoms a clue? Tiredness, dizziness and tummy upset, which could add up to be morning sickness.

Am I reading too much into this? She thought.

Danielle didn't return to the shop that day and she was pleased they only had a few customers. She could shut the shop on time at five o'clock and head home. She had been thinking of nothing else and knew she had to keep her little secret to herself for the time being.

It could be something. It could be nothing. Let's wait and see. May was now upon them and it was a lovely spring morning, so she took Reuben and Oscar for their morning walk before work at the florist. Whilst Louis had been away in Germany and other occasions too, Oscar and Alice had stayed with us, much to Katie's delight.

Although Alice had a carer who looked after her, it had become more apparent that Meg was taking over that role. Katie loved being with Alice and Oscar, so Meg thought it would be very soon that they become permanent residents at Fleurs de Pre.

Strolling along the leafy lane, the grasshoppers talking to each other and the odd bee extracting the pollen from the wildflowers along the country lane, she felt complete bliss. Her mind wandered to the thought that Danielle could be pregnant. If she was, could the father be Phillipe?

Of course, it was. Who else? She must be patient and wait for Danielle to enlighten her with her news. Meg need not have waited too long because as she arrived at the shop, Danielle had already unlocked, the alarm turned off, the kettle was boiling and one happy smiling face was behind the counter.

'Danielle,' I gasped, 'how are you feeling?'

'I couldn't be better, Meg.'

'Come over here and sit down.'

Pausing slightly, she then sauntered to the couch. She knew she had to look surprised if the news was what she was thinking. She had to keep quiet which was becoming increasingly hard for her. Danielle was shaking slightly and Meg could tell the nervousness in her voice. She held out her hand to Danielle and asked if everything was alright.

'Absolutely, Meg! I want you to be one of the first to know. I am pregnant. I am having a baby!'

'Pregnant. You are having a baby?'

'Yes, that's right. We are having a baby.'

'You and who?'

'Well, who do you think, Phillipe of course.'

Meg was ecstatic. She jumped out of her seat and put her arms around Danielle, holding her tightly and not wanting to let go. Meg could see sheer happiness on her face and couldn't be more pleased for her.

'I am eight weeks pregnant and it is looking to be a Christmas baby.'

Unable to control her emotions any longer, tears were steadily flowing with pure delight. Danielle was such a gentle person with a loving nature who would make the most wonderful mother and with Phillipe showing so much kindness and love towards Danielle, they were a match made in heaven.

'We now need to find somewhere larger to live! My little flat is not big enough for the three of us and Phillipe only has a small cottage and again, not large enough to start a family. We have decided to look around for something bigger.'

'What a good idea,' Meg said with slight interest, thinking she may have the answer to this. Danielle mentioned she needed to be close to the florist shop, where hopefully she would be able to take the little one with her and of course, Phillipe needed to be close to the school as well.

'Finding something in the village could take time. There must be something available that suits you both, here in the village or nearby,' Meg told her.

Meg couldn't wait to tell the family and of course, Louis the news. He was due home tomorrow and the excitement was overwhelming. It was so lovely to have wonderful news for a change. Mum said she would start knitting for the baby and may ask everyone at the knitting club to produce a garment or two.

Katie was so excited about the arrival of a new baby and was asking all sorts of questions which Meg couldn't answer.

'Is it a boy, is it a girl? Is Danielle well? When is the baby coming?'

'Let's wait and see, Katie. There is a long way to go and we must keep our fingers crossed that everything will be OK for Danielle.'

Meg rang Phillipe after school and congratulated him on the news. She could tell by his voice he was jubilant at the news of becoming a father. He said it was a surprise and was now getting used to the idea of having a little family of his own, giving him such hope for the future.

'After losing my friend and colleague Simon, I was not in a good place like many others.'

Meg expressed her thoughts by saying, 'Both Simon and you became very close friends and I know Simon would be over the moon at your news.'

Phillipe was mumbling with sheer joy, saying he was getting used to becoming a dad, something he thought would never happen.

'There you go, Phillipe, it has happened and you will make a great Dad,' Meg told him.

Of course, she couldn't wait to tell Louis the news when he arrived home from Germany the next day. She longed to see him and anxiously lingered outside the house when she saw this handsome dark figure walk up the cobbled pathway to the house.

Greeting him with open arms, they just stood for a quiet moment, staring into each other's eyes, embracing and holding each other which seemed like an eternity. They walked into the kitchen and she couldn't control herself.

'They are having a baby.'

'Who,' Louis said.

'Danielle and Phillipe,' I shouted. 'Who do you think?'

There was absolute amazement on Louis's face. He seemed thrilled at the news, asking me if Danielle was feeling ok.

'Oh yes, just a few symptoms like you have but otherwise, she is glowing and thrilled.'

Louis then said, 'Time to open a bottle of bubbly.'

Any excuse for a glass of something. They both sat in the cool of the evening, the dogs sitting beside them.

'It is lovely to have you back home with us, Louis. I have missed you so much. Who would have thought life would have turned out this way?'

Meg went on to say that so much had happened during the last few years and was hoping for better times ahead.

'We are, Meg, we certainly are! How about I take you to see the house tomorrow? The builders told me everything was almost ready for me to move in.'

'Yes, please, Louis; I would like that very much!'

They drove to the house the next day and apart from some landscaping of the gardens, the house was almost completed, looking fabulous. It was enormous and as they walked inside, it was like stepping into a celebrity home. Everything they wanted was there.

There was even a games room with a snooker table. A gym displaying all the up to date equipment. No need for a subscription to the local gym, everything was here! Meg couldn't get over the enormity and luxury of this property. It was a dream house. Louis asked if she liked it.

'Of course, I like it! But isn't it a little big for you and Alice?'

'Well, that is what I was going to ask you, Meg. Would you and the children like to move in with us? There is even an annex built on the side of the property; ideal for your Mum if she wants to join us. The extension has a separate lounge, kitchen, bathroom and bedroom.'

It was, without question, luxurious. I didn't know what to say. Being shocked at the enormity of this new build, she was intrigued.

'What about my home, Louis?'

'Sell it and put the money in the bank for a rainy day!'

It was so much to take in but Meg had to admit it was like nothing she had dreamed of. It was unbelievable! What had I done to deserve all of this?

'Give it some thought,' Louis remarked, 'and let me know what you would like to do because it all makes sense, especially the way our future is looking.'

Agreeing with him, Meg knew the children wouldn't have any issues because of all its facilities; the games room, gym, they would be in absolute heaven. Perhaps a swimming pool one day! So many questions from the children about the move.

Yes, it does have a gym. Yes, it does have a games room. Yes, it has enough gardens to play football. All these questions would be a big step for them too but she could see by the reaction on their faces, they had already moved in!

On the other hand, it was taking quite a bit of convincing for Mum. They both shared so much grief and memories of Dad and Simon at their present home. Mum still had Dad's ashes and that would go with her wherever she went. She must admit she scattered Simon's ashes around the magnolia tree, where he loved and she knew he was with her wherever she went and always would be.

It was a hard decision for Mum to make about the move but she believed that nothing else mattered as long as they were all together. Finally, they all agreed the move would be good for them all and Meg couldn't wait to tell Louis. He couldn't be more pleased and said he would make it a family home with as many possessions as they would like to bring along.

That made Mum feel good. Now the hard work began. She must sell Fleur de Pre and sort out the furniture. It wasn't long before the news got around about Danielle and Phillipe. Baby talk was always something good to hear. The town was excited because they had known Danielle for a long time and wanted to see her happy and settled down.

When Phillipe and Danielle heard about Meg's possible move, Phillipe telephoned her to ask if he and Danielle could look around Fleur de Pre.

Although they had been there many times before, they now appeared interested in buying. It had crossed her mind previously that their home would suit them both admirably but she had to let them make that decision.

'Of course. Come over when you can.'

Meg had only briefly put the phone down before a knock came on the door. It was Danielle and Phillipe. Phillipe remarked by saying that they were both in the area.

'In fact, we were just outside,' he said jokingly, 'when we decided to pop in and have a chat about the house.'

'Well, what do you think?' Phillipe said to Danielle.

'Just beautiful! I have always loved this house.'

'That's settled, then. If the home is big enough for Meg and her family, then it is certainly big enough for us and our little one,' he joyfully remarked. 'We want to put in an offer, Meg.'

'That is wonderful and I couldn't be more pleased that you are my buyers. Danielle told me that we could always come over and visit any time so that memories of Simon and my Dad will always be with you.'

'We will also ensure that the seat around the magnolia tree will be there for you to remember Simon.'

Meg was highly thankful, 'That means so much to the family and me.'

With everything that had happened, Meg couldn't contain herself anymore and broke down into a complete mess. Danielle took hold of her, knowing how upset she was feeling.

'Please don't take any notice of me,' Meg said. 'Feeling emotional now and knowing you will bring up your family here gives me a chance never to say goodbye to this house and has made me the happiest person in the world.'

Phillipe also reminded her that he, too, would be close to his dear friend Simon and for a moment that filled her with so much love and joy towards them both. They settled the price and left the matter in the hands of the Agent.

She couldn't believe this was happening to them so quickly too. Everything was gradually falling into place. They could move into their new home before the holiday, so they had to get their skates on and move fast. Meg could see Mum was somewhat quiet and she asked her if she was OK with the move.

'Of course, I am; it will be strange at first but we will be together and guess what.'

'What Mum,' I said.

'I can now have control of my television programmes,' she laughingly cried out loud.

'You certainly can. No competition now with the boys. Remember, there is an interconnecting door, so you can come to us whenever you want.'

Meg took Mum to the house to show her around; she couldn't believe what she saw.

'Are you sure this is where we are going to live?'

'Yes, this is the house Louis calls home for all of us. I hope we are all very happy here, for a long time.'

'Louis is the perfect man to replace Simon and I know you have much love for each other. So long as he looks after you, now and when I am gone, nothing else matters to me.'

'Mum, you will be with us for many years yet. You aren't going anywhere!'

Chapter 30

The day had finally come and the move was well underway. It was all happening to her again. Moving from one house to another but this time she was without Simon. It was totally different and it did feel strange but the new man in her life was making everything so easy for her.

She left quite a few bits and pieces at the old house for Danielle and Phillipe to start them on their way, although Phillipe had enough to bring from his little cottage, so she knew they weren't short of furnishings. The joy on their faces when they finally took hold of the keys to Fleur de Pre was sheer delight.

They were happy and in love. The little bump was steadily growing and Danielle was a picture of health. Moving to this mansion (as she called it) was something else. Meg had never seen such luxury. Everything went very smoothly and they quickly had Mum's annex the way she liked it, which she approved of immensely.

She even had her very own log burner and the most beautiful en-suite. She told Louis how lucky she was and couldn't thank him enough for making her happy, her daughter and her grandchildren. Mum and Louis stood together in the hallway, which by the way was big enough to hold a party, where she showed so much love and appreciation towards Louis.

The move from the old house was good for all of them; leaving bad memories behind, remembering the good days but making new memories had to be a good thing. Mum went on to say that she had a special place in her lounge for Dad, on top of the dresser and she could show him around whenever she wanted.

'That's what I want to hear, Mum!'

The dogs didn't take long to settle into their extensive garden and surroundings. Katie and Alice had separate bedrooms; both had fairy lights around the headboards and inside the windows. It was like a fairyland and Meg couldn't believe Louis had done this for them.

Louis told her he had arranged for an interior designer to create the desired look of each room and must say, she certainly knew her job.

After a few weeks, they had settled and Meg popped over to see Danielle, who was having a few days off from work due to the fact that she was nauseous. Meg took her the biggest box of chocolates she could find. She didn't think she wanted flowers, as she was always surrounded by them, at work and at home.

She was getting quite big and still had almost four and a bit months to go. Not sure why she bought her chocolates but she did tell her she was there to help with the disposal of them. They both laughed and then began eating the odd chocolate caramel, strawberry cream, truffle delight; feeling quite sick, they decided to put them away for another day.

'I suppose you are now getting ready for the holiday?'

'We are excited, especially the boys. They seem to be growing up so fast now they even talk about girls, which I find quite a little bizarre at the moment.'

'It isn't bizarre, Meg. That's what boys think about at their age. With everything that has happened over the past few years, you have to remember they are almost sixteen years of age. They could even be leaving home within the next couple of years, should they be lucky enough to get into University.'

'It seems strange somehow but I know it could happen,' Meg said in a matter of fact tone.

They took the dogs to Danielle and Phillipe the day before the holiday began. They were at home, knowing every corner of the garden, sniffing and putting their mark where they had once been. They were both delighted to have Reuben and Oscar and told her to enjoy the holiday without worrying about the dogs.

Mum had flown back to Exeter, where her sister greeted her. She was very much like Aunty Gabby in many ways, very thoughtful and extremely kind. Mum phoned to say she had arrived safely and wished us a happy and relaxing holiday.

'Take care, Mum. See you when we get back!'

Very excited, children piled into the seven-seater Audi SUV. They began the 7-hour journey and were well on their way to a very much long awaited holiday. The villa was stunning with its pool and outside eating area. It was pretty and very peaceful, just what we all wanted.

They didn't need to go far. Everything was on hand for them. On a couple of nights, Louis had arranged for a chef to come and cook their evening meal. Meg offered to help pay for the holiday because she did have money in the bank from the sale of the house but Louis insisted the holiday was a treat from him to them.

They walked along the promenade where there were many Michelin star restaurants; oysters and champagne looked the dish of the day! Alongside some of the restaurants was where many celebrities moor their yachts, some must be worth millions. What a life!

She looked back at the boys walking behind, laughing and eyeing up the girls in their short skirts with not much else on top. Giggling schoolboys! It was Danielle, who said to her, they are now growing into young men. Meg's reaction was, not too soon, please, boys!

Katie and Alice were looking at handmade jewellery on one of the stalls and decided they would like to buy themselves a bracelet. They were similar in so many ways and appeared to look out for each other. Was this sisterly love in the making?

Meg had noticed that when one of them needed a little bit of comfort or support, the other was there on hand. Two lovely little girls. They returned to the villa and went to their rooms after a very tiring day. It seemed strange to be sleeping with Louis, knowing the boys and girls were nearby.

Meg hoped they understood that Louis made her very happy and had brought this family together in so many ways. They both lay in each other's arms and stayed cuddled up to each other until morning. She lay there looking up at the ceiling and thinking, who would have ever dreamed moving to France would end up like this?

She was happy and couldn't be happier but sometimes she asked herself if this was real. Would she suddenly wake up and find that it was one very long dream? They had the most beautiful holiday in the south but fourteen days passed quickly and they were heading back to Brittany before they knew it.

Meg told Louis he did nothing but spoil them throughout the holiday and she couldn't thank him enough.

'My pleasure and let's hope more spoiling will come.'

As they drove back, she rested her head on his shoulder and quietly said, 'Thank you, darling.'

They were now settled at their new home and Mum couldn't wait to tell us about her time back in England with Aunt Gabby. She had asked if she could come over and spend Christmas with us.

'Why not?' Meg said, 'That would be lovely; there is plenty of room.'

Louis agreed it would be nice for Mum to have her sister join us for the festive season. Christmas was always very busy but this year was going to be extra special. Phillipe and Danielle were looking forward to the arrival of their new baby and so far, everything was going to plan.

Louis mentioned about finding a Christmas tree for the hallway. Of course, Henri was on hand to deliver the best in the village. He did a good job. It looked stunning! Everyone decided to decorate the house inside and out. Meg had never seen anything so beautiful.

There must have been hundreds of lights and even the trees were glowing brightly with fairy lights in the front garden. Henri was driving past and said, 'You have helped to make the village look spectacular.'

'You helped too Henri, by finding us a most beautiful tree,' Louis shouted out.

The arrival of Aunt Gabby was imminent and the drive to Nantes airport took around two hours. Snow was expected later in the week and the roads were beginning to ice up slightly, so Meg decided to drive a little more carefully than usual.

The flight was on time and it was lovely to see her again. Driving back to the house, she told me that Mum seemed very happy when she last visited her and appeared very happy in her new home. 'I only hope Aunt Gabby that it stays that way.'

Meg told Aunty Gabby that she was always welcome to visit anytime. Christmas Day was fast approaching and everything was in top gear as usual. Meg kept thinking the phone would ring any moment with baby news from Phillipe. Nothing but she was assured that everything was good.

The kitchen was at full speed, with everyone doing as much and as little as possible. To get the boys to make a cup of tea would be a miracle. They were more interested in playing on their Xbox. Katie and Alice were dressing up their dolls.

Aunt Gabby was making pastries and quiches, Meg was ironing and Louis was working a last night at the hospital before having a two-week break. She couldn't wait to sit down, pour a glass of wine and relax when the phone rang. She raced to the phone and could see it was Phillipe.

A very anxious but thrilled voice was on the other end saying, 'Meg, Danielle's waters have just broken and we are on our way to the hospital.'

'Can I do anything?' Meg asked.

'No, we have it all in hand!'

'Don't forget that Louis is on duty at the hospital, should you need anything.'

'Thanks, Meg. I will bear that in mind. Must go-will keep you updated.'

Meg kept thinking and hoping everything would be alright with no problems. Danielle has had a hassle-free pregnancy so far with little or no problems. Let's hope it stays that way. Meg informed the family of events and said Phillipe was keeping us informed as and when he knew anything.

It was a long night and even longer next day. It was now Christmas Eve and looking at the clock, it was midday and still waiting for news. Meg was now beginning to get worried and panicky.

'No news is good news,' Meg kept telling herself.

Louis was due home in the late afternoon, so he could enlighten us on how labour was progressing. Around two o'clock, the phone rang. It was Phillipe. Meg could sense absolute excitement in his voice.

'Well Phillipe, what is the latest?'

There was a long silent pause and then happiness and joy.

'It's a girl. A precious little girl weighing 3.35kgs (7lb 4oz.) Danielle ended up having a caesarean section because the baby had turned and was lying in a somewhat difficult position. It was worth it because she is a beautiful, Meg. We have decided to call her Eve Megan.'

Feeling somewhat emotional, she congratulated them both on the birth of their little daughter.

'What made you choose her name?'

'Well, she was born on Christmas Eve and it made sense but also because you are so very special to us, we wanted her second name to be Megan. When the time is right, we would very much like you to be her godmother.'

'What an honour, Phillipe. It would be a pleasure. The family sends their congratulations with so much love. When can we see her?' Meg asked.

'If everything goes well, I can bring them home late tomorrow morning, just in time for Christmas lunch which will have to be something very simple this year.'

Meg told Phillipe he now had a family to look after and with that in mind, she took a step back, thinking how Simon said much the same thing to her when the twins and Katie were born.

'As they say Phillipe, new house, new baby, nothing could be better. What a Christmas present! Merry Christmas!'

Phillipe told Meg that everyone had been so kind, with lots of presents for Eve and in the corner of the nursery sat a giant teddy bear, the largest he had ever seen which had been presented by Henri from all the villagers.

'What a lovely place we live, Meg.'

'I couldn't agree more.'

She then told Phillipe to get on with finishing the final touches of the nursery.

'Not another bossy woman,' he said jokingly.

They both stood laughing but Meg could sense the pure happiness emanating from Phillipe. Louis arrived home, looking tired and exhausted. The hospital's Immunology Department only had two staff working throughout the past week, which had been absolutely chaotic.

'We coped the best we could and I managed to pop in and see Danielle's little girl. She is beautiful, Meg! They are hoping to come home tomorrow so they can spend Christmas altogether. I have also heard that Danielle's parents are visiting from Belgium to be with them over the Christmas period and help out with the baby and afterwards when Phillipe returns to work.'

'I was so happy about that because knowing how tiring it can be having a young first baby, once the adrenalin and excitement has vanished, you need all the extra help and support.'

Meg wanted to ring Esme and tell her the news about baby Eve. She was delighted and said they made a wonderful couple and who knows, one day, they may even decide to marry, Meg. Wouldn't that be lovely?

Esme told her that her new life in Paris was good and that the Bed and Breakfast was getting very busy, especially with visitors over the Christmas period. 'It is so lovely meeting different people from all around the world and listening to their life stories.'

Esme couldn't wait to tell Meg that she had met someone who made her happy, loved Olivia and was kind and gentle.

'It is early days and I am taking small steps but he has helped me adjust to a new life and is a good listener and for that, I am very thankful. Olivia has settled well into school life and making friends.'

'Esme that is such great news. I hope everything goes well for you. You certainly need your luck to change without a doubt.'

She had been unfortunate in her past love life but perhaps now, she is regaining all that she had lost. Meg hoped so anyway!

'As you probably know, Louis bought your old house and has rebuilt it from scratch. I don't think you would recognise it, Esme. Once completed, he asked us to move in with him and Alice. Of course, we all said we would, even Mum and couldn't be happier. We are now a couple and life has given me back a future for myself and the children. A games room for the boys and Mum has her own annex where she can be on her own if she wants to.'

'Deep down in my heart Meg, I always knew there could be a future with you and Louis. He is quite an exceptional man and you are very lucky to have found someone who not only loves you but will always be there and support you. You have found your happiness, Meg!'

What could she say! Esme was able to express her thoughts exactly. She had to say that she thought they were all moving forward with their lives and with the drama of Greg, the tragedy and death of Simon and her Dad, the future could only get better.

'Can I say that demolishing my old house and rebuilding it was the best thing to happen? All those bad memories have now gone, with good times in front for everyone.'

'You are right, Esme! The past has gone; the future is in front of us.'

'Perhaps one day, Meg, both myself and Olivia will come back to visit. Who knows!'

They said goodbye and reminded each other that they would always keep in touch, even the girls needed to remain friends.

'Totally agree and give my love to all in St Helene,' Esme replied.

'I will pass on your congratulations and get Danielle to send you a photo of baby Eve.'

'I would very much like that, Meg.'

'Goodbye for now.'

Meg sat back and thought about her future with Louis. Would they ever marry one day? She didn't know. Her marriage ended in tragic circumstances and Louis's marriage ended in divorce. Time would tell but she knew she was blissfully happy and truly in love so she hoped it would continue.

They couldn't wait to see baby Eve. It was strange to enter her old house and see a new baby lying in a crib, with Danielle and Phillipe, the proud parents, just sitting there adoring their little girl. It was a very special and magical moment.

She had the most beautiful blue eyes, so much black hair and peachy soft skin. Danielle handed baby Eve to Meg and she just wanted to hold on to her forever. Baby Eve curled her little finger around Meg's finger, which was a very special moment that she would not forget.

Even Louis couldn't resist picking her up and holding her for a few cherished moments. Later that evening and safely back home to the warmth of their new home, she could see snowflakes beginning to fall through the expanse of the large glass windows.

'Christmas is here,' shouted Aunty Gabby, who said, 'it's snowing outside.'

They all sat around the dining room table, enjoying a hot chocolate with the addition of a drop of brandy. It was so good that they could all be together. Not long after all the festivities were over, Mum quietly asked about the future for Louis and her.

Meg told her there was a future but marriage could take longer.

'Please remember, Mum, when I married Simon, I knew it would be forever, not thinking he would ever leave me in such tragic circumstances and I have had to accept that. For Louis, it was different. He married young; life didn't work out for him in many ways and Alice had to be the only good thing to come out of their marriage.

'Having Louis in my life has changed my life in a good way. I love him very much-the children love him and I know you do. We have a future and we must wait for the next chapter in our lives.'

As a family, the boys loved France and the way of life. Katie had a new stepsister who she adored. Reuben had a new playmate and Mum had made lovely friends, joined the local knitting club and was now ready to globe trot around the world, finding the confidence to fly backwards and forwards to the UK-only joking, Mum!

Phillipe and Danielle were now married after a lovely little ceremony in the village, which also coincided with the christening of baby Eve. Meg was given the role of godmother, which she would always treasure. The florist shop was busier than ever, blooming, as they say!

Esme and Olivia were getting on with their lives and Esme had found romance. They all hoped she had found the happiness she so very much deserves. Greg remains in prison with no chance of an impending release.

They were here to stay with a much-loved and respected Louis and a possible beautiful stepdaughter, Alice. A dream had come true. They were a family of seven once again. Whilst holding that thought, Meg felt a shiver go down her spine and a presence within calling her into the cold night air.

Outside, Meg cautiously walked across the frosty pathway and as she looked up, she could see what looked like a white feather slowly mingling within the glistening snowflakes. Meg eagerly jumped up, catching the feather and clasping her hands tightly together.

She knew this had to be a message from Simon, telling her she had his blessing to move on in life and that he was delighted that everyone had all found true happiness. More importantly, she needed to tell him something and her message was:

"Love never dies; we will always be together."

Meg believed his message was:

"There are times in life when we both need to let go.

All I want to know is that you will *catch me when I fall*."